love
unexpected

Books by Jenny Proctor

Romantic Comedy

Some Kind of Love Series

Love Redesigned

Love Unexpected

Love Off-Limits

Love at First Note

Wrong for You

Inspirational Romance

The House at Rose Creek

Mountains Between us

love unexpected

Jenny Proctor

Cover design by The Red Leaf Book Design
www.redleafbookdesign.com

ISBN 9798737160913

For Laura,

who wanted Isaac's story the most

Chapter One

Rosie

Isaac Bishop was not your typical man.

He was more like the kind of man you read about in romance novels and think: *men like this do not exist in real actual life.*

First of all, he was incredibly nice. His entire brand was built around kindness and paying it forward, but with Isaac, it wasn't just an act. He was a natural. He had a knack for making people feel good.

But somehow, he *also* had this incredible sexiness and charm.

It shouldn't be fair. For someone who is genuinely a good person to also look like they just stepped off the set of a body wash commercial. You know the ones. Where a man gets all sudsy in the middle of a forest with a waterfall cascading down his back.

Isaac was totally that guy. With the slightly messy dark brown hair and the bright blue eyes and the jawline that just wouldn't quit. And did I mention his biceps? He had some. He was not an overly muscled dude. But the biceps showed up to work every single morning.

See what I mean? The whole package.

And America loved him for it.

Okay. Maybe not *all* of America. But a very large contingent somewhere in the ballpark of ten million YouTube subscribers loved him. Like me, they started watching his channel, *Random I,* years ago, and they stayed with him as he grew and built his business into a multimillion-dollar operation that employed seventy-five people and released new content daily.

Fun fact. I was one of those seventy-five employees.

I never dreamed I would actually wind up working for Isaac. I was a fan long before I was an employee. But then he posted about a job opening for a web designer and ran a lottery for anyone looking to upgrade their work life. I'd barely been making ends meet in Kansas, designing layouts and writing code for an online clothing company.

An upgrade had sounded perfect.

Plus, Charleston was new and different and . . . *not* like Kansas, where I was from. I'd been talking for months about wanting a change. Why not a warm, coastal city full of fresh seafood, sandy beaches, and centuries-old history?

I'd entered the lottery on a whim, then didn't give it another thought until an HR rep from *Random I* called about my resume.

I'd gotten it. The job was mine.

I only had the courage to make the move because I'd been positive I'd be working at some offsite location writing code in a secluded cubicle with only my spider plant to keep me company. I was comfortable admiring Isaac from afar. But working with him? *No way.*

Ha. Had I only known.

I hovered my mouse over the product description for the latest *Random I* hoodie to show up on my desk. Too many adjectives. The hoodie *was* the softest sweatshirt I'd ever put on my body, but was it cloud-soft? Soft as down? Pillow-soft? Clouds weren't even *soft.* Not technically, anyway.

I sighed and leaned back into my chair, pressing my fingers against my temples. I was a web designer. I could make things *look* pretty all day. But making them sound pretty? I was in way over my head.

"Another product description?" Greta, my first Charleston friend, slid her rolling chair over and leaned into my shoulder, her eyes trained on my screen.

"Wow," she finally said. "That's . . . original."

"This isn't even supposed to be my job," I argued. "I don't write copy. I'm not a writer."

"You're making it too complicated," Greta said, her hand moving to my keyboard. She highlighted and deleted a few words from my description, then swapped a semi-colon for a comma. "But if you must know," she said while she worked, "Isaac did approve hiring a copy writer at this morning's leader meeting. Writing merch descriptions is a part of the job description."

"Seriously?" As team leader, Greta was technically my boss. But it was hard to feel like anyone was much of a boss at *Random I.* Isaac made sure everyone felt like we were all a part of the same team. He shied away from terms like boss and manager and CEO. Even the vast warehouse that housed all *Random I* operations was designed to promote teamwork and connectedness. The actual recording studio where *Random I* videos were shot was downstairs, and the chop shop where the editors and techie people edited and finalized the show had their own space, and Isaac, of course, had his own office, though it was walled in glass, so he hardly felt separate from the rest of us. But otherwise, we were all in one giant room. From the show writers to the web designers to the accounting people. There were no corner offices. No divided floors. It really was an upgrade. Different from anywhere I had ever worked before.

Greta leaned back, a satisfied look on her face. "Of course I'm serious. I know how much you hate writing these things. And there's more than enough content going up on the website to justify hiring a writer." She motioned with her head toward my screen. "See how that sounds. And next time, just pull one of the old descriptions for a product we aren't selling anymore. It's always easier to tweak something that's already written than to write something from scratch. At least until we can hire someone."

"You're good to me," I said as I read over her description. "How did you do this? It's so much better."

She grinned and wheeled back to her own desk. "I deleted five adjectives."

"Five? For real? There are still three in here."

"Yeah," she said, her tone dry. "I know."

"Hey, hey!" Isaac's voice boomed from the elevator doors behind me. "Are we making people happy today?" Isaac generally didn't show up until an hour or two after everyone else was at their desks. A perk of having your name—or at least your initial—on the company logo. Not that I faulted him for it. He worked harder than anyone I knew. And he never cared if his employees needed to arrive late or leave early . . . not as long as they were getting their work done.

I kept my eyes glued to my computer screen as he walked across the warehouse space to his office, his business manager and brother-in-law, Alex, close behind him. I didn't have to watch to know he would high five or fist bump every employee he passed. That he would stop and pick up the beat sheet for that day's episode, that he would ask about someone's new baby or someone else's sick mom.

The man handled people with a grace and skill I couldn't help but admire.

"Greta!" Isaac said, stopping in front of her desk. "How goes it? Where are we with the new hoodies? I was hoping to talk about them on the show today. Are we good for that?"

Greta motioned toward me. "Merch has it well in hand."

Isaac's gaze shifted to me. "Rosie! Talk to me about hoodies."

Side note: I was *not* good at talking to people. I mean, I was a functional adult. I could interact and engage with my coworkers and order food from the local Chinese place and interact with my landlord about cabinet repairs without any trouble. But that hadn't always been the case. It had taken me years to get a handle on my anxiety, resulting in a full arsenal of tools and coping strategies culled from countless therapy sessions, yoga classes, and meditative breathing workshops. All of it had worked. I was fine. Mostly. But sometimes, when I interacted with certain people or felt particularly nervous or overwhelmed, I pretty much lost it.

I willed my nerves to settle. This would *not* be one of those times. I generally avoided one-on-one conversations with Isaac whenever I could out of an absolute certainty that otherwise, I would say something to embarrass myself. Because Isaac definitely qualified as one of those *certain* people.

I swallowed and cleared my throat. "Fifteen more minutes and they'll be live on the site." *Hey look! A complete, coherent sentence!*

"Perfect," Isaac said. "And the ones without the hood? I mean, I have no idea why anyone would want a sweatshirt without a hood, but Dani swears people will buy them."

"I think Dani is probably a smart person to trust when it comes to fashion. And yes. They're good. The sweatshirts, I mean. Not Dani. Though I'm sure Dani is probably fine too. Not that I would know. I never talk to Dani. Or anything." I closed my eyes and winced. "Sorry. I'm . . . the crewnecks are perfect. All good. Ready for lift-off."

Isaac wrinkled his brow, a question in his eyes.

"Launch!" I yelled, loud enough to attract the attention of half the warehouse. "I meant launch," I said, dropping my voice to normal decibels. "The crewnecks are ready for launch. And the hoodies. Can I stop talking now? I'm going to stop talking."

Isaac nodded slowly. "Sure. I think you've told me everything I need to know." He turned as if to walk away then swung back around. "You okay, Rosie? You look a little flushed."

I shook my head, my hands instantly flying to my cheeks. "Nope, I, um . . . I'm good. A-okay."

He shook his head. "Okay. Just checking. You let me know if Greta's working you too hard, all right?" He finally turned and headed toward his office, sparing me the humiliation of having to respond again.

"Wow," Greta said slowly. "That was . . ."

"Shut up," I said. "It's your fault, anyway. You knew the sweatshirts were added to the site and ready to go. You could have just told him for me!"

"And deny myself that little show?" Greta smiled. "Absolutely not."

I dropped my head onto my desk. "Was it that bad?"

"I mean, I don't think he figured you out if that's what you're asking. You just seemed like you're a nervous communicator in general, *not* like you're madly in love with him."

Okay, truth time. I did *not* move to Charleston for Isaac. I'm not that ambitious. Applying for the job had been a leap, accepting it an even bigger one. But I took exactly zero romantic aspirations with me when I left Kansas and moved south.

That didn't mean I wasn't hopelessly in love with my boss. How could I not be? He was Isaac *freaking* Bishop.

I lifted my head and glanced around us, not exactly wanting anyone else in the office to know my secret, but everyone at the surrounding desks seemed preoccupied enough not to be paying attention to our conversation. "I have to figure out a way to get over him. This is getting ridiculous."

Greta rolled her eyes. "Or you could just ask him out."

"I will absolutely *not* ask him out. He's seeing someone right now anyway. And he's my boss. You aren't supposed to date your boss."

"Isaac would hate hearing you call him the boss. You know how he feels about teamwork and collaboration. We're all in this together, Rosie," Greta said in a surprisingly accurate mimicry of one of Isaac's favorite expressions. "And we know he doesn't care about workplace romance. I started dating Vincent when our offices were still crammed into the tiny kitchen house behind Isaac's house on Church Street, and Isaac was our biggest advocate."

"That's because he'd never seen me date anyone before," Vinnie said, coming up behind Greta and leaning down for a kiss. "He couldn't contain his excitement."

Vinnie to everyone but Greta, who insisted on calling him by his given name, had been part of the original team when Isaac started *Random I* in his parents' basement back before he'd even graduated from high school. The studio and headquarters for *Random I* had occupied a few different locations, finally settling into the spacious top floor of a warehouse near the medical complex in downtown Charleston. They'd moved six months before I'd gotten the job and headed south.

Vinnie and Isaac were close friends; it made sense Isaac would have been happy for him. But that didn't mean *Isaac* would be interested in dating one of his employees.

"The point is," Greta said, standing up so Vinnie could drop into her chair before she lowered herself onto his lap, "you have no reason not to consider yourself a desirable option. Just put yourself out there. You'll never know how he'll respond if you don't try."

"I concur," Vinnie said.

I shook my head. "I can't do it. Dating him would just feel weird. Like I'm some weird crazy stalker person that moved all the way to Charleston just to try and be close to him."

Greta rolled her eyes. "You moved all the way to Charleston because you got a job that pays you three times what you were making at the dump where you used to work. So what if you now that you're here, you *happen* to start dating your boss? That doesn't make you creepy."

"*You* know that's why I took the job. But it's still weird. Because I brought . . ." I shot a quick glance around the room and leaned toward them. ". . . *feelings* with me when I came. I have to at least work here long enough that it can look like those feelings started after I got the job."

Vinnie looked from me to Greta then back to me again. "That's not how it happened?"

Greta looked at me sideways, obviously wanting to take my lead on how to answer the question. But how could I explain? I wasn't about to own up to the fact that I'd fallen in love with Isaac when I was still in high school and watching his YouTube channel every day.

"How could that happen for anyone?" Greta finally said, clearly sensing my uncertainty. "Everyone knows who Isaac is. Rosie watched the show just like the rest of us. Even before she met Isaac in person, she still knew who he was."

"I'm telling you," Vinnie said, his voice soothing in a low, melodious way. "He really is the easiest person in the world to talk to. You shouldn't be so terrified of him."

"It's not that I'm terrified," I said. "I guess I just feel like if Isaac were going to notice me, he would have by now. We've even hung out a few times at Jade and Diedre's. He barely notices me. You guys have seen the women that he dates, all tanned and toned and leggy. It's not like I'm exactly his type."

I'd had countless conversations with Greta about my crush, and I'd always known that Greta had likely told Vinnie about my feelings, but this was the first time he'd ever been in on one of our conversations. The reality of his participation, when he was so close to Isaac himself, was a little heady, and I had a hard time keeping my hands from trembling.

"Here's the thing about Isaac," Vinnie said. He glanced up, and I followed his gaze to Isaac's office, where we could see him through the glass deep in conversation with Alex. "He's amazing with people, right?

So good at talking and making other people feel at ease. But he can also be a little clueless. He has a terrible track record when it comes to dating. And everyone close to him knows it's because he's dating the wrong kind of woman. We all see it. Eventually, he'll see it too. But he might need some nudging."

"What kind of woman *does* Isaac need?" Greta asked.

As if conjured by our conversation, Isaac's girlfriend slinked by wearing a tiny denim skirt and a pair of wedges that made her already long legs look even longer. She was sun-kissed and stunning and perfect, making me immediately uncomfortable in my graphic tee and striped blazer. I generally felt pretty good about my look on a day-to-day basis. My dark, curly, chin-length hair. My funky glasses and retro sneakers. But nothing made me feel insecure like a front-row seat to the kind of woman Isaac *actually* noticed.

"He needs someone who understands what makes him happy," I said, my eyes still following the woman across the room. "Who knows Red Renegade and appreciates the depth of his loyalty to such an obscure band. Who can talk to him about books. Who appreciates smart wordplay or a good pun. Who likes scouring yard sales for old vinyl. And who will keep him grounded to reality in the midst of his fame and attention."

Vinnie's eyes widened. "Whoa. That's pretty much dead on." He looked at Greta. "Maybe we ought to get Dani involved. Nobody knows what Isaac needs better than she does. And one conversation with Rosie would probably be enough for Dani to realize it's her." He motioned to me with the hand that wasn't wrapped around Greta's waist.

My chest pulsed with heat at the thought that one of Isaac's closest friends saw me as someone whom Isaac needed, but there was no way I was letting them pull Isaac's twin sister into the mix. I'd met Dani a few times, and she was perfectly lovely. But she was also fiercely devoted to Isaac and married to his business manager. There was no way she'd keep my feelings a secret, and that wasn't a risk I was willing to take.

"Absolutely not," I said, shaking my head and turning back to my desk. "I don't need anyone playing matchmaker. Especially not someone who would definitely tell Isaac that I'm interested." I eyed Vinnie. "And you aren't going to tell him either."

"Don't worry," Greta said, standing up and nudging Vinnie out of her chair. "I've already sufficiently threatened him. He won't say a word. Will you, Vincent?"

"I know what's good for me," he said with a sly grin. "What if we just tell Jade and Diedre? They could help nudge Isaac in the right direction."

"No way," I said, not wanting the suggestion to get even a second of consideration. "Jade knowing would be worse than Dani knowing. You guys know how fierce she is when it comes to Isaac."

Jade was another one of Isaac's original crew. She'd handled his social media until she'd gone off to school to get a marketing degree but had returned as soon as she'd graduated. Now she led the team that handled his social media and was point person for his public relations. Add to all that the fact that she was a loyal friend with strong opinions about what was and wasn't best for Isaac? If anyone had the ability to make or break my chances of ever actually dating the man, it was Jade.

"But Jade likes you, Rosie," Greta said. "You know she does."

I *did* know. Greta and Jade had been quick to welcome me into their circle when I'd first arrived in Charleston. It had only been six months, but I considered them all good friends. Greta, Vinnie, Jade and her wife, Diedre. If I was hanging out with anyone after work, it was them. But that didn't mean I was ready for Jade to know my secret. And not just because she was the only one of us besides Vinnie who was really close with Isaac.

"It doesn't matter," I finally said. "Just because Jade likes *me* doesn't mean she would like *me* to be with *Isaac.*"

Vinnie pushed his hands into his pockets and caught my gaze. "You're overthinking it, Rosie. None of Isaac's friends or your friends need to be involved. Just make yourself a little more available. When we happen to all be hanging out, don't hide like you usually do. Just talk to him."

"I don't hide," I said indignantly. "Isaac rarely hangs out with us anyway."

"He was at dinner last Sunday," Greta said.

"And at the beach bonfire the weekend before that," Vinnie said.

"That's right," Greta said. "Once Isaac showed up, you spent the rest of the night hunting for seashells with Max."

"And it was time well spent," I said pointedly. Max was Jade and Diedre's oldest—four years old and the very best partner for seashell hunting.

Greta sighed. "You're completely hopeless, you know that, right?" She motioned to my computer screen. "Come on. Back to work. I have things to do, and you need to get those sweatshirts live on the site." Greta's tone shifted from her friendly chat voice to her now-I'm-actually-your-boss voice, leaving no room for argument.

I sighed and turned back to face my computer screen, clicking through the last few steps before the sweatshirts were good to go.

My friends made it seem so easy. Like I could just stroll up to Isaac and start chatting like it was no big deal. But I had zero confidence in my ability to not flub up my words over and over again. I had even less confidence that if I *did* try, Isaac would see me as anything other than a slightly quirky girl who happened to be friends with his friends.

Chapter Two

Isaac

"That's just it," I said as I walked up the front walk to Jade and Diedre's home, Bridget following behind me. "I don't *want* a celebrity interview segment. It's not what I do."

"Even if it will bring new viewers? I have a lot of Instagram followers, Isaac, and they're telling me what they want to see from you."

I fought the urge to roll my eyes. The only reason Bridget had a lot of followers was because she hadn't hesitated to use her connection to *me* to build her platform. I hadn't minded at first. But lately, it was beginning to feel like Bridget's online persona was a regular part of our daily interactions. I didn't really have the right to complain. My job was very public. Having a girlfriend who was cool with just how much of my life and time was spent creating content and interacting with viewers made things a lot easier.

But that didn't mean I wanted my girlfriend to change my branding so that it better suited hers.

Jade opened the front door before we even had the chance to knock. "Hey! Everyone is already out back," she said, pausing when her eyes moved from me to Bridget. "Bridget," Jade said coolly. "I didn't think you could make it."

Bridget smiled tightly. "Surprise."

I shot Jade a look, and she grimaced before dropping the ice-queen expression she'd assumed the second she'd noticed Bridget standing beside me.

"We're always glad when you can make it," Jade said with all the warmth of an Icelandic winter. It was no secret Jade didn't like Bridget. But Jade hardly liked anyone that I dated. She acted more like an older sister in regard to my dating life than Dani did. Though, Dani wasn't a big fan of Bridget either.

That probably meant something, but I wasn't in the mood to try to figure out what.

A sparkling blue pool filled the left half of Jade and Diedre's backyard. Vinnie and Greta were stretched out on lawn chairs near the waterfall feature that flowed into the pool. Dani and Alex stood near the grill where Diedre was grilling hamburgers. Baby Nora, Jade and Diedre's newest addition, was in Alex's arms. Max was the only person in the pool, but Rosie, Greta's friend, was sitting on the edge of the pool, her feet dangling in the water. It was only the second week of April, but the temperatures were plenty warm enough to swim.

Bridget brushed past me and headed straight for a vacant lawn chair on the far side of the pool. It took her about five seconds to strip down to her string bikini and stretch out on the chair; she posed for a few selfies—and likely immediately posted them to Instagram—before she put her Air Pods in and her sunglasses on.

"Wow," Dani said, walking up beside me. "Bridget's feeling social today, huh?"

I ran a hand through my hair. "She's annoyed I won't do a regular celebrity interview segment for the show. She says her followers keep talking about how much they would enjoy it."

"Her followers, huh? You mean all the people who just like to look at her fashion choices and her sexy body?"

"That's not—" My defense of Bridget died on my tongue. That hadn't always been all Bridget was. But it definitely felt like that's all she'd been lately. "You're one to talk," I said instead. "Your Instagram is all about fashion."

Dani rolled her eyes. "Fashion *design*," she said pointedly. "It's totally different. My purpose is to feature the clothes, not the body inside them." She folded her arms across her middle. "You're scraping the bottom with that comparison, little brother. But lashing out at me will not make what I say any less true."

She was right. Dani had more than earned her right to have an Instagram account about fashion. She'd gone to design school, worked for one of New York's most prestigious designers, and was now building an impressive business of her own. I just didn't like it when she called me out on stuff. Which she was absolutely about to do.

"Why are you still dating her, Isaac?" Dani asked. "Does she really make you happy?"

Yep. There it was.

I shrugged dismissively. "The fans like her."

"Oh, right. The fans. They should definitely have a say in whom you do or don't date."

"They don't get a say. I'm just saying, if we break up, it has to be a whole thing. Fans would wonder why she suddenly stopped showing up in videos. I'd have to address it. It's a lot of work."

"Here's a thought," Dani said. "Next time you're in a relationship, how about you just keep things private? Then no one needs to know when and if you break up."

"Oh, wow, what a novel idea," I said, matching her tone. "Then I can just watch my entire career go down the drain."

"Oh, whatever. You're being dramatic."

"Am I?" I shrugged. "I gave up my right to privacy a long time ago, Dani. It's just part of the job."

She pursed her lips like she wanted to disagree with me, but then she stilled, her face turning an alarming shade of green.

"Hey, you okay? Morning sickness again?"

She breathed in and out slowly. "Why do we even call it morning sickness? I swear I am sick every hour of the day."

"What do you need?" I asked. "Water? Ginger ale? Alex?"

She shook her head. "Not Alex. He's enjoying baby Nora. Some ginger ale would be good, though. Then I'll just sit and distract myself from how terrible I feel by admiring the incredible retro vibe of Rosie's swimsuit."

I glanced back toward the water. Rosie was in the pool now, pulling Max around like a tugboat while he laughed and kicked his legs. I grabbed a ginger ale from the cooler for Dani, then dropped into a chair beside her. "She really seems to like hanging out with Max," I said.

The last few times we'd all been together outside of work, it seemed like wherever Max was, that's where Rosie was, too.

"She's good with him," Dani said. "But it could also be that she's the only one who doesn't have a significant other, so hanging out with Max feels easier than dealing with all the happy couples." She shot me a pointed look. "Or not so happy couples."

I ignored Dani's jab, instead focusing on the interesting part of the conversation. "Rosie's not dating anybody?"

Dani shrugged. "I mean, I guess she could be. But she's never brought anyone to any of our get-togethers. So, probably not."

"Should we set her up with somebody? She's still pretty new in town, right?"

"I think so. It's been less than a year, for sure."

"She seems cool." I watched as Max turned and wrapped his arms around Rosie's neck, eliciting a grin from Rosie that unexpectedly tugged at something deep in my gut. She had a really gorgeous smile. "Maybe she'd get along with Tyler."

Dani sipped her ginger ale. "Maybe. I don't think I know her well enough to judge. She does seem nice though. And her fashion sense is spot on."

"Isaac!" Max called from the water in his little boy voice. "Come swim with me. I want you to throw me in the air."

I glanced toward Bridget, who looked as though she had no intention of moving anytime soon. Would it be weird if it was only me and Rosie in the water with Max? We'd only spoken a couple of times, and it had almost all been work-related.

"Please, Isaac?" Max called. "Please, please?"

Jade walked up to the table and put down a big bowl of tossed salad. "Don't you disappoint that child, Isaac. His mamas have been buried under new baby stress. He needs all the attention he can get."

"Fine, I'm getting in," I said, knowing better than to disappoint Jade. I stood up and yelled across the pool. "Hey, Vinnie. Are you getting in?"

He held up his drink as if that were justification enough for him to stay exactly where he was. I rolled my eyes and peeled off my shirt, tossing it back on the chair.

"You better watch out, Max!" I yelled before running toward the pool and landing a cannon ball in the deep end that I realized a minute too late was going to splash Bridget even more than it would splash Max.

I came up out of the water to a laughing Max and a spluttering Bridget. She stood on the deck now, her hair wet and her mascara running down her face.

I looked at Max and winced. "Oops," I said playfully, which only made Max laugh harder.

"Seriously, Isaac?" Bridget said, her arms folded across her toned and tan stomach. "Oops?"

"It's a pool party, Bridget, and you're wearing a swimsuit next to the pool. How was I supposed to know you didn't want to get wet?"

She grumbled something unintelligible as she stomped toward the house. It wasn't the last I'd hear about it, but with the bright spring sun warm on my shoulders and a giggling four-year-old looking for my attention, I couldn't bring myself to care.

I lowered my shoulders into the water and made my way over to where Max bobbed in the shallow end, a pair of arm floaties keeping his head above the water. A few feet from where he floated, I dropped into the water and swam after his ankles, grabbing them before popping up right in front of him. Max erupted into another round of full-bellied laughter, making an annoyed Bridget well worth it.

Out of the corner of my eye, I saw Rosie moving toward the stairs. I hadn't meant to scare her away. Also, her swimsuit really was stellar. Black and retro in a twenties pin-up kind of way.

"Should we go get Rosie?" I whispered to Max, not knowing exactly what I wanted to accomplish, only that I didn't want her to get out of the water.

"Yeah, let's be sharks," Max said.

I grabbed Max by the waist and propelled him toward Rosie, even as he raised his hands to his head to make a shark fin and started humming the theme song to Jaws.

Rosie's eyes widened as she saw us approach, and she smiled as she scrambled a little faster toward the stairs.

"I'm getting you, Rosie!" Max called.

She was on the top step by the time we reached her.

Max reached out and grabbed her ankles. "Got you!" he said with unrivaled enthusiasm.

And unrivaled strength, apparently.

Rosie immediately lost her balance, toppling backward into the water. I barely had time to shove Max out of the way and lift my arms up before she fell on top of me. The unexpected force of her fall knocked me off my feet and we both ended up under the water. My hands snaked around her waist on instinct and stayed there until we were both on our feet and upright, water streaming off our faces.

"Are you okay?" I asked.

She looked up, her eyes finally meeting mine. Only then did I realize how close together we were standing. Her hands were on my arms, just above my elbows, as if she'd used them to brace herself and find her balance.

A sudden awareness prickled my skin, heightening my senses, amplifying every sensation coursing through my body. The warmth of her fingers on my arm. The softness of the skin at her waist where my hands still held her steady. The rise and fall of her chest, only inches from mine.

Rosie broke away first, releasing my arms and taking a huge step away with a slight shake of her head. "I'm good," she said hastily. "Thanks for breaking my fall." She turned and looked at Max, leaving me motionless where I stood. "You got me!" she said playfully, hoisting Max into her arms. "You are one scary shark."

I turned away, only to catch Dani staring at me, her eyebrows raised quizzically. I lifted a shoulder in her direction, already knowing what she was thinking. She'd pair me off with *anyone* if it meant getting Bridget out of my life. But it wasn't that easy. Bridget fit my lifestyle. She didn't mind the attention. The fans. The frequent live streams and interactions. And that mattered.

An uneasiness settled into my gut, my sister's words sounding in my brain without her even needing to speak them.

It isn't all that matters, Isaac, and you know it.

Chapter Three

Rosie

Well, *that* had been a close encounter.

I could still feel the warmth of Isaac's strong hands around my waist, could still see the beads of water dripping down his surprisingly ample chest.

I'd never seen Isaac without a shirt on.

Wait, that wasn't true. I'd seen him in *Random I* videos over the years when his antics had required swimming, but I'd never seen it in person. Definitely not from only six inches away.

And then the way his eyes had searched mine. He'd genuinely been concerned about me. But of course he had been. If I knew anything about Isaac's nature, it was that he genuinely cared about people.

"All people, Rosie," I muttered to myself as I changed out of my swimsuit. "Isaac cares about *all* people. Not just you."

Still, there had been *something* in his eyes. Something that made me think . . .

A sharp knock sounded on the door. "Are you finished?" Bridget called, annoyance clear in her tone. "I'm literally dying out here."

I sighed. I gave myself one final once-over in the mirror above the sink. My hair was already starting to dry, my mass of curls looking more like a frizzy helmet than an actual style. I'd been warned about Charleston humidity, but this was ridiculous. Maybe I'd ask Dani what product she used on her curls. They always looked perfectly contained and controlled. And her hair was twice the length of mine.

"Just another minute," I called to Bridget. I stuck my head under the sink, gasping when the cold water hit my neck, and worked the water through my wild hair. A few minutes later, I finally emerged from the bathroom, my hair tamed into being presentable at least, if not quite fantastic.

Bridget leaned against the wall across from the bathroom door, her eyes trained on her phone. She'd finally put clothes on—something I immediately noticed because she wore a Red Renegade t-shirt. Could she like the band as much as Isaac did? The t-shirt was definitely vintage, featuring the cover art from the band's 1983 limited release album. It was the kind of t-shirt *only* a true fan would wear. Maybe I hadn't given her enough credit.

"Sorry to keep you waiting," I said, motioning to the bathroom behind me. "I'm done now."

She glanced up from her phone for a split second but otherwise didn't move. "No worries," she said, her fingers still flying over the screen.

Why had she seemed so annoyed before if she wasn't in a hurry? Still. I wanted to like this woman. To believe there was a reason that Isaac liked her.

"That was their best album, in my opinion," I said, motioning to her shirt.

She looked up one more time, her eyes blank. "What?" She motioned to her phone. "Sorry. I was . . . preoccupied."

"Red Renegade," I said. I pointed to her shirt yet again. "The '83 limited release. It's their best one."

She looked down, as if seeing her shirt for the first time. "Oh. Right. I wouldn't know. I pulled this out of Isaac's laundry basket. I liked the colors, so he said I could keep it."

I stood there, unsure if I was more offended by her lack of awareness or that Isaac would give something so valuable to someone who would cinch it up and tie it in knots to the point of obscuring the image on the t-shirt in the first place. "You know it's Isaac's favorite band, right?"

Her eyes had dropped back to her phone, and she responded without looking up. "I tried to listen, but . . ." She shrugged. "I don't know. It just sounded like noise to me."

Noise?

I had absolutely *not* given the woman too much credit.

"Right," I mumbled under my breath as I moved past her in the hallway. "Well, the bathroom is all yours."

I settled into the overstuffed chair in the corner of Jade and Diedre's living room. Everyone outside had already started to eat, but I needed a minute. My close encounter with Isaac had left me reeling in a good way, but then my run-in with Bridget had done the opposite.

She was so obviously wrong for him. How could he not see it? True, couples could get along with different tastes in music. But it was more than that. I'd seen enough of her in his live streams and other videos to at least have a basic opinion. It was possible she was totally different on camera than she was in person, but she just didn't seem like she got him. Like she understood him. Not like I did.

Although, fans did seem to love her.

Maybe I was the one who was out of touch. Or it was all just wishful thinking—some misplaced hope that *I* would be better for Isaac than she was.

I pulled up Isaac's Instagram account and scrolled through his last few posts. He'd already posted a selfie of himself and Bridget by the pool. They looked perfect together. All attractive and sun-kissed. But her words about Red Renegade kept pulsing through my mind. How could Isaac let something like that go? If he just knew what it was like to be with someone who understood, who felt the significance of the band like he did . . .

The way he'd looked at me when he'd caught me in the pool flitted through my mind. There *had* been something there. I didn't want to steal Isaac away from his girlfriend. I would never be that girl. Even if I was, I wasn't deluded enough to think, with my retro fashion vibe and my love for colorful sneakers, that I could ever compete head-to-head with a woman as gorgeous as Bridget. But if I could just suggest the possibility that there might be something *more* out there, some*one* more . . .

But how?

I could just go outside and start reciting song lyrics. Red Renegade had a deep backlist. It wasn't hard to find lyrics that applied to most situations in life. But that felt a little desperate. Plus, I was nothing if not an introvert. I hung out with Max whenever I was hanging out with my friends because Max was easy. He had very low expectations, and I didn't have to spend near as much time worrying about what I said or what other people thought of me. I knew my friends liked me. But I was still the new girl. My confidence had not grown quite enough for me to put myself out there in that way. Especially not in front of Isaac.

But maybe I didn't have to put myself out there in person.

Isaac got way too many direct messages and emails to read them all. But I had an in.

Jade was the one who led the social media team that read everything that came in and decided what was interesting enough for Isaac to see. If I told her I'd sent something I wanted in front of Isaac's eyes? She could make it happen.

Of course, I'd have to admit to her how I felt about Isaac. And so far, Greta and Vinnie were the only two people who knew that particular secret. Well, the only two people in *Charleston.* My parents knew, of course, and my cousin, Marley. I was an only child, but Marley and I were as close as sisters.

Was I willing to let Jade know, too? She'd tell Diedre, of course. But if I asked her not to tell anyone else, she wouldn't. Jade was intense, but she was a true and loyal friend. She'd respect whatever I wanted.

Still. It was a risk.

My hands trembled as I pulled up my old Instagram account, the thrill of possibility humming beneath my skin. I'd loved Isaac from afar for a very long time. But now I was *doing* something about it. Sort of. And that felt amazing.

The account was one I'd used as a teenager and was all art, cartoons, and graphics I'd designed. The username associated with the account, @briarsandthorns, was both part of a line from a Red Renegade song and a subtle nod to my middle name, Rose. Because roses had thorns. But the official name on the account was my first name, Ana, even though I'd always gone by Rosie. I'd tried to switch over to Ana as a teenager, believing Rosie was too cutesy, but the only place it had ever stuck was on Instagram. At least that worked to my advantage now. Ana C. was vague enough that Isaac wouldn't have any reason to suspect it was me.

I scrolled through all the old posts. There was a touch too much existential angst woven through for my current tastes, but I'd done some good work. It at least wasn't anything to be ashamed of.

I pulled up a sketch I'd done of one of Red Renegade's album covers, the same one Bridget had been wearing when I'd run into her outside the bathroom. I'd washed out the colors, deepening the grays and blacks behind each of the band members so they stood more starkly against the skyline behind them. It wasn't half bad. Especially since I'd only been seventeen when I'd done it.

On impulse, I called Marley. I glanced outside while the phone rang, noting that everyone but me was outside now—even Bridget, who must have passed back through the living room without me noticing.

Marley answered on the first ring, just like I knew she would. "Talk to me, but talk fast," she said. "I've got a meeting in minutes."

In many ways, Marley was my polar opposite. She was vibrant and boisterous and loud and wasn't afraid of anything, and she was my very best friend. She worked from her home in Nashville, running a business that recruited and trained virtual executive assistants, a career born out of necessity since she was raising her kid—my eleven-year-old nephew, Shiloh—alone and needed both a steady income *and* a healthy measure of flexibility.

"Seriously? It's Friday night. Why are you working?"

"A lot of my trainees are currently working full-time jobs. Sometimes I have to train on the weekends. We're wasting minutes, Rosie. What's up?"

"I need you to tell me to do something brave," I said.

"You're doing it? You're finally talking to him? Do it, Rosie. Be brave!" Funny. She had known immediately that my something brave had to do with Isaac.

"Come on," I said, my tone flat. "You know me better than that. But I *am* going to send him a message. I think."

Marley was silent for a beat. "What kind of a message?"

"Some Red Renegade artwork I did a hundred years ago. That part doesn't matter. What matters is that I'm doing this. I'm reaching out. I should, right? This is a good idea?"

"Absolutely, this is a good idea. Still no in-person interactions?"

I sighed. At least Marley's tone was free of judgment. She really did know me better than anyone. She'd lived with my family for the last three years of my high school experience and she'd witnessed the extent of my anxiety firsthand. She'd never push me.

"We talked about sweatshirts earlier this week."

"Well that's . . . something," she said.

"Sure. I turned tomato-red and told him the crewnecks were ready for lift-off. He told me I looked a little flushed and asked if I was working too hard."

Marley chuckled. "I mean, it could have been worse."

"True. We could have been talking about the *Random I* boxer briefs that are for sale in the store. They have his face on them, Marley. Can you imagine?"

"I absolutely can. I bought Shiloh a pair for Christmas last year. They are totally ridiculous, but he loves them."

"How is Shiloh? I miss him."

"Grouchy. I swear the kid is eleven going on seventeen. He's more like a teenager every day."

"I can't even believe he's eleven."

"Me neither. K, I gotta go in just a sec. But first tell me how much time you're spending doing your visualization exercises."

I rolled my eyes and dropped back into the chair. "Please don't start talking to me like my therapist."

"Oh, come on. You know they work. The more you practice, the less awkward you'll be when you talk to him again. Then you won't have to hide behind Instagram messages."

"I'm not hiding."

Marley didn't respond, but her silence was plenty of accusation on its own.

"Fine. I'm hiding," I said. "But it still might work. You know how funny I am when we're texting."

"Yes. A real riot. Come on. Let's practice. I'll do one with you right now."

"I thought you had a meeting."

"I can be five minutes late. Let's pretend . . . like you're talking to

Isaac about the boxers he sells in his store."

I scoffed. "That is a conversation that will never actually happen."

"You never know," Marley said. "Besides, talking about underwear has to be as awkward as your occasional run-ins at work will get. If you're prepared for that, you're prepared for anything."

I huffed, glancing over my shoulder one more time to make sure I was still alone. "Fine. We're talking about underwear. You start."

Marley cleared her throat, dropping her voice an octave to sound more like Isaac. "Hey, Rosie. Are the boxers up on the site yet?"

"They are. In ten different colors. Everything is ready to go."

"I've heard they're pretty comfortable," she said. The inflection in her voice actually sounded a lot like Isaac. Though, as big a fan as Shiloh was, she'd probably heard dozens and dozens of Isaac's shows playing in the background of her life. "And hey, look at that," she continued. "Five-thousand five-star reviews."

"Amazing," I said. "How does it feel to have five-thousand people sleeping with your face on their junk?"

"Rosie!" Marley said, laughing. "You would not say that to your boss."

"No, but it's a valid point."

"Just remember that you really are funny, Rosie," Marley said. "The next time you're talking to Isaac, channel your inner actress and act like you're talking to me."

"But I don't want to *act* in front of Isaac. I want to be myself."

"I would argue that the *you* you are when you're with me is way more real than the bumbling dummy you are when you're talking to him."

"Okay. That's fair."

"I really have to jet now," she said. "But yes. You should absolutely do something brave. Send the message. Better yet, *sign* the message. Don't hide, Rosie. Everyone needs more Rosie in their life in whatever form they can get it."

"Tell Shiloh I'll call him this weekend."

"You got it," Marley said. "Love you, Ro."

I scrolled back to the image on my Instagram profile and saved it to my camera roll, then pulled up my direct messages; I quickly searched for and found Isaac's *Random I* profile. One finger tapped against my lip as I thought about what to say. But no. That's exactly what I didn't need to do. No thinking. I'd been *thinking* about Isaac for years. It was time to actually *do* something.

Channeling Marley's courage and optimism, I hastily typed out a message. *Found this image among my old posts and thought you might like it. My own interpretation of the limited-edition album in '83. Notice the faint outline of wings behind the clouds at the top. My personal nod to "Wings that Weep," definitely Renegade's most underappreciated song.*

I dropped in the image, hesitating only a moment before deciding that, despite Marley's confidence in me, I was not ready to sign my own name to the message. Before I could second-guess myself, I hit send, suddenly feeling more alive than I had in months.

I'd done it. I'd put myself out there.

Now I just had to make sure Isaac saw the message.

Chapter Four

Rosie

"So let me get this straight," Greta said, swiveling her chair to face me. "You sent a direct message to Isaac's *Random I* Instagram account, and you want Jade to make sure he sees it?"

It had been three days since last Friday night when I'd sent the message to Isaac, and I still hadn't mentioned it to Jade. I'd convinced myself it was a work thing and Jade would be more willing to discuss it . . . *at work.* But that was a fancy delay tactic if ever there was one. The truth was, I was terrified I'd made a colossal mistake and it was too late to undo it. It was only Marley's continual reassurance that had given me the courage not to abandon the whole plan.

I nodded. "She can do that, right?"

"Of course she can," Greta said. "But why didn't you just show it to Isaac yourself? We were all together this weekend. You could have just pulled it up on your phone and said, 'Hey, Isaac, look what I made.'"

"Oh, sure. That wouldn't have been risky at all."

"What would you have been risking?" Greta said.

I struggled to keep from rolling my eyes. Greta was almost as extroverted as Isaac and had a natural confidence that I couldn't even dream of having. She was the kind of person who arrived at a party believing that everyone in attendance already wanted to be her best friend. If she caught a man staring at her, she automatically assumed it was because he found her attractive. If I caught a man staring at me, it could only be because there was something wrong with me. Spinach in my teeth or a chocolate stain on my shirt or an unzipped zipper.

"Oh, I don't know. Embarrassment? Humiliation? Rejection?" I said. "Not to mention the fact that Isaac has a girlfriend. Who was *in* attendance when we were last together. I would have just looked . . . desperate."

"You would have looked like a friend who happens to like the same band he does."

"No, *you* would have looked like a friend who likes the same band he does. I would have looked ridiculous. Like I was trying too hard."

She shook her head. "You don't give yourself enough credit."

I huffed. "Look, can we just celebrate the fact that I've done *something*? That's a good thing, right?"

"Fine, yes," Greta conceded. "I like the fact that you're finally putting yourself out there. But this barely counts, Rosie. Did you even sign the message? I mean, what's your goal here? What are you wanting to come out of this?"

I shrugged. "I want him . . . to respond, I guess. So we can get to know each other a little bit. So he can see there are women out there who don't think Red Renegade sounds like *noise*."

"Ah. You've been talking to Bridget."

"She's so wrong for him, Greta."

"I know. But if he doesn't know the message is from you, why does it matter? Who cares if some faceless woman on the internet doesn't think Red Renegade sounds like noise? We want him to know *you* feel that way, right?"

I shook my head. "No. I mean, yes. Eventually. But not yet. I don't want to seem like I'm trying to break him and Bridget up."

She narrowed her eyes. "But that *is* what you're trying to do."

I folded my arms across my chest and leaned back in my chair. "Not directly, though. I'm just trying to suggest the possibility of something . . . different. And a direct message conversation is way less threatening than doing that in person, right? I don't want to look like a homewrecker."

It was the one part of my plan I'd been struggling with. I *didn't* think Bridget was right for Isaac, but that didn't mean I had a right to meddle in his relationship. –

She rolled her eyes. "They aren't married, Rosie. And all you did was send him an album cover. You're not a homewrecker. And you wouldn't have been if you'd done this in person, either."

"I know I'm ridiculous, okay? I should have the courage to just go after what I want, to trust I'm good enough, and everything else I know comes so naturally to you. But this is what I've got right now. Can you please just help me?"

She sighed. "Of course I'll help you. But I'm still not sure this is a good idea. Because he might not respond. He gets a lot of messages. I don't want that to disappoint you."

Greta had a point. But something in my gut told me Isaac *would* respond. Red Renegade had a pretty devoted cult following, but even among their most dedicated fans, the limited-edition album didn't get much love. That Isaac had a t-shirt featuring the album cover had to mean he loved it too. Those shirts were not easy to come by.

But then, he *had* given the shirt away.

I sank back into my chair. "Maybe this was dumb."

Greta's face softened. She leaned back into her chair, mirroring my position, and studied me for a long moment. "Let's go talk to Jade," she said, as if having finally decided to be on my team. "You'll never know unless you try, right? If this is the way you want to try, I support you."

She stood and extended a hand. "But then we have to get back to work. I swear, you're the worst at getting me talking and then my to-do list just goes out the window."

"But I'm twice as productive as everyone else when I *am* working, so you love me anyway, right?" I said as I followed her to Jade's end of the warehouse.

"And you're lucky you are," she said. "It's the only thing that saves you."

Jade was in a meeting.

With Isaac, no less, which only made me feel more twitchy and nervous. Two agonizing hours later, she dropped into Greta's desk chair and swiveled to face me. "Fine. I'm here. What on earth has you so worked up?" she said, crossing one pin-striped leg over the other.

My eyes darted to Greta, who stood cautiously behind her. "What? I texted her. You've been so preoccupied, I just told her to escape the meeting as soon as she could."

"I was happy to escape," Jade said. "Nobody's happy in there right now."

My brow furrowed in concern. "Is everything okay?"

"Things are fine. Just . . . creative differences on the team."

"The Drake Martinson interview?" Greta asked.

Jade nodded. "Isaac still doesn't want to do it."

"That makes sense," I said. "He's never interviewed celebrities before."

"He's also never dealt with tanking numbers before," Jade said. "Celebrities bring new viewers, and Isaac could use an infusion of those." She clapped her hands. "Anyway. I didn't make up an excuse to leave the meeting just to keep talking about the same thing. What can I do for *you*?"

My eyes darted to Greta as if she could give me the strength I needed to tell Jade my plan.

"Um, I—" I what? I had no idea where to even begin.

"Just tell her, Rosie," Greta said. "Jade is your friend. You shouldn't be freaked out about this."

"I'm in love with Isaac," I blurted, squeezing my eyes closed even as the words tumbled out. I peeked one eye open. "And I have been for a very long time."

Jade reached out and placed her hand on top of mine. "Look, I get it," she said, her voice soft and Southern and lyrical. "I'm a lesbian who's been married for three years, and even *I'm* a little in love with Isaac. He's as good as they come."

Heat flooded my cheeks, not so much from embarrassment as from relief at having finally told Jade how I felt. I quickly launched into an explanation of the message I'd sent and how I hoped she'd work her magic to get it in front of Isaac.

She studied me for a long moment after I finished my explanation.

"I've known Isaac a long time," she finally said. "I was managing his social media for free when he was still recording in his parents' basement. He's the one who encouraged me to get a degree in marketing, and when he expanded *Random I* into the warehouse and realized he needed more help, I was the first person he called. We're tight, Rosie. Did you know he was the one who introduced me to Diedre? He was in my wedding party when she and I got married."

I swallowed. Suddenly, involving Jade seemed almost as risky as involving Isaac's twin sister, Dani. "I didn't know that."

She eyed me warily, her silence nearly pushing me off the edge of reason.

"You know what, it was a dumb idea," I said, holding up my hands.

"I just . . . I'm not really good at the whole in-person thing with guys. Not at first. And I thought . . . if he could just get to know me . . . but forget it. It's really fine."

"You know how many women reach out to him every day?" Jade said. "I get it all. Photos, invitations to hook up, photos that *are* invitations to hook up, if you get what I'm saying. People asking for money, people asking for mentions or likes or shares. It's all made me a little protective of Isaac's privacy."

"I get that. I really do. But I didn't send him an invitation to hook up," I said. "You know me well enough to know I would never do that. I just sent him some artwork. It's a Red Renegade album cover, and I genuinely just thought he might appreciate it."

Jade's perfectly sculpted eyebrows went up. "You're a Red Renegade fan? That's . . . different."

I looked from Jade to Greta. "Seriously? Does no one else around here have decent taste in music?"

Jade chuckled. "You thought he might appreciate it? Or you also hoped he might respond?"

"Of course I hoped he'd respond. If he could just get to know me a little bit . . ." I shrugged. "I think we could be friends."

"Friends?"

I was going to start sweating if she didn't ease up soon. "Or more than friends. What else do you want me to say? I really like him. I just want a chance to get to know him. For him to get to know me."

Jade eyed me up and down in a way that made me feel like a contestant on American Idol. "What's your favorite tv show?" she asked.

"Mine?"

She gestured for me to answer as if it was obvious why she needed to know.

"Um, that's hard. Probably *Chasing Rainbows.* The last season in particular."

Jade nodded. "Favorite book."

"That one isn't hard. *A Chain of Tomorrows*, by Peyton West," I answered without hesitation.

Jade tugged at the sleeves of her oversized sweater and leaned forward. "Okay. How do you feel about Valentine's Day?" she asked.

"You totally know the answer to that," Greta said. "You were there when she went off on her rant about overpriced roses and the commercialization of human emotion."

Jade grinned. "That's right. I'd forgotten." She studied me a moment longer, her expression giving away little as to whether she liked my answers or not. Had I known it would lead to such a thorough vetting, I never would have asked for Jade's help. I might have stood a better chance hitting up one of her team members who wouldn't care quite so much.

"Last question," Jade said. "How do you feel about high heels?"

An image of Bridget parading through the warehouse in wedges taller than my morning latte flashed through my mind. Did that kind of thing really matter to Isaac? It had to be why Jade was asking. But it couldn't matter. Isaac wasn't that guy. I didn't know him as well as Jade or even Greta. But I knew enough to make some guesses, and I just couldn't imagine him caring about what kind of shoes a woman wore.

Either way, I wouldn't lie about it. I was me, and I liked me. I wouldn't change who I was, even for Isaac Bishop.

I glanced down at my Converse. "Um, I *think* I own a pair? I maybe haven't worn them in years, though. Not since my uncle's wedding."

Jade looked at Greta, a smile lighting her face. "Okay, you're right. I see it."

"See?" Greta said. "I told you she'd be perfect for him. Vincent thinks so, too."

Apparently, Greta's text to Jade had revealed a little *more* than she'd let on.

I couldn't decide if it was validating to have an entire team of people rooting for me or humiliating that I *needed* an entire team of people rooting for me just to connect with a man. Either way, I was too far in not to see this thing through.

Jade held out her hands, palms up, and motioned for me to take them. I slipped my hands into hers, her deep brown skin a contrast to my own, and wondered where this was headed. "Rosie," she said, "I love the idea of you and Isaac together. Truly. Forget the message. Diedre and I will have another get-together this weekend. We'll find a way to get you two alone so you can spend some time talking."

I pulled my hands away and shook my head. "I can't. I . . . this stuff doesn't come as naturally to me as it does to the rest of you. Plus, he's with Bridget. That's the whole point of doing it this way. Less pressure."

Jade gave me a good, hard look before her shoulders finally dropped and she leaned back in Greta's chair. "Fine. We can do it your way. Tell me more about this message. What was it, and when did you send it?"

I couldn't stop myself from smiling. "Friday night. And it was a picture of a Red Renegade album cover."

Jade pulled up her phone. "You're saying you sent it Friday? Have you gotten a response yet?"

"No. Not yet."

She looked up. "Are you sure?"

"I think I'd know if Isaac had responded."

"Not from Isaac. I just mean a general form response thanking you for reaching out, blah, blah, blah."

I grabbed my own phone off my desk and pulled up my Instagram account just to make sure, but there was nothing, no form message or otherwise. "I haven't gotten anything," I said again.

Jade chuckled. "Then you don't need my help after all. We're already responding to messages sent on Sunday, which means if you haven't gotten the form response back, someone on the team already saw your message and decided it was worth forwarding on to Isaac. He's probably already seen it."

A sudden pulse of fear tightened my gut. "Really?"

"I mean, maybe not yet. But he checks them every day, usually before he films so if there's something he wants to mention on the show, he can."

I nodded. That made sense. I'd heard him do shout-outs to fans and viewers who had messaged him in the past.

Jade stood. "Just because he's seen it though doesn't necessarily mean he'll respond. If he doesn't, you're going to have to try to chat him up like the interns do."

I nodded. "Got it. Fair enough."

She scooted out of the way, making room for Greta to drop back into her chair.

"But . . ." I hesitated, and Jade paused, turning back to face me. "I just . . . he won't know it's from me, right? You won't tell him? If he doesn't respond, I'd rather he not know I tried."

Jade shook her head. "I got you, Rosie. I won't tell him anything."

Chapter Five

Isaac

@briarsandthorns: Found this image among my old posts and thought you might like it. My own interpretation of the limited-edition album in '83. Notice the faint outline of wings behind the clouds at the top. My personal nod to "Wings that Weep," definitely Renegade's most under-appreciated song.

I pulled up the image that accompanied the DM my social media team had dropped into my primary inbox on Instagram. With hundreds of messages coming in a day, there was no way I could look at them all, but at least one person on the team read every single message. And when it was something they thought I'd like to see, they'd move it over.

They'd made the right call this time around. The artwork was incredible. Nuanced and emotional. I would disagree that "Wings that Weep" was the most underappreciated Renegade song, but whoever this person was, they had wicked talent.

I pulled up the profile and looked it over. "Ana C.," I read out loud to my empty office. "Let's see what else you've done."

I scrolled through a few more of her posts, stopping on a digital rendering of a mass of people walking on a busy street. In the middle of the crowd, one girl stood out, the colors making up her clothing and hair vibrant against the muted grays and blues of the people surrounding her. She looked totally different from anyone else, but the expression on her face said she didn't really care. That she even liked it that way.

"What has you so engrossed?" Bridget said, leaning on my desk right next to my chair.

I looked up. I hadn't even heard her come in. "Oh. Nothing. Just some artwork done by a fan."

"It's so cute that they send it to you," she said. "Can I see?"

I turned off my phone and lay it face down on the desk. "Don't worry about it. It was nothing too impressive." That was the farthest thing from the truth, but weirdly, I didn't want Bridget to see Ana's artwork. She wouldn't get it.

Bridget scooted a bit closer. "So I hear the Drake Martinson interview is officially on the books. So glad you decided to go with it."

I clenched my jaw. I still wasn't excited about the interview, but Alex had insisted I only had to commit to one, and the numbers he and Jade had presented about how it might boost the show's ratings had been compelling. I just hoped I wouldn't get flack from my tried and true fans over it. "Yeah. We'll see how it goes," I said.

"Way to sound excited, Isaac. You should be thrilled Drake Martinson even agreed to come on your show. He's like, the hottest thing in Hollywood right now."

"Well, why don't *you* interview him, Bridget?" I said, suddenly weary of the conversation. "You guys would probably get along great."

"Whoa. What's with the hate? I just want your show to be successful. You know that."

When Alex and Jade had made the argument in favor of bringing on Drake, I'd believed they had the best interests of the show in mind. But with Bridget? I wasn't half as convinced. "Actually, I think what you want is whatever is going to frame *you* in the best light."

She scoffed. "What's so wrong with that? Of course I want to look good. My followers count on me always looking my best."

"Is that even real, though? Always looking your best? What about bad days when you feel horrible, and you just want to stay in your pajamas? What about when you've got food poisoning, or your dog just died?"

Bridget rolled her eyes. "I don't even have a dog."

I was picking a fight. And that wasn't fair. Bridget didn't deserve to be chastised for things which ultimately didn't matter. Not when we actually needed to have a much bigger conversation.

One I'd seen coming for weeks.

One I'd been putting off for just as long.

Bridget and I had grown too different over the past couple of months. Her presence rarely did anything but make me feel more stressed, more out of touch with who I wanted to be. It was time to end things. But here? Now? In my office where my entire staff could watch through the glass walls?

"I need to get back to work, Bridget. Did you come by for a specific reason?"

"Only for a selfie," she said. "It's been a while. I want to remind my followers how cute my boyfriend is."

Oh, geez. Her timing couldn't be worse. "You know what? I'm not feeling it today."

"Seriously? I came all the way down here. I have full make-up on right now. Do you know how long that takes?"

I did know. I'd waited for her to armor up plenty of times.

"I know. But I'm not feeling great. And I have a lot to do before filming, and that's scheduled to start in less than an hour." I stood up and pushed my chair into my desk. "But let's do dinner later, okay? I think we . . ." I almost told her we had some stuff to talk about, but that would have made her ask questions. Questions I wasn't ready to answer.

"You think we what?" she said, as if sensing the weight of what I'd meant to say.

"I think we could get a table at Husk," I said casually. "I'll call and see what I can do."

"Oh," she said, mollified. "Fine. But wear something nice because I'm definitely taking a selfie then." She blew me an air kiss then turned and left, walking through the warehouse with the confidence of an Avengers star on a Hollywood red carpet.

Tonight was not going to be fun.

I ran into Rosie in the elevator on my way down to the second-floor studio, her arms full of . . . boxer shorts? They *were* boxers. In at least ten different colors.

I shot her a sideways glance. "Going someplace special?"

She rolled her eyes. "Very funny."

"I assume you're going down to the store?" I said, my fingers hovering over the elevator button that would take her to the ground level. The entire first floor of the *Random I* warehouse was where merchandise was stored and packaged for shipping. Since Rosie handled the merch website, it made sense that's where she was headed.

"I'm definitely not headed to lunch with all of these," she said dryly.

I grinned. "You know, I've heard they're pretty comfortable. You should keep a pair. Sleep in them, maybe."

She looked at me for a long moment, a look of surprise on her face.

Had I said something wrong?

"With all due respect," she finally said, her tone playful, "I think I'd feel weird about sleeping in boxer shorts featuring my boss's face. I appreciate the suggestion though."

"I can definitely respect that position. It's not so different from the reason I don't sleep in them either. I mean, I'm a pretty confident guy. But you gotta draw the line somewhere, you know?"

She lifted an eyebrow. "And that line for you is not wearing underwear with your own face on it? How grounded you must be."

It was only the teasing glint in her eye and the perfectly dry delivery that kept her words from actually sounding critical. I smiled. Rosie was *funny.*

The elevator doors slid open on the second-floor studio, but instead of leaving, I pushed the button that would hold the doors open and turned back to Rosie, following an impulse I hoped didn't lead me astray. "Hey. Can I ask you a question? Totally not work-related, and actually kinda personal. Which means you can say no, and I wouldn't hold it against you at all. I just feel like I need a woman's perspective."

Her eyes widened, making it easy for me to see their dark blue shade. Like the sky at dusk. Almost navy, but not quite that dark. "Um, sure, I guess. But, wouldn't you rather ask Dani? Or . . . Jade?"

I shook my head. "Nah. They're too close to the situation. And their opinions are already firmly anti-Bridget, so they don't have the ability to be objective."

"Ah," she said. "So we're talking about Bridget."

I ran a hand through my hair. "Right."

"Okay, I guess. What did you want to ask?"

"So, I'm breaking up with her tonight, and I just want to make sure I do it in a way that will cause the least amount of damage."

Rosie stilled. "Oh." She took a deep breath, visible even from across the elevator. "I, um . . . okay?" she said.

"So we're supposed to meet for dinner, right? But I don't want to pretend like everything is fine through an entire meal, and then break up with her at the end. But I also don't want to do it at the beginning of the meal, because then she'll get upset and leave, and she won't get to eat. I know I have to do one or the other, so which is worse? Or better, I guess. Which way would *you* rather be broken up with?"

She stood silent for a long moment, long enough that I started to feel awkward just standing there holding the elevator doors open.

"I don't have a ton of experience in this arena," she finally said, "but I don't think I'd like either of those options."

My shoulders dropped. I didn't want to hurt Bridget. And I'd already promised her dinner.

"Do you know her well enough to order for her? Like, from the restaurant?"

Bridget and I had eaten at Husk together a few times. I could probably guess at what she'd order. "Probably," I answered. "Why?"

"Order ahead of time, and get it to go," Rosie said. "Get there early, pick up her dinner, and then meet her in front of the restaurant. If the weather is nice, talk outside somewhere. Not inside, with tons of people watching. Especially since you're you, which means people will definitely be watching. Then when all is said and done, offer her the meal you picked up for her. She might not take it, but at least you tried."

It was good advice. The only thing Rosie had gotten wrong was that Bridget probably *would* rather have the break-up happen with people watching. She'd likely get a lot of mileage out of the sympathy it would generate if someone happened to record the entire thing.

I lifted my shoulders, suddenly feeling the weight of all the drama the break-up would cause. I'd have to address it with the fans at some point and deal with the fallout of people emailing and messaging and tweeting how they felt about it. There was some merit in what Dani had suggested—about keeping my next relationship off-screen. But that was so much easier said than done. So little of my life was actually private. "That's really good advice."

She shrugged. "I think it's good you're trying to be kind about it."

I nodded. "Yeah, I guess so. I mean, it's still going to suck."

"As break-ups usually do," she said. "At least you're on the better side of it this time."

I wasn't so sure. No matter who initiated the break-up, we would both have to wade through all the inevitable untangling of our lives, both on and off the show. But none of that was Rosie's fault. "You're a good friend, Rosie," I said. "Thanks for the advice."

She smiled, her lips pressed into a tight line. "Friends. Of course," she said.

I finally released the button holding the doors open and stepped into the annex outside the studio. "Hey, have you met Tyler yet?" I said before the elevator doors slid closed.

Rosie only stared.

"Next time we're all together, I'll introduce you," I said. "I think you might like him."

The doors closed on my words so I couldn't see how Rosie responded, but hopefully I'd played up the *friend* aspect enough that it wouldn't feel weird that I'd asked her such a personal question. Plus, maybe she really would like Tyler.

Tyler would definitely like her.

He'd be crazy not to.

Chapter Six

Rosie

You're a good friend, Rosie.

The stupid words repeated over and over in my head as I dropped off the boxers I'd finished adding to the website and made my way back up to my desk. *Friends.* And then he'd asked if I was interested in meeting Tyler.

It had totally killed the thrill I'd felt over learning he was breaking up with Bridget. As well as the thrill of actually making it through an entire conversation without saying anything stupid.

Actually, I still felt pretty proud of that. Even if he'd friend-zoned me before even giving me a chance. I pulled my phone out of my back pocket and texted Marley. *THE UNDERWEAR CONVERSATION ACTUALLY HAPPENED AND I WAS NOT AN IDIOT. You would be so proud.* I sent the message and dropped the phone on my desk before dropping myself into my chair.

"What's wrong with you?" Greta asked. "You look like someone stole your puppy."

"I'm a cat person," I said dejectedly.

"Okay," Greta said slowly. "You look like someone stole your kitten. What's wrong?"

I lowered my head onto my desk, my forehead pressed up against the cool glass. "I just ran into Isaac in the elevator."

Greta's eyebrows went up. "And it didn't . . . go well?"

"It went fine, at first," I said, sitting back up. I picked up my mouse and wiggled it a little too forcefully to wake up my screen. "You should have heard me, Greta. I did so great. I didn't flub up my words at all. We talked about sleeping in his boxers, and I was funny and witty. And then he told me he's breaking up with Bridget, and I gave him real, actual advice."

Greta frowned. "I'm going to pretend like the first half of what you just said made sense so we can talk about the break-up. He told you that? They're breaking up?"

I nodded. "Tonight. He asked me for advice on how to do it, and I gave it in whole complete sentences."

"I don't understand why this is bad news," she said. "They're breaking up. And you're talking to him. This is all good, right?"

She made a few clicks on her own computer, and an email immediately popped up in my inbox. "Those are the colors of the new logo," she said in her business voice. "We're supposed to adjust the rest of the site to complement. Can you take care of that this afternoon?"

I nodded and pulled up the log-in page that would allow me to access the site's code. "You don't understand," I said to Greta, jumping right back into our Isaac conversation. "He told me I was a good *friend.* And then he asked me if I was interested in meeting Tyler. He's the camera guy, right? The tall one?"

"Yes. And he's super nice. You might really like him," she said.

I scoffed. "Yeah. And since now it's obvious that I am only *friend* material in Isaac's eyes, that's probably what I ought to do. He put me firmly in the friend zone, Greta. And he wants to set me up with one of his friends. This is not good news."

She reached out and put a hand on my back. "Okay. It's not *great* news. But just because that's how Isaac is feeling now doesn't mean that's how he's always going to feel."

I rolled my eyes. "Why would his feelings change?" I looked down at myself. "*This* isn't going to change."

"You're doing it again," Greta said, shaking her head. "Not giving yourself enough credit. Just because you don't have Bridget's long legs or perfect boobs doesn't mean you don't have anything to offer. Stop selling yourself short."

"She does have perfect boobs, doesn't she?"

"Yes. But Isaac is still breaking up with her. Because he is not the kind of man who cares about stuff as shallow as that. That's why you care about him, right? Because he isn't like that?"

I wanted to believe her, but a doubt still niggled in the back of my mind, one I didn't even want to voice. Because I was just too afraid that if I said it out loud, I'd realize it was true.

"What?" Greta said. "What are you not saying out loud?"

"What if—" I said, cutting myself off. I forced a breath out through my nose. "What if he does care about stuff like that? Look at the women he's dated over the years, Greta. They all look like Bridget."

"He hasn't dated *that* many women."

"Enough to have established a pattern," I said.

"That's just it, though," Greta said. "None of those relationships have lasted. That has to be the most telling thing."

There was likely truth to Greta's words, but I couldn't bring myself to feel any optimism as I drove myself home at the end of the day. It had been almost a week since I'd sent Isaac my message, and even though Jade insisted he'd seen it, he still hadn't responded. What more could I do? I'd hit a dead-end digitally, and now, it appeared I'd hit a dead-end in person, too.

An hour later, I pulled on my fuzziest socks and crawled into my bed with a bag of Twizzlers, my laptop, and my cat, Reggie, who was excellent at distracting me from my own woes with his very important need to have his ears scratched in just the right way. The day had been somewhat of an emotional roller coaster, and bingeing an entire season of *Schitt's Creek* felt like the perfect way to recover.

I picked up my phone and scrolled through my notifications, making sure there wasn't anything important enough to distract me from the binge session I was eager to start.

And then I froze, my hand hovering over the screen as my heart leapt into my throat.

I had a new message on Instagram from *@RandomIOfficial.*

I dropped my phone onto my bed, too afraid to read the message, and nearly hit Reggie. He scrambled to the side and jumped off the bed with a disgruntled meow.

I stared at the phone, forcing air in through my nose and out through my mouth, just like my mother had always taught me. Social interactions had been crippling for me as a kid, so she'd armed me with as many coping mechanisms as she possibly could. "Whatever you're dealing with," she'd always said, "it's never going to be made better by not breathing."

Three deep breaths later, I was ready to reach for my phone. This wasn't a big deal. It was what I wanted. For Isaac to respond. To give me the chance to talk to him, to let him see the real me.

The message was longer than I expected.

Okay. You've got my attention. Your artwork is impressive—impressive enough that I'd love to buy a print to hang on my wall, if you do that sort of thing. But first, we need to have a serious conversation about Red Renegade's most underrated song. "Wings that Weep" is amazing, yes. And I'd give it the number two spot on the list of Renegade's "should have been loved more" tracks. But it isn't number one. I'll give you three guesses.

I scrambled onto my bed and pulled the covers over my legs, anticipation making me jittery. I had no idea how to respond. Or *when* I should respond. Were there rules to this sort of thing? Reasons I needed to wait a day or two to reply? Would it look too desperate to respond right away?

And only three guesses? That hardly seemed fair. Red Renegade had released nearly two dozen albums over the span of their career, including two different collections of their greatest hits. I opened the music app on my phone and scrolled through their track list, eliminating any of the songs that had made it onto either of their greatest hits albums. Obviously, none of those could be considered underrated. It took ten more minutes of searching before I'd narrowed down my choices to five songs that, in my mind, were both brilliant and under-appreciated.

I swiped back to Isaac's message, hardly believing he was on the other side of it. I gnawed on my lip wondering which song to guess first. I could make a compelling case for all five if I had to.

Okay. I'll play, I typed, willing my hands not to tremble. *But don't think that by doing so I'm rescinding my belief that "Wings that Weep" really IS number one.*

I sent the message then looked over my list of potential contenders.

Butterflies at Night, I typed.

Isaac's reply came through almost immediately. *Ohhh, good guess. But no.*

I huffed. Who made him the expert?

@Briarsandthorns: Red 87, I tried next. *And I might fight you over this one. The guitar solo alone is pretty much priceless.*

@RandomIOfficial: Hmm. I'd forgotten about the guitar solo. You're right. But I'm still not sure it can dethrone the song I have at the top of my list.

I grumbled, debating which of my three remaining songs I wanted to try. They were all amazing songs . . . but were they songs Isaac would think were amazing? A bolt of inspiration shot through me and I abandoned my list, instead opting to guess a song with a low, brooding melody and an extended piano part. It was the most melancholy of all of Red Renegade's work, its lyrics raw and revealing.

The song was about fame and how it ate away at the most important aspects of your life. I always felt sad when I heard it, but I'd never felt much emotional connection beyond that. I'd never been famous; in fact, I spent a good amount of effort every day making sure I didn't do *anything* that thrust me into any sort of limelight. But Isaac had been famous—at least in some respect—since he was sixteen years old. If there was any song that connected with him on a visceral level, it had to be this one.

The Truth About Lies, I guessed, hesitating just briefly before sending the message.

@RandomIOfficial: I have to be honest. I didn't expect you to figure it out.

The thrill of victory pulsed through me.

@Briarsandthorns: It's a good song. I wish I could see them perform it live.

@RandomIOfficial: I think they only performed it live once. At a show in the early nineties. I'm not sure they actually liked the song.

@Briarsandthorns: A little too close to home, maybe?

@RandomIOfficial: Maybe.

@Briarsandthorns: Is that why you like it? Cause it resonates for you?

Isaac didn't respond right away, and I immediately regretted the boldness of my message.

@Briarsandthorns: Sorry. I shouldn't have asked that. I'm a stranger and it isn't any of my business. It's possible I'm just still reeling over the fact that you actually responded.

I grabbed a Twizzler while I waited for Isaac's response, welcoming Reggie back onto the bed when he decided to like me again. I scratched under his chin. "It's only been three minutes, Reg, and I already might have blown it."

My phone buzzed and I jumped; Reggie shot me a look that clearly implied if I didn't settle down he was absolutely finished with our relationship.

@RandomIOfficial: Like I said, your art impressed me. And I don't mind you asking the question. It only took me by surprise because I've never really thought about why I like the song. But yeah. When I dig deeper, it does resonate in a personal way. Not that I'm complaining. I wouldn't trade what I've got.

@Briarsandthorns: But there are occasional downsides?

@RandomIOfficial: You get it.

@Briarsandthorns: No. I am the farthest thing from famous. But that's what the song says, right? The pinches of pain hiding in the praise.

@RandomIOfficial: Keep quoting lyrics to me, and we might be friends forever.

I dropped back onto my bed and pulled a pillow over my face, squealing into the pillowcase. This couldn't actually be happening. Reggie didn't flee this time, but he did dig his claws into my thighs, a final warning that he would not tolerate any more of my giddiness. It was good I had someone as sensible as Reggie to keep me in check.

Before responding to his message, I pulled up Marley's Instagram profile and sent her an all-caps message. This was definitely an all-caps kind of occasion. I briefly hesitated when Reggie, who clearly couldn't decide *how* he felt about me, nestled up against my chest, demanding attention. *HE ACTUALLY RESPONDED AND NOW HE IS FLIRTING WITH ME AND I AM DEAD SEND HELP IMMEDIATELY.*

"What do you want?" I said to Reggie, dropping my phone and scooping him up. "First you claw me and now you're demanding love? You think I love you enough to deal with this back and forth, huh?"

My phone buzzed with a message and I glanced at the screen, letting out an audible gasp. "Reggie! Look at what you made me do!" Somehow, in my fumbling right before sending the message, I had managed to *not* send my all caps message to Marley.

@RandomIOfficial: Um, did you mean to send that last message to me? I'm guessing not. Do you still need me to send help?

This. Was. Not. Happening. At least Isaac couldn't see the heat flaming my cheeks. At least there was that.

@Briarsandthorns: Um, no. That message was not meant for you. And now I'm REALLY dead. I'll just go now. Have a very nice life.

@RandomIOfficial: Haha. I don't think I can let you go yet. Not until I'm sure you really haven't died. I would hate to know I'd caused such a thing. Especially when I wasn't actually flirting.

@Briarsandthorns: THIS IS NOT HELPING WITH THE DEAD SITUATION.

It was fifteen minutes before Isaac responded again. Fifteen torturous, awful minutes in which I was positive I'd ruined everything. When another message from him finally popped up, I'd eaten more than half of my bag of Twizzlers.

@RandomIOfficial: Are you still there?

@Briarsandthorns: I'm sorry, what? I can hardly hear you through the fog of my own existential dread.

@RandomIOfficial: Did it freak you out? It's just a safety thing. Sorry if it was weird.

I stared at the message trying to make sense of what he'd just said. Sorry if what was weird?

A text message popped up from Jade and I pulled it up. My phone had gotten more action in the last ten minutes than it had in months. Or, you know, ever.

If he brings it up, you heard from me, Jade's message read, *I verified your age, and had you text me a picture of you, holding your driver's license. Also I emailed you a nondisclosure agreement, which you digitally signed.*

So that's what Isaac had been talking about. Was that really what Jade had to do when Isaac interacted with people? I mean, I understood.

For all Isaac knew, I could be twelve.

Or in prison.

Okay, maybe not in *prison* prison. I doubted Instagram was a thing in prison.

Another message from Jade popped up. *I actually will send you a nondisclosure agreement in a few minutes. Annoying, I know. It'll just say you won't post any of the messages he shares with you privately in any public places.*

An actual nondisclosure agreement? Things suddenly felt . . . real. And weird. But it made sense. Isaac had messaged me from the official *Random I* account. His image was his business. It made sense that he had people around to protect it.

Got it, I texted to Jade, double and triple-checking that the message was going to the right person.

Don't worry, she responded. *I didn't tell him who you are. Just that you're female, in your twenties, and you'd rather keep your name private.*

Is this standard protocol? I texted back, suddenly curious if she had files and files of driver's license photos of everyone who had ever interacted with Isaac.

Not standard protocol, Jade replied. *He's never actually done this before.*

I paused. He'd never responded to a direct message before? *Never done what, exactly? Never responded at all?*

No, he responds, Jade clarified. *But only briefly. He's never asked me to vet someone so he can KEEP responding. Way to grab his attention.* She followed her message with a winking emoji and a gif of Rosie the Riveter flexing her muscles.

I get it, I finally messaged to Isaac. *It wasn't weird. But you DID get a little flirty.*

@RandomIOfficial: All the more reason for me to make sure you aren't my grandmother's age.

@Briarsandthorns: Or in the seventh grade.

@RandomIOfficial: Nah. You knew too much about Red Renegade to be twelve. And your art reflects too much maturity. But I am relieved that you aren't a balding security guard in his fifties.

@Briarsandthorns: Haha. I guess I do have the advantage here. Since I know exactly who you are.

@RandomIOfficial: So let's level the playing field. Tell me who you are. Ana, right?

It wasn't technically a lie, was it? My name *was* Ana. I snuggled back into my covers, *Schitt's Creek* and even my Twizzlers completely forgotten. *All of who I am? That might take a while,* I messaged back.

@RandomIOfficial: I've got all night.

Chapter Seven

Isaac

I leaned back on the couch in my office and scrolled through the last few messages Ana and I had exchanged the night before. It had been a week since I'd first responded to her message, and we'd been texting back and forth almost nonstop.

Last night, we'd texted back and forth for almost an hour about the latest Peyton West novel. Coincidentally, it was the last book that we'd both read. And we loved it for all the same reasons. But it wasn't just taste in books and music that we shared. Everything Ana said, the way she viewed the world, the way she talked about her friends and what they meant to her, the way she talked about her parents . . . it all felt so in sync with how I felt. I liked her. *A lot.*

"Isaac." Alex's voice flitted into my brain sparking a sudden awareness that it wasn't the first time he'd called my name.

I sat up and turned. "Sorry, what? Did you need me?"

"Dude. You've been lying on your couch with a goofy grin on your face for half an hour. The entire warehouse is starting to wonder what's wrong with you."

I couldn't stop myself from smiling. "So I'm in a good mood. That's not a crime."

"Are you messaging *her* again?" Alex said, his expression taut. It was possible my brother-in-law didn't think communicating with a stranger on the internet was a good idea.

"Her name is Ana," I said defensively.

"It could be," Alex said. "But you can't know for certain, no matter what Jade says."

I rolled my eyes and stood, moving to my desk. "Why are you so cynical about this? Where would she have found someone willing to hold up their driver's license and pose for a picture in the ten minutes it took for her to respond to Jade? She is who she says she is. I'm sure of it."

Alex shook his head, his expression making it clear he was hardly convinced. "You can't be sure. Not unless you've met her in person."

"Okay. I'm mostly sure. Sure enough to keep getting to know her."

Alex sat on the edge of my desk, his posture rigid, his face stern. I got the distinct impression that he was infused with his own worry as my business manager, combined with *Dani's* worry as my sister. "Is she the reason you broke up with Bridget?"

I immediately shook my head. "Not at all. I got the first message from Ana before we broke up, but I didn't respond until after. And Bridget and I were destined to break up anyway. Ana didn't have anything to do with it."

Alex's shoulders dropped a tiny fraction. "That's what Dani said, too. That breaking up with Bridget was a good thing regardless of whether or not this new woman had anything to do with it."

I reached a hand out and squeezed Alex's shoulder. "I don't want you guys to worry about it. I've got a good feeling about Ana. And I promise I'm being careful."

"You think you're being careful," Alex said. "But if you're spending hours chatting with her every night, you're bound to tell her things. Things she could use against you if she felt compelled to do so."

"She could, but Jade had her sign a nondisclosure agreement. If she tried, we'd have reason to sue her. Not that she would," I said. "She isn't like that. I just need you to trust me on this one."

He shook his head, his arms crossed firmly across his chest. "Dani doesn't like it."

"That should be a feeling she's used to." I settled into my chair and turned on my computer. I didn't have anything specific to do, but if I looked busy, Alex might quit with the interrogation. "She didn't like Bridget, either."

"Your sister just wants what's best for you. And you can't say you have the greatest track record. You always date the same kind of women, and so far, none of them have been right for you."

I abandoned my email and swiveled to face Alex head-on. "You and Dani are always saying that, and I still have no idea what you mean. What kind of women do I date?"

Alex paused like he was giving the question serious consideration. "Beautiful ones who love the glow of your spotlight?"

That was it? That was the thing they were focusing on? "Why is that a bad thing?" I smirked. "I am *also* beautiful and love the spotlight."

"Maybe *that's* the problem," Alex said. "You're dating women too much like yourself."

I tried not to let his observation sink too deep, not wanting to consider what his observation said about me. Bridget had definitely loved the glow of the spotlight. Is that why I'd broken up with her? Because she was stealing some of it from me? I pushed the thought away, immediately recognizing it as false. I hadn't minded that Bridget liked the spotlight. I just hadn't liked how much she'd wanted me to change, to conform to what she thought our relationship should look like.

"So what's Ana like?" Alex asked. "Is she like Bridget? How does she feel about your celebrity status?"

"Actually, I think she likes me despite my celebrity. She's not like Bridget at all."

He ran a hand over his jaw. "I'm willing to concede that it's *possible* she's a real person and she might be good for you. But I still want you to be careful. Letting someone in that you don't know, telling them things, personal things, it isn't safe."

That sounded like something my very professional business manager would say. "I hear you. And I heard you when you said the same thing five minutes ago. I promise I'm being careful."

He nodded. "Fine. Just keep me in the loop, all right? If she ever says anything suspicious—

"Alex," I said, cutting him off. "I got it."

He sighed and nodded.

"How's Dani feeling, by the way?"

Alex frowned. "Horrible. She pretty much throws up every morning like clockwork. It's painful to watch, but she says she doesn't mind it because it makes her feel better enough to eat. Otherwise, she just feels nauseous all the time."

I liked to think of myself as a pretty chill guy. But the thought of becoming an uncle when Dani and Alex's baby was born ignited a level of excitement inside me that I'd never experienced before. I already had a stack of toys that I'd collected back at the house and Dani wasn't even three months into her pregnancy yet. At least *that* part of my life wasn't up for public consumption. Dani's rules. No public discussion of my soon-to-be niece or nephew until Dani was past the six-month mark in her pregnancy. It was killing me not to talk about it, but I'd only recently rebuilt my relationship with my twin sister; I wasn't about to screw it up.

"That sucks, man," I said. "Will it last the whole time?"

He shrugged. "Her doctor says it might, but for most, it eases up in the third or fourth month."

Steven knocked on my office door briefly before sticking his head inside. "Drake Martinson is *in* the studio," he said. "You ready to get started?"

I nodded, willing my face to remain impassive. "Give me ten minutes. I'll be right there." I looked back at Alex. "Anything else you need from me?"

He looked down at his phone, scrolling through the notes app he lived and died by. I couldn't fault him for it. He brought a measure of organization to my life I'd never managed to maintain on my own.

He finally shook his head. "I don't think so. You'll get your travel plans for this weekend's on-location shoots—Vinnie, Steven, and Mushroom are going with you—so make sure you approve those, but otherwise, I think you're good."

I nodded. "Cool. Hey, tell Dani I'm going to bring you guys dinner tonight. Whatever she's in the mood for, I'll pick it up."

Alex nodded. "I'm sure she'd love that. But don't ask what she's in the mood for until right before you pick it up. If you ask now, it'll likely change before tonight."

"Noted. Just tell her I'll text her when I leave the studio."

Alex headed for my office door but then turned around, shooting me a very serious look. "Isaac, please be nice to Drake. You might not think this will help, and you might be right about that. But it *will* hurt you if you're rude. And we can't afford for anything to hurt you right now."

I suppressed a sigh and nodded my head. "Noted. Thanks for the reminder."

Alex pushed through the glass door and headed to his desk, visible just outside of my office, where he would do all the things that kept my business running smoothly. I still wondered how something I'd randomly started ten years ago in my parents' basement had turned into a content-creating machine that reached ten million viewers on a daily basis. Or, it *had* reached ten million viewers on a daily basis. Before our numbers had started to slip.

Before heading downstairs, I pulled out my phone and messaged Ana.

@RandomIOfficial: True story. I'm interviewing Drake Martinson in fifteen minutes.

@Briarsandthorns: Drake Martinson. Is he the Robinhood guy? From the movie? Have you ever interviewed celebrities before?

I swallowed my irritation, remembering Alex's warning that sharing stuff with an internet stranger wasn't a good idea. Ana wasn't a stranger, odd as that sounded, but maybe in this one part of my life, a little caution was justified.

@RandomIOfficial: Not usually. But he's originally from Charleston, so we managed to book him for an interview while he was in town to visit his family.

And I was happy about that. Maybe if I kept telling myself as much, it would start to feel true. *My publicist is a genie,* I added to my message.

@Briarsandthorns: Would it make you feel less proud if I told you I hated the movie? (Because I hated the movie.) I won't tell you if it will make your interview harder.

@RandomIOfficial: Haha. I didn't love it either. The cinematography was awesome. And the story was fine. But . . .

@Briarsandthorns: Don't leave me hanging here, Isaac. I'm curious to see if our complaints are the same.

I glanced at the time on my phone. I probably didn't have time to answer. But I decided to answer anyway.

@RandomIOfficial: Okay. I guess I just feel like for having such a strong female cast, none of the female characters got to do anything significant. They just sat around and waited for the men to save them. It felt like a waste of talent. And a waste of good storytelling opportunities. When Jesslyn was right there and could have saved her little brother herself, why did she have to wait

for Henry to come and do the saving? There was a freaking sword hanging on the wall. And she'd been training with her brother in the countryside for a decade. She could have handled that sword.

@Briarsandthorns: I am both stirred and compelled by your feminism. I had the exact same thoughts about Jessyln's character. Why was she even there but to look pretty and swoon into Henry's arms?

@RandomIOfficial: I have never understood why swooning is a thing. Can that even really happen when it isn't fake?

@Briarsandthorns: In today's modern world? It shouldn't. We wear modern underwear that allows us to breathe. But back then, with corsets and what not? I think swooning was totally real.

@RandomIOfficial: What are you doing right now?

@Briarsandthorns: Um, pretending to work? Hoping my boss doesn't notice that I'm actually sending messages on Instagram?

@RandomIOfficial: Whenever I imagine web designers, you're all working in dark basements with dim lighting, staring at screens that are flashing with green code.

@Briarsandthorns: Um, is that what it's like for YOUR web designers? We have moved past the days of War Games, you know.

@RandomIOfficial: I have so much love for the fact that you just referenced that movie. And you're right. My web designers work in a regular office just like the rest of us. They even get real, modern computers.

@Briarsandthorns: You're so good to them.

@Briarsandthorns: You should go do your interview. Your fifteen minutes are officially up.

@RandomIOfficial: Yes. Yes they are. But I think I'd rather chat with you.

@Briarsandthorns: Than interview a movie star? I'm flattered.

@RandomIOfficial: You should be. I'm holding up the entire afternoon because I'd rather be here with you.

When a response didn't immediately come through, I typed out another message.

@RandomIOfficial: Did I just scare you away? Because I was thinking about asking you if we could talk on the phone sometime, but if it's too soon, I won't ask.

This time, her response popped up almost immediately.

@Briarsandthorns: You didn't scare me away before. But I'm not gonna lie. That last message is a tiny bit intimidating.

@RandomIOfficial: Why? Talking isn't all that different from texting.

@Briarsandthorns: It's entirely different from texting. You can't delete things you say . . .

@RandomIOfficial: Very true.

My phone buzzed with an incoming call from Steven. I rejected the call even as I walked toward my office door. I shot Steven a quick text letting him know I was on my way.

@RandomIOfficial: Just think about it. No pressure.

Ana had told me she had her reasons for keeping a low profile, and so far, I hadn't pushed her. Just because my life was an open book didn't mean that other people had to live the same way. Plus, there was something a little magical about getting to know someone through nothing but text. I didn't know her voice or what she looked like. And yet, I felt a connection anyway. It was strange. And humbling, in a way. I'd dated a lot over the years. An upside to relative fame and plenty of money. But that ease often made it hard to find anyone whom I felt really connected to. It was hard not to wonder about people's motives, about whether or not they were actually interested in me, or just interested in the notoriety of dating me. But Ana wasn't like that. She didn't even want *me* to know who she was. She for sure wasn't interested in the world knowing we were talking.

I looked back over our last few messages, wondering how to persuade her to give me just a little more.

@RandomIOfficial: The thing is, I like you. Which means I've started

talking about you with my family and closest friends. They already think I'm crazy for wanting to be friends with someone I met on the internet. If we talked . . . it might make them worry a little less.

@Briarsandthorns: You like me?

@RandomIOfficial: Enough to make a movie star wait for his interview.

@Briarsandthorns: I promise I'll think about a phone call. Now go! Tell Drake I said hi.

@Briarsandthorns: Also, I like you, too. I don't have Drake Martinson waiting on me, but if I did, I'd probably stand him up altogether if it meant more time to chat with you.

One more message popped up before I closed out my phone and crossed the warehouse to the elevator.

No words, just a single red heart.

I smiled all the way to the studio.

Chapter Eight

Rosie

I dropped my phone into my purse and scooted closer to my screen just as Isaac left his office and headed toward the elevator that would take him downstairs to the studio. It had been all I could do not to keep glancing at his office while we were messaging back and forth. The few times I did sneak a peek, he'd been smiling. Staring at his phone and *genuinely* smiling.

"You know, you do actually have work responsibilities around this place," Greta said, eyeing me from her desk.

I grimaced. "Sorry. He just told me he likes me. And asked if we can talk on the phone some time."

Greta's eyebrows rose. "What did you tell him?"

"I . . . deflected. I mean, obviously we can't actually talk. There's no way I could disguise my voice enough for him not to recognize me."

Greta shook her head. "Are you not worried that he's going to make the connection anyway? You're a web designer, Ana is a web designer. You both like Red Renegade . . ."

I grimaced. "Actually, he doesn't know I like Red Renegade. That's Ana's thing. A small concession I've had to make, because man, my wardrobe is limited when I knock my *Renegade* shirts out of the rotation."

"One of these days, you're going to slip up, Rosie. And I'm going to say I told you so."

I waved a hand dismissively, even though I'd nearly worked myself into a panic attack more than once over that very issue. "I will not. He thinks Ana lives in Kansas. There's nothing that would make him connect her to me."

"Except that you're *also* from Kansas."

I rolled my eyes. "It's a big state. And believe it or not, hundreds of female web designers live there. I'm not worried about it."

(I was totally worried about it.)

I pulled up the afternoon's to-do list and read through the items, looking for the one that would be the easiest to tackle. Progress in and of itself was motivating. Better to check off two or three small things and let that push me to the harder tasks rather than start with the hardest thing and have it take all day. I was a girl who liked checked-off check boxes. I'd even been known to write something onto my list *after* I'd already finished it just so I could check it off and feel like I'd accomplished something.

"Hey, will you be there for pizza tomorrow night?" Greta asked, her eyes trained on her screen.

"I'm planning on it. We're trying Garfield's, right? The new place over at the end of King Street?"

"That's the plan. I've heard it's really good."

"Did Diedre ask you to bring anything? I offered, but she said I could just show up."

"You know Diedre. She loves to play hostess and mother us all. She'll never let you bring anything."

"Hey, didn't we already fix the Check Out button on the shopping cart page?" I asked. That item had been on our to-do list yesterday, too. "Is it not working again?"

"It's not, but it isn't something we can fix. It's something on the money side. I called the e-commerce people this morning, but apparently, it's a problem that's affecting multiple sites, and I haven't heard anything back yet. Actually, I was just going to head down to the studio to see if Alex can use his magical Southern charm powers of persuasion to get a faster answer for us. You want to go instead?"

I stared at her like she'd just asked me to kiss a hedgehog. "Why would I ever want to do a thing like that?"

She rolled her eyes. "Alex doesn't bite. Besides, he's downstairs right now. In the studio. Where Isaac is."

"Yeah. That's exactly my point."

"Come on. What is your actual plan here, Rosie? Are you just going to hide on Instagram forever and never tell Isaac who you really are?"

"It's been a week," I said emphatically. "That's hardly forever. And Alex may not bite, but he is still very scary and professional." I wasn't actually scared of Alex. But being in the same room with Isaac was hard enough with a wall of glass between us. I felt connected to him through the conversations we'd been having over the past week, enough that it felt perfectly natural to glance his way, to catch his eye and smile, as if he'd know, just by looking at me, that I was thinking of a joke he'd shared with me earlier or remembering the story he'd told me about him and Dani getting trapped in the attic when they were kids.

But Isaac had zero reason to feel connected to me. All I would accomplish by staring was freaking him out and making him think Alex had hired a nutso to work on his web design team.

Greta paused. "Okay. Alex is a little scary. But this is an important question. If he knows we haven't made any sales today because e-commerce is down, he will want it fixed. And he will know all the right people to call to make sure fixing *our* site is at the top of the priority list."

"Ugh. Fine. You're sure Alex is downstairs?" I looked toward his desk. He'd been there a few minutes before when Isaac and I had still been chatting.

"Positive. Drake Martinson is too important for him not to hover and make sure everything goes smoothly with his guest appearance."

I stood and pushed in my chair, mostly terrified but a tiny bit thrilled now that the option of avoiding the encounter had been taken away. I didn't often have reason to be in the studio, and the magic of how everything pulled together still fascinated me.

I took the stairs down to the second floor and stepped into the annex outside the studio. The light above the door was still green, so I pushed my way inside, at least unconcerned that I would be interrupting an actual shoot. They were close to shooting though, Drake Martinson already seated on a stool next to Isaac while one of the techs adjusted his mic. Safe in the dimness that surrounded the brightly lit stage, I let my eyes linger on Isaac a beat longer than I ever did upstairs and, by default, on the movie star sitting beside him. Drake Martinson was arguably one of America's hottest up-and-coming actors; I wouldn't deny that he had all the marks of a classically attractive movie star. But in my eyes, he still paled in comparison to Isaac. Isaac was good-looking in his own right, but more than that, he had this light about him. He saw people. Made them feel comfortable and accepted and happy. And that happiness seemed to constantly radiate from him. One of the segments of his show that had stuck around the longest was his daily kindness challenge. Every day, he challenged his viewers to spread kindness in a new way. Paying specific compliments. Buying someone's coffee. Returning someone's shopping cart. It was never big stuff—he wanted the challenges to be accessible to everyone and not just people who had extra cash to burn—and it was a strategy that had paid off. The challenges had developed their own cult following, with people filming their experiences and sharing them online on a daily basis.

With others, I might wonder if it was all manufactured for appearances, but I didn't doubt Isaac's sincerity for a minute. In person, it was easy to see in his eyes how much he liked bringing joy to other people, and how vulnerable he was willing to be to make that happen.

I thought again of how readily he'd told me how he felt in our earlier messages. *I like you,* he'd said. Just like that. He'd owned his feelings without hesitation.

He'd inspired that same boldness in me, which was no small thing. Usually, just the thought of being that forthright had the potential to break me out in hives.

"Are you a Drake Martinson fan?" a voice whispered beside me.

I looked up to see Alex standing beside me, his arms crossed across his ample chest.

"Oh, um, actually, I was looking for you," I said, doing my best to squelch a sudden irrational fear that Alex had seen me staring at Isaac and immediately figured everything out.

"Everything okay?" Alex asked.

I paled. Was my discomfort so obvious? "I'm good. Thanks for asking."

Alex leaned forward, an expectant look on his face. "Okay. But . . . you said you were looking for me?"

Right. That's why he asked if everything was okay. He hadn't noticed me staring at Isaac; he was asking about *work.* "Oh. Right. That. Something's up with e-commerce. We've checked everything on our end, but it looks like the problem is something CyberWorks needs to fix."

"Quiet on set," a voice called out.

Alex motioned me toward the studio door.

My gaze darted back to Isaac's smiling face for a brief second before I turned and followed Alex into the annex between the elevator and the second-floor studio.

"Have we called CyberWorks about this?"

"Greta did this morning," I said. "But she hasn't heard anything back, nothing except that it's a problem that has affected multiple sites. They didn't give us any indication of when it might be up and running again. Greta was hoping you might be able to call over and do the Southern charm magic thing you do to make things happen. Those were her words. Not mine."

Alex grinned. It suddenly occurred to me that if something happened between Isaac and me, I would get to know this man on a much more personal level. We'd be friends, even. Go on double dates. The thought brought a flush to my cheeks that I only hoped Alex hadn't noticed. I was thinking way too far ahead. Like dial-it-back-creepy-stalker level ahead.

"I'll see what I can do," Alex said.

I breathed out a sigh of relief. "Perfect. Thanks."

He moved toward the elevator, his cell phone already in his hand, but he paused, looking my way and motioning toward the studio door. "Have you ever seen them tape an entire show?"

I shook my head.

"You should go watch. It's fun to see it happening live. I'll let Greta know you'll be back up in a bit."

Never one to argue with my superiors, I crept back toward the studio, hesitating as I looked up at the light, now red, that hung above the door.

"Just sneak in quietly," Alex said from behind me. "If you make any noise, they'll be able to edit it out."

I offered him a quick nod over my shoulder—he really wasn't so scary—and snuck back into the studio.

The show was in full swing, Isaac and Steven, his occasional in-studio co-host, tech news specialist, and frequent field correspondent, sat on either side of Drake at a long countertop where all three worked to assemble three-dimensional puzzles of a building I couldn't quite identify.

A timer running off to the side indicated it was supposed to be a race, but none of them seemed very determined to beat the others. They joked and laughed as they built, none of them making very good progress. When the timer dinged, they all lifted their hands from their models, Isaac with a particularly dramatic flourish.

Isaac's brand of entertainment definitely wasn't for everybody. His channel deserved the name *Random I*; individually, the show was filled with things that a lot of people might consider pointless. But there wasn't a randomness to Isaac's purpose. He loved to make people happy. And he was good at it.

After the puzzle building, they transitioned to a trivia game with questions that covered everything from Drake's latest movie to his childhood growing up in Charleston. His fans would love it, and Isaac was being charming enough, he'd likely gain a few hundred thousand new subscribers because of it. Maybe more.

Sensing that the filming was coming to a close, I pulled out my phone and snapped a quick photo of the set, making sure it included a clear shot of Drake Martinson's profile. Marley would never forgive me if I managed to get this close to one of her favorite actors and didn't do anything to document the moment. With photo—and phone—securely in hand, I moved back to the studio door, only stopping when I heard Isaac say my name.

Well, sort of my name.

"My friend Ana and I were talking about your movie this morning," he said to Drake. "She says hi, by the way, and we decided we only have one complaint about how things went down in the final few scenes."

He'd said my name. On air. He'd called me his friend. Not a fan. Not a follower. But a friend.

Only Isaac could manage to joke his way through explaining to Drake, without insult, why it would have been more satisfying to see Jesslyn wielding a sword to save her brother herself rather than swooning into Henry's arms. Especially since Drake had played Henry. Isaac's wordsmithing was impressive, but I could hardly appreciate it for how distracted I was by the thrill of hearing my name from his lips. Our messages were completely secret and totally private, assuming Jade wasn't reading them—I should ask Isaac about that—and I liked it that way. At least for now. It was almost as if the Isaac that existed inside my phone was a totally different person—an Isaac in some parallel universe. But this, hearing Isaac in the flesh speak of me, reference me by name, was a worlds-colliding kind of moment, and it completely stole my breath away.

Back upstairs, I dropped into my desk chair with a dramatic sigh.

"How did it go?" Greta asked. "Alex told me you were watching the taping."

I leaned my head back into my seat. "I got it so bad, Greta."

She smiled, sympathy evident in her eyes. "I know, sweetie. When are you going to *tell* him?"

I pulled my glasses off and dropped them onto my desk, cursing the mascara that kept me from rubbing the heels of my hands into my eye sockets. A week ago, I'd been absolutely certain that I would never know Isaac personally—that our relationship would always remain strictly professional. My daydreams obviously included more elaborate interactions, but I was a realist. I didn't actually expect them to ever happen.

But then, that wasn't exactly true. I hadn't moved all the way from Kansas City just so I could chill with my cat and admire Isaac from afar. Which is exactly why Bridget and her sacrilegious use of Isaac's Red Renegade t-shirt had compelled me to action. Because fears aside, I really *did* want Isaac to know me.

So what was I so afraid of?

It was easy enough to realize, even if I didn't want to admit the truth out loud.

I liked me well enough. I was happy in my not particularly toned but still functional body. I liked my quirky, dialed-down fashion sense and felt confident of my value, even when I spent Friday nights in fuzzy socks, snuggling with my cat.

I didn't *need* Isaac's approval.

But I still recognized that attraction couldn't be forced. And there was no guarantee that Isaac wouldn't take one look at me in person and decide I wasn't what he was looking for after all. He'd been so quick to put me in the friend zone. Why would he feel any differently if he found out Ana was actually me?

Still, the longer our online relationship went on, the harder it would be to tell him the truth. Because at some point, it would start to feel like I was being dishonest. Like I was intentionally keeping secrets from him.

Alex stopped in front of Greta's desk, handing her a sticky note. "This is the guy at CyberWorks that you need to call. They've figured out the problem. It's just a matter of implementing the fix. If you call him and tell him Harrison gave you his number, he'll get us up and running within the half-hour."

"Perfect," Greta said. "Thank you."

"Sure thing," Alex said. He looked my way. "Did you enjoy the show?"

I nodded. "You were right. It is fun seeing it live."

"The energy's a little different, right?"

"Isaac definitely knows how to light up a room," I said. "It's even more obvious in person."

Alex narrowed his eyes in a way that made me wonder if I'd said too much. "Yeah. That's a good way of saying it."

He tapped his knuckles on Greta's desk. "You let me know if this doesn't get things fixed and I'll call Harrison back."

She nodded. "You got it."

She shot me some side-eye as soon as Alex was out of earshot. "Try to get the stars out of your eyes before you talk about Isaac with any of his family members again, k?"

My hands flew to my cheeks. "Was I really that bad?"

Greta smirked. "I'm not going to lie to you. But it's possible Alex only saw you as an adoring fan instead of someone who's actually in love."

She picked up her phone and dialed the number scrawled across the sticky note Alex had handed her. While she waited for the call to pick up, she nudged my chair with her foot and motioned to my to-do list still pulled up on my screen. She covered the mouthpiece of her phone and widened her eyes. "I'm pretty sure you've done exactly nothing off that list today. Get busy. And as long as I'm giving orders, tell him, Rosie. You know it's inevitable. Just do it now and save yourself some drama."

I did know it.

That didn't mean I wanted to admit it.

It definitely didn't mean I had to like it.

Chapter Nine

Rosie

I lay on the floor in the middle of Jade and Diedre's living room while Max rolled matchbox cars up and down my arms and legs.

"This one is the fastest," Max said matter-of-factly. "Because it's blue. And blue cars are always the fastest."

"They are? I didn't know that."

"Yep. Followed by red cars and then black cars. Yellow cars are the slowest. Mama says when I'm old I can drive a blue car. But Mimi says my car has to be yellow."

I stifled my laughter, recognizing the parenting styles for Max's moms immediately. Jade was Mimi and Diedre was Mama. They hadn't really decided that's how it would be—Max hadn't been talking yet when they'd gotten married—it's just the way things had evolved, and they'd stuck with it. Jade was definitely the more cautious of the two—more inclined to hovering and covering with band-aids. Diedre, on the other hand, was pretty chill. She was warm and nurturing, but not super worried about climbing trees or skinned elbows. "You're a kid, Max," I'd heard her say more than once. "Getting scuffed up is part of life."

For my part, I was content to be the fun friend who never had to worry about making parenting decisions. At least not for the time being. If I could guarantee I'd get a kid like Max, I'd consider having children sooner rather than later. It had only taken about five minutes the first time we hung out for him to become one of my favorite tiny humans, second only to Shiloh. I loved that Max talked like a grown-up—with big words and long sentences, all with his tiny boy voice. Cutest thing ever. An image of Isaac flashed through my mind, and I wondered what his kids would look like. Whether or not they would have his dark wavy hair or be blond like his sister. Would they have his blue eyes?

"Knock, knock!" a voice called from the entryway.

I sat up, suddenly hyperaware that I had *just* been thinking about what Isaac's very not real hypothetical children might look like. And now he was here. Walking into the kitchen. A blush crept up my cheeks, and my heart started pounding. My friends usually warned me when Isaac was going to be around as well.

"Rosie, your face is red," Max whispered, his face only inches from mine.

My hands flew to my cheeks. "That's weird," I said, trying to play it off. "Hey, do you have any more cars in your room? Want to go see?"

Max lit up like a Christmas tree. "Yeah! Come on. I can also show you my dinosaurs."

I followed Max down the hall to his room, not even caring if I missed the pizza. I couldn't hang out with Isaac. We'd been messaging for nearly three weeks now. And save Isaac's growing persistence in trying to schedule a phone call—I was running out of reasons to refuse him—things had been going *great.* Amazing, even. Isaac was flirty and engaged and interested. But hanging out with him in person was a whole different mess. Because I had to treat him like a stranger. And he definitely didn't feel like one. Maybe allowing my anxiety to reign would work to my advantage in this regard. As long as I was an anxious, sweaty mess, I wouldn't want to get anywhere near him in person.

Ten minutes into my epic dinosaur battle with Max, Isaac appeared in his bedroom doorway. So much for not getting near him.

Max jumped up, his triceratops forgotten, and ran to greet him. "Isaac!"

"Hey, little man. Who's winning the battle?"

"The Spinosaurus, of course," Max said. "He's on a team with the Triceratops. Rosie's Tyrannosaurus just got beated bad."

I glanced up to see Isaac looking at me. "Hi, Rosie," he said, his deep voice washing over me like gentle waves on a quiet beach.

"She fought her hardest," I said, holding up the T-rex. "But in the end, the Spinosaurus outsmarted us all."

Isaac grinned. "I've always heard those Spinosauruses were wily."

"You want to play, too?" Max asked. "You can be on Rosie's team."

Oh, please no. Or maybe *oh please, yes?* I'd never been so conflicted over a dinosaur battle.

"Actually, I just came up to tell you guys the pizza is here. Want me to eat your piece? Or . . .?"

"Pizza!" Max yelled, launching himself from the room like a tiny rocket. His footsteps were pounding down the stairs before I'd even put down my dinosaurs.

Isaac crossed the room and crouched beside me, scooping the dinosaurs into the plastic bin where they lived. "He's a fun kid, right?" He stood and offered me a hand.

I only hesitated a second before sliding my hand into his, willing myself not to react to the solid warmth of his touch. This was casual, easy, a hand he would have offered to anyone. And yet, my body did *not* react like it was a casual touch.

I held his hand a moment longer after I stood, long enough to look directly into his eyes and say, "Yeah, he is." My voice was breathy and soft and not at all like it should have been while talking about Max. I dropped Isaac's hand and took a giant step backward. "I mean, Max. Max is fun. Super fun. The best fun." *Stop. Talking. Rosie.*

Isaac's expression morphed into one of confusion. "Yeah." He looked toward the door. "Um, you want to eat?"

"Yeah," I managed to squeak. I hurried past him and out the door, only hoping the fire in my face would cool before we were downstairs and facing everyone else. I made a detour through the living room, mumbling something about grabbing my water bottle, in hopes that Isaac would take the more direct route to the kitchen and give me a tiny reprieve.

Isaac did just that, and I collapsed onto the sofa, lowering my head to my knees and taking slow, deep breaths. I was fine. Things were fine. I just needed to eat, say as little as possible, and then escape before I could do anything else to embarrass myself.

Jade stuck her head into the living room. "Hey, there you are. You okay?"

I grimaced. "Oh, sure. Fine. Great. So, so great."

She sank onto the sofa beside me. "I swear I would have warned you had I known he was going to be here," she said. "It was Diedre. They were texting about something else, and the pizza came up and it just sort of happened. She didn't even think about how it might make you uncomfortable."

I shook my head. "It's fine. You guys are friends. And you've been friends with him a lot longer than you have with me. I can't expect you to choose between me and Isaac. That would be ridiculous."

Jade eyed me warily. "You know, you could just tell him. Then this wouldn't be a big deal. We could just all hang out together."

I sighed. "If you had heard me five minutes ago, you wouldn't have made that suggestion. I can't do it, Jade. I'm literally the most ridiculous person on the planet whenever I'm within five feet of him." I could almost hear Marley's voice in my head, reminding me that if I would just visualize, channel my inner actress, I'd be fine. But that took a measure of mindfulness I couldn't always claim. Sometimes, Isaac caught me off guard. What was I supposed to do then?

"But it won't always be that way. If you just talk to him, remember how he makes you feel when you're texting, you'll eventually relax. What did your therapist always tell you about making situations that cause you anxiety *less* anxious?"

First Marley, now Jade? I shot her a look and she rolled her eyes. "It's not my first time around the mental health block, sweetheart. Answer the question."

I huffed. "She said I had to confront the situation instead of hide from it."

"Right. If going to the store freaks you out? You gotta go to the store enough times to *stop* freaking out. Normalize it. Visualize yourself having normal conversations. That's all you gotta do here."

"Except, the grocery store can't decide that I'm ridiculous and never let me come back. Isaac totally can."

"He's not that kind of guy, Rosie. And you know it."

He wasn't the kind of guy who would decide he didn't want to be my *friend.* But he could absolutely decide he didn't want to be *more* than friends.

"Come on. Come eat. Isaac is already sitting with Max. He'll talk his ear off long enough for you to fix a plate and find a corner to hide in."

We walked into the kitchen side by side, and Greta immediately looked up, her eyes filled with an unvoiced apology.

I smiled and gave my head a slight shake. My friends were good to me. A little pushy, but good to me.

After dinner, I took baby Nora and the bottle Diedre had prepared for her and settled into the rocking chair in the corner of the living room while Diedre and Jade put Max to bed. Greta settled in across from me.

"Are you hiding behind a baby?"

I nuzzled Nora's fuzzy head. "Possibly. But can you blame me? She is the sweetest."

"You look good with a baby in your arms."

"Yeah? I like kids, though I haven't spent much time with one this tiny. Not since I was in high school."

"Your cousin, right? She had a baby while you were in high school?"

I nodded. "And she lived with us, so I got lots of baby Shiloh time."

"Do you want kids someday?" Greta asked.

My earlier Isaac-themed daydreams flitted through my mind. I willed myself not to blush. Greta was asking a *general* question. Not a specific question. She had not asked: *Do you want to have Isaac's kids someday?*

"I for sure do," I said. "Two or three, maybe? I was an only child for most of my life, until Marley moved in with us, but I always wished I'd had siblings."

"I was the oldest of five," Greta said. "If I have any, it'll only be one or two. My house was an absolute circus growing up."

"What are we talking about?" Isaac asked, leaning over the back of the couch.

"Kids," Greta said. "Do you think you'll have any?"

"I hope so," Isaac said. "I think being a dad sounds like fun."

It was a very Isaac answer. He would be one to recognize the fun parts without necessarily worrying about all the hard that came along with it. Not that he couldn't handle the hard. It just wouldn't be the part he focused on. At least, that's the impression I'd gotten from years of watching his videos and weeks of exchanging secret messages with him. Which obviously made me a very reliable expert.

"Hey, just a heads up. I'm going live in the next ten minutes, so if you don't want to be a part of it, you better find a place to hide."

Greta groaned. "Seriously? Right now? What on earth could you possibly need to say to people right now?"

"It's the name of the game," he said dismissively. "I speak when inspiration strikes. It isn't always convenient, but it's paying your salary, so . . ."

"Fine," Greta said. "But I'm still going to whine about it. I hate it when you invite ten million friends to dinner." She glanced at me. "You better take the baby back to the bedroom. Diedre and Jade won't let the kids be in any of the videos."

"Oh. Okay. Got it."

"I do need someone to be in it with me, though," Isaac said. "Rosie? You game? I just got Drake Martinson's answers back from the viewer-submitted questions that came in after the show. I need someone to read the questions so I can respond with the answers he sent over."

I paused at the hallway that led back to the bedrooms, Nora resting against my shoulder. "Me? I . . . I don't think so." I'd never actually considered the possibility of putting myself on camera with Isaac. But it stood to reason that if I struggled to keep my cool when it was only *him* in the room, I for sure shouldn't be trusted with ten million viewers watching.

"Are you sure?" Isaac said. "You don't even have to say anything on your own. You just read the questions right off the email. It's pretty simple."

The look in his eyes made me want to say yes. I could channel my inner actress and read questions off a card. And even though I claimed I wanted to avoid face time with Isaac, the reality was, he was pretty hard to resist. But it wouldn't just be face time with Isaac. It would be face time with Isaac . . . and millions of his fans. "I don't think so," I said. "You want me to send Jade down?"

Something that almost looked like disappointment flitted across Isaac's expression, but it was gone so fast, I wondered if I'd imagined it. A tiny spark buried deep in my heart flamed to life. It wasn't much, but it was something. And I was desperate enough to cling to anything.

"Sure," Isaac said. "Jade will probably do it. Or Vinnie, if she isn't up for it."

I turned down the hallway but paused after only a few steps when Isaac called my name again. "Hey, Rosie, what about acting as camerawoman? Total behind the scenes work."

I nodded. "Okay. I can handle behind the scenes."

He smiled. "Great."

Greta raised an eyebrow as we turned into Nora's room. "Sounds like someone wants to spend a little time with Rosie."

I rolled my eyes. "He's just being nice."

She hmphed. "Maybe. Or maybe he likes you."

"He does not like me. He likes Ana."

She shot me a dry look. "Oh. Right. That's entirely different."

I lowered a sleeping Nora into her bed and set the empty bottle on the dresser beside the crib. "Does he do this a lot?" I asked, my voice low so as not to wake the baby. "Random live streams when you guys are all hanging out."

Greta rolled her eyes. "All the time, though less so now that baby Nora is here. We don't hang out as much as we used to because so much revolves around the baby. It's the nature of his business, though. It's important he stay connected to his fans."

"But on a Friday night? Do people really care that much?"

She huffed a laugh. "Someone *always* cares. And he probably wants to do the question/answer follow-up tonight since the Drake Martinson episode just aired today. I swear his typical viewer has an attention span of about fourteen seconds. If he doesn't strike now, interest will wane, and the video won't get as many views."

I shook my head. "I cannot imagine having to think about all of those things all the time."

Greta shrugged. "Isaac could probably think about it less. But he didn't build *Random I* into what it is today by doing things halfway."

I couldn't stop thinking about Greta's words for the rest of the night. While holding Isaac's phone as I filmed his live stream, marveling at his easy on-air demeanor. While I hugged all my friends goodbye and drove the short distance to my tiny house in Park Circle.

I'd never really spent much time imagining what *Random I* looked like from the inside—to his friends, his family members, the people who were around it every day, constantly accommodating Isaac's filming. I'd been pining after Isaac for a long time. But somehow, the impossibility of our relationship had always kept me from imagining what it would be like to actually date someone who lived his life in the public eye. I loved the limelight about as well as I loved the thought of getting a Pap smear. I didn't want people—especially the nameless people on the internet—to care about me at all.

Of course, it hadn't been a big deal to just say I wasn't interested in being in the video. The only person obligated to be on camera was Isaac. And he definitely wasn't the guy who was going to pressure anyone. But still. A little bit of *Random I* magic had dimmed. And I wasn't sure how I was supposed to feel about that.

Chapter Ten

Isaac

Jade was sitting at my desk when I showed up to work on Tuesday morning. And she did not look happy.

"What's up?" I asked as I dropped my bag onto the chair in front of my desk. "Long night? Is Nora okay?"

She shook her head. "Nora's fine. It's you I'm worried about."

"Uh-oh. What did I do?" I shifted my bag onto the floor and sat down in the chair, sensing that Jade might want to talk to me about more than the interns leaving their leftovers in the warehouse fridge.

"Did you talk to your little Instagram friend about sharing her artwork on your show?"

"Her name is Ana," I said, wishing my friends would take my relationship with her a little more seriously.

"Right. Ana. But did you?"

I frowned. "No," I said slowly. "But it's on her public Instagram profile. Public is public, right? Should I have?"

"Public for someone with less than five hundred followers is a little bit different than public for someone like you, Isaac."

I ran a hand through my hair. "You're right. I get it. What does this mean? Has there been fallout?"

"Not necessarily. The internet loves her stuff. I've gotten hundreds of messages from people interested in buying a print of the Red Renegade cover, wanting to know how they can reach out to the artist and commission their own stuff."

"But that's good, right?"

"It might be. If that's the kind of attention Ana is looking for. But what if she isn't?"

"Okay. I see your point. I should have asked her first. Surely she'll be excited, though. Selling her artwork would be legit."

"I think so, you think so, but that doesn't automatically mean she'll think so. You just have to think, Isaac. You've given me the sense that she's a pretty private person, right? And your life is anything but. You gotta ease her in slowly, you know?"

"Understood. I'll talk to her."

"And tell her to consider cleaning up her social media profiles. Make sure there's nothing on any of them that she wouldn't want the world at large to see. If she's connected to you, and there's any kind of dirt out there? Somebody will dig it up. You know they will."

I sighed. I'd seen it happen enough to know that Jade was right. I was not the kind of famous that got me mobbed in the street or had crowds of screaming fans congregating outside my house. But I did have a base of fans who were so loyal, so thorough, it sometimes seemed like they knew more about my life than I did.

It wasn't a conversation I looked forward to. Ana *was* a private person. I wasn't sure how she'd react knowing that one, I'd shared her stuff without asking—if she hadn't watched the show and figured it out already—and two, if we kept talking, there was no way to prevent her from becoming the subject of public scrutiny.

Still, I couldn't pretend like my life was anything other than exactly what it was. It was the nature of the game. For better or worse, I couldn't change it.

After Jade left, I settled into my desk chair and pulled up my message thread with Ana. I tapped my phone against my hand, wondering how to start the conversation. She watched the show; I knew that much. Who's to say she hadn't already seen yesterday's episode?

@RandomIOfficial: Sooo, did you see yesterday's episode of Random I?

@Briarsandthorns: Not yet. Why? Did I miss something amazing?

@RandomIOfficial: Here's the thing. I kind of, maybe, or actually did share your album cover artwork on the show. The good news is that we've gotten a lot of messages from people who are interested in buying a print. The bad news is that I should have talked to you about it before I shared your stuff online. And now Jade says I need to talk to you about cleaning up your social media profiles in case there's anything you might not want the Random I *fandom to discover about you.*

@Briarsandthorns: That . . . is . . . I don't know what that is. I'm glad people are liking my art. But yeah. The other part. That doesn't sound fun.

@RandomIOfficial: I wish I could say it didn't really matter. But unfortunately, it's just the downside of being a part of my life.

@Briarsandthorns: What does Jade mean by "cleaning up my social media profiles?" I don't know what that looks like.

@RandomIOfficial: I can have her message you about it. I'm sorry about all this. I was just excited about your work, and I like talking about the things I love, and . . . I didn't think about what this would mean for you.

@Briarsandthorns: I get it.

I waited for another response to come through, but that's all she said. She got it. What did that even mean? *I get it and I will never want to meet you in person? I get it and I agree with you? I get it, please never message me again?*

After filming tomorrow's episode—we always filmed in mid to late afternoon on the day *before* the show would actually air—I wandered down to the back patio. The studio had felt crowded today, like the interns had somehow multiplied, but it probably had more to do with me feeling stressed out by my conversation with Jade, and the exchange of messages with Ana that had followed. The patio was almost always empty, and the afternoon was warm. Hopefully, it would give me a little space to clear my head and figure out how to make sure Ana wasn't upset with me.

Except, the back patio *wasn't* empty.

Rosie sat at one of the picnic tables, her cheek pressed against the tabletop and her eyes closed. I paused, not wanting to wake her if she'd fallen asleep, but she must have heard me approach.

She sat up, her eyes widening like I'd startled her.

"Sorry. I didn't mean to scare you. There's not usually anyone out here."

"No, no, you're fine," she said, offering me a warm smile. "I was just . . . breathing."

"Something I generally recommend." I lowered myself onto the bench across from her. "Is everything okay?"

She shrugged. "I . . . I think so. Just a weird morning, is all."

I pursed my lips in mock consternation. "Is it your boss? I've heard he's a monster."

She chuckled. "Absolutely. He's the literal worst."

I winced dramatically. "That's too bad. You know, I've heard the same thing from a lot of people. From what everyone is saying, his only saving grace is that he's really handsome. So even though his personality is the complete pits, people keep him around because he's pretty on the TV."

She laughed, her smile brightening her entire face and making her eyes sparkle. "You're terrible."

"Ha," I said. "There it is. I knew I could make you smile."

"Mission accomplished, huh?"

"I do my best."

There was something supremely satisfying about pulling a smile out of Rosie, especially since I could tell she'd been feeling down about something. I generally liked to make people happy no matter the person or the situation. But the smile Rosie had just given me? It was worth a thousand smiles from strangers.

Which didn't make any sense. Rosie was a friend. Almost more like a friend of a friend. Unless we were hanging out with our mutual friends, we didn't really talk.

So why had her smile done such strange things to my heart? It left me feeling uneasy. And a little like fleeing. But I tamped down the urge. Just because I noticed the woman had a nice smile didn't mean she was anything more than a friend. Jade had great hair. And Diedre had nice skin. Noticing those things didn't mean anything. It was fine for me to notice that Rosie had a nice smile.

Wasn't it?

Chapter Eleven

Rosie

It was the weirdest sensation for Isaac to both feel completely familiar to me and utterly foreign at the same time. I knew this man. We'd been chatting every night for almost a month, and yet, we'd spent very little actual time together in person. It was my turn to speak, but I was afraid to say anything. What if I ended up mentioning something that Ana knew, but Rosie didn't know? But then, *Rosie* hardly knew anything at all. I just needed to act like I was sitting across the picnic table from a stranger.

And yet, Isaac *wasn't* a stranger. My heart knew that. I was bad at words when my heart and mind were in agreement. I had no idea how I was supposed to manage my brain doing one thing while my heart did something else entirely.

I took a slow, deep breath quietly enough that I hoped Isaac wouldn't notice. He still looked at me with his penetrative gaze, his eyebrows lifted in expectation. *Right.* I still hadn't said anything. What had he said again? Something about his best? About making people smile?

"It's your gift, I think," I said, almost without thinking. "Making other people feel good."

He studied me closely, his expression contemplative. "Thanks. I think sometimes it makes people think I'm just silly all the time. That I can't be serious."

"I don't think you seem that way at all. You definitely have a fun-guy vibe, but . . . fun guys can be serious, too. And I mean, you *are* an entertainer. It's your job to make people happy. You have to be serious about that."

His eyebrows went up. "Serious about making people happy?"

I shrugged. "Exactly." I pursed my lips, suddenly itching to ask the question I'd been pondering for the past half hour. After our last instant message conversation, I'd been trying to process all kinds of things. "Is it worth it?" I asked. "The fame?"

He thought for longer than I expected. Somehow, I'd thought his answer would come as swiftly as his smiles.

"Most of the time," he finally said. "Honestly, I'm still blown away with everything I've been able to build and do because of my fans. The fame is a natural consequence of that, so I try not to feel salty about it."

"I sense there's a but to that sentence." I realized that I was talking with Isaac with much more ease than was typical. And I wasn't even having to try. But then, of course I wasn't. Because Isaac wasn't a stranger to me anymore. We talked every night.

"You are perceptive, Rosie," he said.

My heart clenched at the sound of my real name coming off his lips. For a moment, I wondered if I ought to just tell him right there on the spot. *Surprise! It's me. I'm Ana. Ana Rose, actually, and I've been in love with you for years. Message you after dinner?*

But the unease that had accompanied our earlier conversation wouldn't leave me alone. Cleaning up my social media accounts, worrying about people finding out who I was, digging up information about my personal life. Not to mention the many ways in which Isaac opened his life up to his fans. If I were *a part* of his life, that openness would inevitably include me.

"Can I ask you a question?" Isaac said. He leaned forward, propping his elbows up on the table.

I nodded, grateful for the distraction from my own swirling thoughts. "Sure."

"I get the sense that you're a little more of an introvert than I am. Would you say that's safe to say?"

"I'm not going to overthink about what you have observed to lead you to that conclusion and just go with yes, you have surmised correctly. I am definitely an introvert."

"So, I have this friend," Isaac said. "And she's also an introvert."

Oh, no. He was not going to do what I thought he was going to do.

"Okay," I managed to squeak out.

He ran a hand through his hair. "So here's the situation. This woman is an artist. An amazing one. And she shared this thing that she drew with me, and I was just really blown away by it. So I shared it on the show, and my publicist *and* my social media manager seem to think that was a bad thing. That I shouldn't have mentioned it, or her, without talking to her about it first."

I wracked my brain for a question I thought someone that knew nothing of the situation might ask. "Did she send it to you hoping you might share it? Fans do that kind of thing, right?"

I hadn't thought about him sharing my art at all. I'd only wanted to get *his* attention. I suddenly wondered how he'd interpreted my intentions.

"I don't actually think so. It felt more personal than that. I really think she just wanted *me* to see it."

I tried not to smile, happy he'd at least read the gesture for what it was. "Then I'm not sure why you're asking me for help."

He turned his head, his eyes thoughtful. "I see your point. But why wouldn't she want me to share it? It's amazing. I really think she could be making money off of stuff like this." He picked up his phone and swiped a few times before turning it around and showing me the *Weeping Wings* album cover I'd drawn. "See? It's a rendering of an album cover from a band we both like."

I nodded, schooling my expression into something that reflected surprise. "She's very good."

"Right? You should see the rest of her stuff. She's just got this cool vibe that is . . . anyway. I just thought she'd appreciate me talking her up. She's really good at what she does."

"But she didn't appreciate it?" I asked.

"I don't actually know," he responded. "I messaged her about it and told her I'd be sure to ask her before mentioning her or her stuff on the show again, and she seemed fine. Maybe a little less chatty than normal."

I folded my hands on the worn table in front of me, hoping he couldn't see how they trembled. "Why are you worried, exactly?"

He turned his phone over and over in his hands. "I don't know. On the one hand, I'm not sure I really understand why she *wouldn't* want me to share her stuff. But I also don't want to screw things up. Our friendship is kinda new. If this were your artwork, would you be upset?"

Ohhhh, boy. The number of women who would kill to have the opportunity to tell a man exactly how she felt without having to own *any* of the feelings. It was too much. I felt a sudden urge to laugh bubbling up inside of me. Not like a ha-ha-ha funny kind of laugh. More like a HA-HA-HA-I'M-LOSING-CONTROL kind of laugh. The kind that even Mom's breathing couldn't tame.

I focused on Isaac's eyes, willing the warmth and sincerity there to leech into me and give me the calm I couldn't find on my own. Somehow, the steadiness of his gaze actually *did* calm me. "I don't know that I would necessarily be upset. But I would definitely ask her before you share her stuff on the show again. Not everyone loves . . ." I hesitated, suddenly realizing if I finished the sentence like I'd intended, it might sound like an insult.

He raised his eyebrows. "What? Loves attention like I do? I know what I am, Rosie. You won't hurt my feelings by pointing it out."

A knot of tension formed in my gut. "Are you always like that? Isn't there anything you keep private?" The second I'd asked the question, I wished I could call it back. It was the kind of question Ana could have asked, but not Rosie. Not the web designer who handled Isaac's merch store and had only ever had a couple of conversations with him that hadn't been about work.

Still, I craved the answer like I craved a deep lungful of air. It mattered in a way it hadn't a few weeks ago. Before my unrequited crush had turned into something that looked a lot more like possibility.

Isaac didn't even flinch. He just smiled, his eyes sparkling. "Some things. Dani is pretty particular about her privacy, for example, so I'll always respect her boundaries. But other than that? It's all about the connection, you know? People like to feel like they're getting the real me. And the only way for that to happen is for me to give it to them."

I admired his dedication and sincerity. It was likely the very thing that made him so good at what he did. He really *did* connect with people. That he was so transparent, so open, had to be largely why so many people loved him. And yet, I couldn't help but wonder how that affected his personal relationships. Dialing into the needs of ten million viewers was a tall order.

But at least he had *some* self-awareness. The fact that he was concerned about whether or not he'd crossed a line in sharing my artwork was encouraging. Even if his concern had been prompted by his friends. It was flimsy reassurance, but I clung to it just the same.

"It's admirable that you're willing to be so open with your fans. I'm sure it's why they like you so much," I said, my gaze focused firmly on my hands. If I looked him in the eye, he'd likely see the question I *really* wanted to ask.

"I sense a but to that statement," he said.

I winced.

He was good.

I looked up to meet his gaze.

"I'm an open book, Rosie," he said with no small measure of chagrin. "You can ask me whatever you want."

Willing courage into my words, I asked, "But you have to consider the possibility of collateral damage, right?" I thought about his friends and the way they'd all scattered when they didn't feel like being in one of his videos. "Have you ever worried that living so publicly might have a negative influence on your private relationships?"

Isaac only stared. There wasn't malice in his expression, but neither was their warmth. It was the most impassive I'd ever seen him look.

"Sorry. That was probably impertinent. It's just . . . the idea of living so publicly is so far outside of *my* comfort zone. Take your new friend, for example. You said she's more introverted, right? And Jade was concerned she might not like you sharing her stuff publicly?"

"I see where you're going. Do I worry that the public nature of my life would be off-putting to someone like her, eliminating the possibility of us having a relationship?"

I squelched the sudden desire to squeal over the fact that he'd used the word *relationship* and settled for an encouraging nod.

"It's a reasonable question. But honestly, I don't. It's not like people don't know what they're getting into, you know? My career is very public. And I can't change that."

The hope beating in my heart dimmed the tiniest bit. Surely he didn't think that *every* aspect of his life had to be shared with the world at large.

"I mean, obviously I'll always respect people's boundaries. But I also expect people to understand that *I* don't really have any. And that works for me." Isaac stood and reached for his phone. "On that note, I should get back to work."

I nodded and stood. "Me too, actually."

"Yeah, with that monster of a boss you've got, you're probably nervous to take breaks at all." He shot me a sideways grin. "Thanks for your help," he said before I could reply.

I followed him across the patio toward the door that led back into the warehouse. "I don't think I actually—"

"No, you did help," he said cutting off my protests. "I *can* respect Ana's boundaries, so I'll for sure ask before I share her stuff on the show again. But you've also helped me recognize that I can't apologize for the public nature of my life or pretend like it isn't my reality. It is what it is. And if this is going to go anywhere"—he waved his phone in front of him, referring to, I assumed, his online relationship with Ana—"she's going to have to be okay with that." He opened the door and held it for me as I crossed in front of him. "Collateral damage or not."

Isaac pushed the button for the elevator while I waited silently beside him. Would I be okay with Isaac's love for the spotlight? With him having ten million best friends?

I'd been watching Isaac's videos and live streams for years and had seen the countless photos that went up on various social media accounts multiple times a day. Those avenues of content had shown me the inside of his house, the car he drove, every corner of his studio and office. Loving him from afar, all those windows into his life had made it easier to feel like I knew him, but now, up close, close enough to reasonably imagine having an actual relationship—at least a friendship—with him, all those windows were terrifying.

Despite the surreal thrill of knowing Isaac was actually considering *me* as a possibility, one stark reality was crystal clear for the first time: I would never be the girl okay with living life in front of a camera.

Chapter Twelve

Isaac

I sat in Alex and Dani's living room, my feet propped up on their coffee table and Dani's feet resting on my lap. She leaned against Alex, whose arms were around her and resting on her stomach, which was just starting to show signs of the baby she carried.

It was weird seeing her pregnant. Not bad. Just . . . weird.

"I'm not saying I'm disappointed in the interview," I said, resurrecting an argument Alex and I had been having for weeks. "Drake was a nice guy. I just don't want to do another one. That's not who I am."

"But you've seen the numbers from that episode, Isaac. You can't argue against them. Your new subscriber rate has tripled since the episode aired."

I shook my head. Alex was thinking like a numbers guy. But I sensed in my bones that this wasn't the change we needed. I couldn't explain beyond that. I was willing to admit we needed a change, but I wouldn't pander for attention with celebrity interviews. We just needed something exciting—something that made viewers who had been with us for years as excited to watch as they had been when they'd first started. I just had to figure out what it was.

I'd been doing this long enough to trust that the answers would eventually come, but it didn't usually take this long for inspiration to strike.

"Maybe you just need to get out of the studio more," Dani said. "I know you went out to California a couple of weeks ago, but even that was a pretty controlled shoot. You used to just go out on the streets and talk to people."

"That was easier when fewer people knew who I was," I said, wishing it wasn't the truth. "With Captain Practical over there"—I motioned toward Alex—"it's hard to get out and really engage like I used to."

"My job is to protect your assets," Alex said, his tone unapologetic. "And believe it or not, you are actually the show's most valuable asset."

I sighed. "Yeah, yeah. But I do like the idea of getting out of the studio."

"What about the road trip idea you've been talking about for so long?" Dani asked through a yawn. "Just take your camera crew and drive somewhere. Stop at little no-name diners, talk to people who are off the beaten path enough that engaging won't pose the same risk as, say, hanging out at Waterfront Park."

"A road trip?" I repeated. I really had been talking about doing some kind of road trip segment for years. But the timing or reason for going on a trip had never felt right.

Alex nodded. "It would take a little arranging, and we'd have to carefully plan your stops, but a road trip could work."

I rolled my eyes. "A spontaneous road trip that isn't actually spontaneous," I said. "Sounds fun."

"You're too big to put people on camera otherwise," Alex said. "You want to be spontaneous? Don't film anyone but yourself. Then you can be as spontaneous as you want."

"Alex?" Dani reached up and cupped her hand around her husband's cheek. "You're kind of a buzz kill."

I grinned. It was nice having Dani on my team.

No matter how planned out and precise Alex would need a road trip to be, the idea was growing on me. We were close enough to summer that the weather would be good no matter what direction we decided to drive. I just needed a destination. And a reason for going.

"Hey." Dani nudged me with her toe, exchanging a quick look with Alex—one of those weird couple looks where they had an entire conversation with only their eyeballs. "What if you went to Kansas to meet Ana?"

My eyes jumped to Alex, his expression telling me he wasn't at all surprised by Dani's suggestion. So that's the way it was.

"You guys are good," I said. "I mean it. It didn't seem scripted at all the way you worked it right into a conversation about the show. Well done."

Dani smirked and lifted her shoulders in a little shrug. "We practiced. But that doesn't mean the suggestion isn't valid. You *should* go to Kansas. It's time, Isaac. You've been messaging this girl for over a month, and you haven't dated anyone else the entire time. You obviously like her."

I did like her. We weren't messaging quite as feverishly as we had those first weeks, but we'd settled into a predictable routine, sending messages once or twice throughout the day, then chatting for a few minutes late at night. I'd given up suggesting that we talk on the phone; for whatever reason, Ana didn't seem to want to do it. Whenever I pushed, she quickly retreated, either changing the subject completely or ending our conversation altogether. I worried she was hiding something, but I was afraid pushing her might push her away. Despite the things I still didn't know about her, I really liked talking to her. She was funny and smart and had really good insight about music and books and people. And I didn't want to ruin that.

Plus, when I'd shared her artwork on the show, the follow-up conversation we'd had made me think that even though that circumstance had worked out to her benefit, she might not be the kind of person who would appreciate an on-air ambush as our first meeting. "I don't think Ana would go for it," I said. "I get the sense that she's a really private person."

Dani shifted, pushing herself up a little. Probably to make it easier for her to give me the evil, twin-stink-eye she'd used when we were kids to try and make me do what she wanted. "I love that you're being so respectful of Ana's wishes. I really do. But Isaac, this is who you are. Unless you're planning on a career change, at some point, Ana is going to have to decide if she's willing to be a part of *all* of your life, and not just stay safely tucked away inside your phone. Besides, it's not as if you'd have to film the *entire* road trip. You could pick and choose what you put on camera. Make it more about the journey and less about the destination. That way, you can just turn the camera off when you actually meet Ana for the first time."

Dani had a point. But the fans wouldn't be nearly as invested if they couldn't also be excited about the destination. Like it or not, the content that sold best was always the content that made viewers feel the most connected.

But the segment didn't need to be about *my* connections. It could be about viewers' connections. Online friendships and online dating was an enormous part of modern culture. The thrill of meeting someone in person for the first time that you'd only ever met online was definitely the kind of thing that would get people excited.

"I think you woke him up," Alex whispered to Dani. "It's like I can see the actual wheels turning in his brain."

I shot Alex a bored look, but he wasn't exactly wrong. If I'd had paper in front of me, I would have been scribbling down notes for how fast the ideas were flying through my brain. "That's it," I said, standing up.

Dani's feet dropped from my lap and thudded onto the floor. "Hey," she said. "A little warning next time."

"What if we turn it into a whole segment?" I said, pacing around their living room.

"Turn what into a whole segment?" Alex said. "So far, you haven't actually said any of your ideas out loud, man. Back up and bring us up to speed."

"Right. Okay. What if we create a new segment for the show based on making connections? We find people who have known each other online for years but have never met in person. We could send two separate crews, one to each person, and then we road trip to a designated location in the middle so they can meet."

"Why not just fly?" Dani asked. "Wouldn't that make things a lot easier?"

"There's nothing magical about flying," I said. "The road trip would be what we use to get to know the people we're connecting, highlighting their life, getting to know the ways in which this relationship they've formed has mattered to them. We can stop at roadside motels. Eat in old diners. Do all the road trip things, but with the express purpose of bringing two people together. Any two people. Gaming friends. Potential couples. Old ladies who have been playing scrabble together for years. Whatever. We could do anything."

"You and Steven would each lead a crew?" Alex said.

"Totally. Steven would love it. And we definitely wouldn't have to drive everywhere. We could fly to wherever the two people live and then rent cars to drive to the designated meeting spot. It would require some logistics getting it set up, but it wouldn't be anything the team couldn't handle."

Alex nodded, even as Dani stood, her brows furrowed and her mouth taut. "Stop, stop, stop," she said, putting her hands on her hips. "You're getting way off course." She stomped toward the kitchen, coming back with an open bag of Cheetos, wielding a Cheeto like a miniature orange-dusted sword. "The whole point of suggesting a road trip was so you could go to Kansas and meet Ana. If this woman is going to be something other than an online pen pal for the rest of your life, I'd appreciate it if you could go ahead and figure that out. Because if she isn't, you need to kick it into gear and start dating other people. I'd like for my kid to have cousins to grow up with, preferably close in age, which is going to be entirely impossible if you don't get a move on." She looked down at the Cheeto in her hand and groaned. "Ugh. I can't eat this."

She handed the Cheeto to Alex, who ate it without even flinching, then dropped the bag onto the coffee table. "Why does everything in this house have to smell so gross?" She ran a hand down the front of her stomach. "I hate everything. Especially you and your stupid idea that isn't going to get you any closer to Kansas so I can have a new sister and this baby can have real friends." She sniffed. "I'm going to go throw up. And then I'm going to take a bath."

I watched her disappear down the hallway until the click of her bedroom door sounded at the end of the hall. "Wow," I said. I looked at Alex; he had the whole bag of Cheetos now and was eating them with apparent nonchalance, but the lines of tension on his forehead told me he was anything but relaxed. "Is she gonna be okay?" I asked.

He sighed, dropping the Cheetos onto the table. "She's been sick all day. The morning sickness has been more like all-day sickness the past couple of weeks and it's really messing things up at work. She's got a couple of custom wedding dresses she's been working on for months and the deadlines are looming and . . . I don't know. If I thought it would actually help, I'd learn how to sew just to feel something besides completely useless."

"But like, she's okay, right? Healthwise? Is she really supposed to feel this sick? I just feel like there should be something we could do to help." I didn't have a ton of experience with morning-sick pregnant women. Dani looked okay on the outside, but I'd never seen her turn down a Cheeto.

Alex stood up and crossed the room to where I stood, placing a bracing hand on my shoulder. "Dani's tough. She'll be fine, and the baby is fine, too. But there *is* something you can do to help."

I nodded. "Anything."

"Go to Kansas, man. Give Dani something to be excited about, something to be *distracted* by. On the show or not, figure out what Ana means to you and do something about it."

I spent the next forty-eight hours mulling over the problem. The more I thought about it, the more I wanted to launch the idea of a road trip segment designed to connect people. I had that tingly reassurance deep in my gut that told me it would be a hit with the viewers. I'd been trusting that creative intuition for years. There was no reason to start doubting it now.

My intuition also told me the very best way to launch it would be to make a connection of my own. A road trip to meet Ana, especially if viewers thought I was romantically interested in her, would be a huge hit with the fans.

But what would Ana think?

Random I and the public nature of my life wasn't going to change anytime soon. If she didn't want to be a part of it, then maybe Dani was right, and I did need to move on. But I couldn't make that decision until I'd at least tried to meet her. It was time. If there was any chance the connection we felt online could develop into something more than friendship, I had to give it a shot. I had to find out for real.

And I was not a man that ever did anything by halves.

Still, it was a risk. What if saving the show meant losing Ana's friendship?

I looked up from my desk; Jade was across the warehouse talking to some interns. I stood up and moved to my office door, opening it long enough to call her name. "Hey, Jade? You got a second?"

She met my eye, nodding before saying something else to the interns then turning to head my direction. The nearer she got, the more I motioned for her to hurry.

She eyed me warily as she passed in front of me into my office. "What's got you all worked up?" she said, her dark eyebrows raised.

I closed the door and dropped onto the sofa that sat in the corner of the office, not wanting to have this conversation across a desk. "I'm ready to meet Ana in person."

"Well it's about time," she said with a smirk. "What's the plan?"

"I've got one, and the whole team will find out about it at our meeting tomorrow morning, but for now, I'm hoping you can show me the picture that Ana sent you."

"What?"

"She gave you one, right? When you vetted her before we started talking? You told me you confirmed her identity and said she checked out."

"I did say that," Jade said hesitantly. "But I can't show you the picture. I accidentally deleted it."

I ran a hand across my face. "What? How?"

Jade shifted, her gaze darting sideways before it settled back on me. "Oh, you know. I was just deleting photos I didn't need, screenshots, documents, that sort of thing and I guess I accidentally selected *that* photo as well. Sorry, boss."

I narrowed my eyes. Jade never called me boss. Was she hiding something? It also wasn't like her to randomly delete pictures. "Don't call me boss. Did it not back up to the cloud or anything?"

Jade shook her head. "My backup was turned off for a little while. I don't know how that happened. But I'd already deleted the photo before I turned it back on. Why do you need to see it?"

It was a relevant question. I leaned back in my chair and shrugged. "I guess I just want to know what she looks like."

Jade pursed her lips. "You couldn't just ask her to send you a picture?"

I could. But there was something about not having our pictures involved in getting to know each other. We'd talked about how old we were, and she'd given me a vague description of herself, but I hadn't really felt the need to make it an issue.

"I feel like it'll ruin things."

"But seeing the photo she sent me *won't* ruin things?"

"I don't mean seeing her picture will ruin things. I mean *asking* for it might. I get the sense that she appreciates that I haven't asked for one. That it isn't important to me."

Jade rolled her eyes. "Easy for *her* to feel that way. Your face is all over the internet. You have the right to ask her to send a picture, Isaac. It's only fair." She stood up and pushed her hands into her back pockets. "Honestly, I'm surprised you haven't taken the plunge before now. You can't have a relationship with a faceless person forever."

"No, you're right." I shook my head. "Forget it. It doesn't actually matter. I'm going to meet her regardless of what she looks like. Going in blind will probably make things better anyway."

"Isaac," Jade said, her tone serious. "What are you planning?"

I grinned and headed toward my office door. "I need to go buy a car."

"Isaac," Jade called after me as I headed across the warehouse.

"Tomorrow," I said, turning and taking a few backward steps. Jade stood in my office doorway, her arms folded across her chest. "I'll explain everything tomorrow."

"I'm calling Alex," she said, loud enough for the entire warehouse to hear, but I didn't care. Alex was the one who had given me the idea in the first place.

In the elevator, I pulled out my phone and messaged Ana.

@RandomIOfficial: So . . . I'm going to be in Kansas next week. Can we meet?

Chapter Thirteen

Rosie

I set my phone down on the bathroom counter and sighed. I'd gotten Isaac's last message the afternoon before and I still couldn't figure out how to respond. I'd thought about calling Marley but had decided that was the last thing I wanted to do. She'd tell me in no uncertain terms that I had to tell Isaac the truth. But how?

It wasn't that I hadn't known this moment was coming. But the moment had become more than just me finally admitting to Isaac who I was. It was also me admitting to Isaac why I'd been lying to him for over a month. Well, almost lying. I'd been very careful to choose my words wisely and avoid telling outright lies, but that didn't mean Isaac hadn't made some erroneous assumptions. It wasn't so much that I was scared Isaac would be mad that I hadn't been forthright about my identity. He wouldn't be. He'd proven himself over and over again to be the kind of man who simply rolled with things. He was, in every sense, unfailingly optimistic.

But that didn't mean he wouldn't be disappointed when he learned that Ana was actually Rosie the web designer. Disappointed that I wasn't leggier or blonder or whatever. There was nothing mysterious about Rosie the web designer. I was just me. And *me* was rather ordinary.

There was also the issue of what I actually *wanted* in a relationship. I'd been thinking a lot about the public nature of Isaac's life. Navigating the whole situation with him sharing my stuff on the show, cleaning up my social media profiles, worrying about strangers finding out who I was . . . it had given me a lot to think about.

Maybe it wasn't *just* a matter of what Isaac would want once he knew the truth.

It was also a matter of what I wanted.

No matter what, the truth would force our relationship to change. We lived in the same city. Worked in the same building. There was no way things could stay the same. The thought of things changing, of possibly losing the friendship that we'd built, left me feeling untethered in a way I didn't like.

If things didn't work out, would I leave Charleston? Tuck tail and move home to Kansas?

Aside from the boost in my pay, which was awesome, I really liked my new job. Greta and Vincent, Jade and Diedre, they'd all become really good friends. And even if the city was getting hotter by the minute as summer approached, I was in love with having the ocean so close. I didn't really *want* to leave.

Still, I couldn't stay silent. Otherwise, Isaac would show up in Kansas expecting to meet a woman that didn't actually exist.

Reggie rubbed against my leg, his meow insistent enough that I knew his food bowl had to be empty. Tugging my towel closer around me, I followed Reggie to the kitchen, jumping back when I came face to face with my landlord, Joe, the door to the cabinet below the sink in his hands.

My half-gasp, half-scream must have startled him because the cabinet door nearly slipped out of his hands; he struggled to catch it before it dropped onto the floor, or worse, onto his toes. When the door was safely in his hands once more, he lowered it onto the floor and leaned it against the wall. "Sorry, Rosie. I didn't mean to scare you."

I tucked my towel a little closer around me. To Joe's credit, he kept his eyes trained directly on my face. "What are you doing here?"

"Just finally taking care of the cabinet doors. To be honest, I didn't think you were still home. If I'd known, I would have knocked."

"I'm not usually home this late. It's just . . . been a weird morning." If avoiding work by staring at a text message I couldn't respond to for two hours counted as weird, that's exactly what it had been.

Suddenly deciding that Reggie could wait to eat until after I was fully clothed, I backtracked toward my bedroom. "I do have to get to work though, so I'm just going to . . ." I closed my bedroom door, not even waiting for Joe to respond. Reggie followed, begrudgingly so, jumping onto the counter and dropping himself onto my phone as if to punish me for my lack of consideration.

"No more phone for me this morning, huh?" I said, scratching behind his years. "Fine by me, Mr. Grumpy Pants. I need to get ready for work anyway." I was already an hour late.

By the time I'd worked my way around Joe to feed the cat and toast myself a bagel for the road, I was almost two hours late. Unusual for me, but Greta would understand. I'd never been late before. I didn't doubt she'd be forgiving when I explained why I was feeling out of sorts.

Before I had even backed out of my driveway, the phone rang, Greta's face filling the screen.

I answered the call, waiting for the Bluetooth in the car to pick it up.

"Hey," I said when the connection was complete. "I'm sorry I'm late. It's been a dumb morning."

"I can imagine. What are you going to do?"

I paused. I hadn't told Greta, or anyone, about Isaac's question.

Could she know about his trip to Kansas, too?

"Wait, what are you talking about? What am I going to do about what?"

"You haven't seen Isaac's video?"

My hands clenched the steering wheel a little tighter. "What video?"

"Oh, man," Greta said. "She hasn't seen it," she said, her voice a little further away.

Jade's voice sounded through the phone. "Well, tell her to watch it," she said.

"Watch what?" I said to Greta. "I'm driving. Please just tell me what it was."

"Pull over and watch it, Rosie. Now. Before you come into the office. I'll see you when you get here." She hung up the call without another word.

Heart pounding, I pulled my car into the parking lot of a corner gas station and pulled up Isaac's YouTube channel. There was nothing new posted, so I switched over to his Instagram profile. Sure enough, there was a live video—one he'd filmed the previous afternoon. It already had over two million views.

My hands trembled as I held my breath and hit play on the video.

Isaac leaned against the hood of a car, something that looked old, but . . . *not old.* Like it had been fully restored. It was a hatchback of some sort, a Volkswagen, maybe? Despite the fear squeezing my gut, I couldn't help but chuckle. The car was very Isaac.

Isaac talked about the car for a few minutes, giving a shout-out to the mechanic who had done the restoration work and retrofitted the car with an all-new engine. From there, he launched into an explanation of a new segment he'd be featuring on the show about online friends taking cross-country road trips to make real-life connections. His enthusiasm was contagious, and the idea was solid. People were going to love it. But I knew as well as I knew anything exactly what was coming. Exactly *why*

Isaac was going to be in Kansas.

The end of his video confirmed my fears. "I can't wait to help viewers connect with friends from all over the country. But first, I'm going to make a connection of my own. I have an online friend who I've never met in person . . . and she's become pretty special to me. She lives all the way up in Kansas, so I'm taking this bad boy"—he patted the car behind him—"and I'm driving north to find her." He looked right into the camera and smiled. "I'll admit, I'm a little nervous to meet her. But win or lose, I'll never know what happens next if I don't take the plunge. So I'm doing this. And I'm taking all of you with me." After a promise to provide further details in future videos, Isaac signed off.

I leaned back into my seat and dropped my phone onto my lap.

What on earth was I supposed to do now?

My mind reeled as I drove the short distance to the warehouse. When I pulled into the parking lot, I could see Greta and Jade standing outside the front door waiting for me. I parked and willed my nerves to calm. Things were going to be fine.

My phone rang as I climbed out of my car, Diedre's face filling the screen. I wasn't sure Diedre had ever called me. We'd only ever texted.

"Hey," I said after picking up the call. "You okay?"

"Have you talked to Jade yet?" she said without preamble.

"I just got to work, so no, but she's waiting for me. She and Greta both."

"Honey, listen to me," Diedre said in her best mom voice. "You don't have to do this if you don't want to."

I stopped in my tracks. "Do what? I don't know how much you know, Diedre. I only found out about Isaac's video seconds ago."

"Jade is going to ask you to go to Kansas. Because it will be better for the show, better for numbers. But that isn't on you. It isn't your job to save *Random I*, and I just wanted to make sure you had a friend who told you as much."

My heart warmed from her concern. “Thank you for saying so.”

“If you want to go to Kansas and put yourself out there, then do it. But if you don’t, that’s your right. Don’t let anybody guilt you into feeling like you don’t have a choice. Especially not Jade. I know better than anybody how persuasive she can be. She could persuade people the sky was purple if she had to. But this decision isn’t about her. Or the show. Or even Isaac. You’re the one taking the risk here. You make the decision that’s best for *you.*”

It was a lot of information to process. I hadn’t yet considered the possibility of going to Kansas—of letting the road trip play out. I’d just assumed I would confront Isaac, tell him the truth, and that would be that. No road trip necessary. But logically, it made sense that Jade and the others would want the road trip to happen. Especially with the way the show’s numbers had been sliding lately. If the video was already getting a good response—and my quick review of the comments after watching it made it seem like it was—it wouldn’t be good to abandon the idea now. Of course, that wasn’t my fault. Isaac had been the one to presumptuously assume he could even *find* Ana in Kansas when I hadn’t yet responded to his message telling him I was willing to meet.

“Rosie? You there?” Diedre asked.

“Yeah, I’m here. Thanks for calling. I didn’t know it until you said it, but I needed to hear someone remind me it’s okay to make this decision about me.”

“I’m on your team, Rosie. Call me again if you need moral support.”

“Thanks, Diedre.”

I hung up the phone and walked slowly toward Greta and Jade.

Jade shook her head as I approached. “That was Diedre on the phone, wasn’t it?”

I lifted my shoulders. “Good guess.”

“So what are you going to do?” Jade asked. Clearly, she knew exactly what Diedre had told me.

"I walked up here thinking I was going to go find Isaac and tell him the truth."

"And now you know why I think that's a terrible idea."

I nodded. "And I get it. It's your job to think about what's best for the show."

"The reaction to his video has been huge," Jade said. "Online forums are full of speculation about who this mystery friend is and about whether or not she had anything to do with his breakup with Bridget."

"Sponsors have also been reaching out," Greta said. "Food, drinks, restaurants, hotels. They all want in."

"I know you don't pay attention to the numbers because it isn't your job to do it, but *Random I* has been in a little bit of a slump lately." Jade folded her arms. "We haven't seen this kind of excitement in a long time."

"People think it's romantic," Greta added.

I shook my head. "It is *not* going to be romantic when he gets to Kansas and he finds *me* instead of Ana. He's going to be disappointed, and that will not translate well to viewers. Has anyone thought about *that* possibility?"

A new wave of nausea washed over me at the thought of ten million viewers watching Isaac learn that I was the person on the other side of his online relationship.

Greta was silent for a beat. "Is that really what you're afraid of? You're amazing, Rosie. Isaac is going to see that."

I wanted to believe that they were right about Isaac. But insecurities aren't always rational. And the reality was that no matter how things played out, this would mean change. And I'd been spiraling from that realization even before I'd watched Isaac's video.

I looked from Greta to Jade. "I've made some really good friends lately," I said. "I like my job. I like the life that I've built for myself here."

Jade nodded. "Okay."

I shrugged. "Messaging is easy. It's safe. What if I tell him who I am, and it screws everything up?"

Jade's face softened. "We'll still be your friends no matter what. You know that."

"I know. But if things don't pan out with Isaac and me, there's no way it wouldn't make work weird." My eyes dropped to the pavement at my feet. "Besides, I . . ." The words stalled in my throat. After the ruckus I'd made about wanting to reach out to Isaac in the first place, I wasn't sure my friends would understand what I'd been about to say.

"Besides what?" Jade prompted.

I had to tell them. I wouldn't be able to extricate myself from this situation without their help. Not now that it included *Random I.*

"What if it isn't what I want?"

Greta's eyebrows went up. "Are we still talking about going to Kansas?"

I shook my head. "What if *Isaac* isn't what I want?"

"Oh, geez." Jade pressed a hand to her forehead. "You cannot even be serious right now."

"That's not fair," I said, holding my ground. "I've never even been on a real date with the man. I like him, yes. But his life is a little overwhelming. *This* is a little overwhelming. It's a lot to sign up for based on nothing but a month of direct messaging."

"But it *is* based on more than direct messaging, isn't it?" Greta asked. "You've been watching Isaac's show for a long time, Rosie."

"But this is different," I insisted. "A personal relationship is different. His life, his fame . . . it's big."

"And you didn't know that when you *started* messaging him?" Jade asked, frustration infusing her words. "That'd be like me looking at Diedre six months into our relationship and saying, I'm sorry, I knew you had a child, but I just assumed he wouldn't be a part of things once we started dating."

I rolled my eyes. "That's not a fair comparison. Besides, I never thought dating Isaac would actually be a possibility. I sent that message on impulse, but I don't think I actually expected him to respond. I'm . . ." I hesitated and looked down at myself, my arms held out as if for inspection. "I'm a nobody."

"Oh, honey," Greta said, wrapping an arm around my shoulders and shooting Jade a look that could only be interpreted to mean *chill the hell out.* "You aren't a nobody."

I pushed the heels of my hands into my eyes, not even caring what it would do to my eye makeup. "What do I do now?"

My friends were both silent for a long moment.

"I think I have an idea," Jade finally said. "But I'm not sure you're going to like it."

I scoffed. "At this point, the only thing I could possibly like is rewinding my life six weeks so that none of this ever happened."

"Don't be saying that," Jade said. "Come on." She held out her hand and tugged me gently forward when I slipped my fingers into hers. "We need to tell Alex what's going on."

My feet turned to lead inside my shoes, immediately halting our progress. "What? Why Alex? What does he have to do with this?"

Jade didn't answer, but she was too formidable a woman for me to argue with her once she'd set her mind to something. She tugged me again, unsticking my feet and dragging me up to the third floor, where we found Alex sitting at his desk. Luckily, Isaac was nowhere to be seen.

"We have an issue," Jade said to Alex, quietly enough that hopefully, no one else heard.

Alex looked from Jade to me, and then to Greta, who had followed us up. "Okay," he said hesitantly. He stood and opened the door to Isaac's office, motioning for us all to precede him into the room.

Even with the door firmly closed behind us, I could still feel the stares of everyone else in the warehouse. They had to be wondering why we'd stormed into the office and demanded an audience.

"What's up?" Alex asked, his arms folded across his chest.

"It's me," I blurted out before anyone else had the chance to speak. I'd suddenly grown weary at the idea of Jade or Greta speaking for me.

Alex looked at me warily. "Who is you?"

"I'm Ana," I explained. Sweat broke out across my upper lip. "Which is, actually, my real name. Ana Rose Crenshaw. And I am from Kansas. I didn't lie about that part either." I lifted my shirt away from my body and shook it a few times, willing my body temperature to cool. Anxious sweating was possibly the worst part of having social anxiety. Nothing made me *more* anxious than worrying about whether or not everyone could tell that I was anxious. There were all kinds of strategies I'd learned to cope. Dark clothing. Layers. Industrial-strength antiperspirant. My life was such a party.

Understanding dawned on Alex's face. "You're the one who's been messaging Isaac all this time? I thought you lived in Kansas."

I bit my lip and nodded. "I did. My parents still do. And that's the location still listed on my old Instagram profile. When Isaac made the assumption it was still true, I didn't correct him. I know I should have told him, but I'm not . . . I'm not good at this. At talking. At . . . *dating*."

Alex started to laugh. "This . . . this is amazing," he finally said. "It's perfect. You're perfect."

I froze. That . . . was not the reaction I'd been expecting.

Alex shook his head, his smile wide and his hands on his hips. "Do you know how worried his family has been about this? About him spending so much time talking to some faceless woman on the internet? Dani will sleep so much better knowing you aren't a psychopath trying to take advantage of her brother."

Oh. Well then. I was perfect in that I *wasn't* a psychopath. Glad Alex had set the bar so high.

Apparently, Alex's reaction wasn't what Jade had been expecting either. "Alex. Isaac just told ten million people he's driving to Kansas to meet someone. If Rosie tells him who she is? There's no point in him making the trip."

"And the internet is so in love with the idea of Isaac's road trip, our social feeds have been more active in the past twelve hours than they have been in months," Greta added. She shot me an apologetic look. "Not that that's the most important thing."

Alex's face fell. "Right. You're right. I've been watching the numbers myself." He looked up at me and ran a hand across his face. "So you just need to go to Kansas to be there when he shows up."

"Or," Jade said, casting me a sideways look before I could repeat my earlier protest. "She can catch a ride *to* Kansas. With Isaac."

I scoffed and held my hands up. "Absolutely not," I said, a pulse of panic building inside me. "That's completely crazy."

"Hear me out," Jade said, lifting her palms in a placating gesture. "You need to spend more time together, right? What better way to see if you can handle life in the fast lane with someone like Isaac than actually *getting* in the fast lane? I know it can be overwhelming thinking about the cameras, the attention." She shrugged. "But he's worth it, Rosie. He is to the rest of us."

"So, Rosie co-pilots the road trip," Alex said, his voice suddenly business-like and practical.

Jade nodded. "Then when you finally arrive in Kansas City," she said, her eyes on me, "you go in first, telling Isaac you're going to scout out the situation, but then when Isaac comes in, it'll just be you."

This was a terrible idea. A horrible idea. A terrible, horrible . . . maybe not impossible idea.

"So I would be in the car with him. In the video segments, the live streams . . ."

"It wouldn't be the entire time," Greta said. "Think about the videos and things Isaac posts. They're what, five, ten minutes long? That's not very much time when you compare it to twelve hours of driving."

"It's sixteen hours," Alex said, ever practical. "And you'd probably be doing more like two or three hours of total filming every day. There is always way more content than what actually makes it into the videos. You're right about the live streams though. Those are always pretty short."

"Two or three hours of filming?" I dropped onto the couch in the corner of Isaac's office and was momentarily distracted by how comfortable it was.

"Two hours of editable filming," Greta said. "So all the stupid things you say or do can be edited out."

I huffed a laugh. "Oh, well that's comforting. Will I be able to edit the stupid things I say or do out of Isaac's brain?" I leaned forward and pressed my forehead into my hands, my thumbs massaging my temples. "What if he's disappointed?" I said, almost too softly for anyone to hear. "Or what if I spend a week in the car with him, I hate being on camera, and I'm disappointed?"

"He won't be disappointed," Alex said matter-of-factly. "You're beautiful, smart, funny. And you've already formed a connection that I know means a lot to him."

The kindness of Alex's compliment almost brought tears to my eyes. His words were brotherly and sincere and acted as a cool balm to my frazzled nerves.

"I'm biased, obviously," he continued, "but I don't think you'll be disappointed either. Isaac is a lot. I get that. He's impetuous and impulsive and he doesn't always spend enough time thinking about the unintended consequences of his actions. But he's also genuine and kind and would do anything to make other people happy, particularly the people he's closest to."

Greta dropped onto the couch beside me and took my hand, squeezing it with hers. "It's a risk," she said softly. "But if it works? What a way to start a love story."

"And talk about good television," Jade said. "His viewers are going to love this."

I took a deep breath, in through my nose then out through my mouth. This was crazy. Too crazy. "What if I can't do it?"

"Then you don't have to," Alex said quickly, the certainty in his voice reassuring. "You have a choice, Rosie, and we'll support you whatever you decide. But either way, you'll still have to tell Isaac the truth." He ran a hand across the back of his neck. "And while I realize this is a personal decision, the sooner you could decide what you're doing, the better. There are already wheels in motion setting up sponsors and planning the details of the trip. If all that is going to have to stop, I'd rather do it sooner than later."

Maybe Jade was right. Maybe the road trip could actually function as a trial run. A no-stress way to see what life with Isaac would actually be like. After all, he would believe he was on his way to meet Ana, which would definitely take some of the pressure off me. "You guys won't tell him, right? That it's me?"

Alex shook his head. "Isaac is an open book, and believe it or not, a terrible actor. He won't be able to lie if he knows the truth. If the road trip is going to happen, the *entire thing* needs to happen, which means Isaac stays in the dark until the end."

"I don't understand," I said. "Why would the whole thing have to happen? Because of the sponsors?"

Alex nodded. "This won't be a regular road trip, Rosie. I get that this is personal for you, but it is also Isaac's business. There will be stops you'll have to make. Restaurants you'll visit. A specific hotel where you'll stay. We've even had a company reach out about the road trip snacks you'll buy along the way. All that will be planned ahead of time and there will be agreements in place regarding the time you spend and the things the viewers see."

I hadn't ever considered that aspect of *Random I.* Of course there were sponsors and advertisers involved. Isaac just always made everything seem so seamless, so organic.

"So if I told him early, or someone else told him, it could potentially ruin the trip."

Alex shrugged. "I'm not going to stand here and tell you the business is more important than your personal life. Deals fall through all the time and Isaac has deep enough pockets to handle the fallout. But on the surface, yes. That's a fair assessment."

"So, I tell him before we go, and there's no trip, or I go on the trip and commit to keeping the secret until we get to Kansas."

"Pretty much," Alex said.

I had made a lot of choices in my life, most of them practical and reasonable and dictated wholly by my desire to avoid anything that might cause my anxiety to flare up. I had isolated myself through most of high school, avoiding activities that weren't absolutely essential. I'd skipped homecoming, prom, all the after-graduation festivities. I had chosen a university close to home so that I could keep the same therapist and be close to my parents should I need them. It was only in my college years that I had finally gotten better at taking small risks, at letting people in and forming real friendships. But even then, I still spent a lot of time watching other people do fun and exciting things. I became known as the responsible one, the one to keep everyone else from getting too crazy.

It wasn't so much that I had felt driven to be responsible. Mostly, I'd just been terrified.

I was so damn tired of running scared. Of letting the threat of an anxiety attack keep me from *living.*

"Okay," I said, surprised that I'd managed to get the word out for how dry my mouth suddenly was.

"Okay?" Alex asked.

I nodded. "Okay. Let's go to Kansas."

Jade grinned and Greta clapped her hands. "This is going to be amazing," she said.

"We just have to figure out one thing," I said. I instinctively looked around the office for a water bottle. My tongue felt a little like sandpaper. "Who is going to persuade Isaac to take me with him? An on-air road trip with a random web designer that has never been in front of the camera seems like a ridiculous decision."

"Leave that part to me," Alex said. "I can handle Isaac."

Later, I texted Marley an update. She'd been getting regular information regarding my moonlighting as Ana and would, I was positive, find this particular development absolutely hilarious. Even I had to laugh when I read back over my message.

So. Exciting news. I'm going on a road trip with Isaac, as Rosie . . . so that we can drive to Kansas City . . . to meet Ana. Did I mention the car we're driving is tiny? It's a very tiny car. So tiny I'm worried there won't be enough oxygen inside.

WHAT, Marley texted back. *I need more details. He's making the trip . . . and you're making it with him? Why you? That feels random. Amazing, but random.*

I texted back a quick summary of my conversation with Alex and the orchestrations that had landed me in such a weird situation.

This is so amazing, Marley texted when she finally understood the whole picture.

And ridiculous, I texted back. *Don't forget the ridiculous part.*

Rosie. The period after my name was enough for me to know she was asking for my attention, preparing to say something big. I bit my lip while the blinking dots bounced along my screen.

I'm so proud of you, her next message read. *This. Is. Brave.*

Marley knew better than anyone how huge—how intimidating—this would feel to me.

I'm scared, I texted back.

I know. But you got this. You're going to do great. And also, HE IS GOING TO FALL IN LOVE WITH YOU. She followed her message with a heart eyes emoji and seventeen red hearts.

No one would ever say Marley wasn't optimistic.

If only a little of her optimism could rub off on me.

Chapter Fourteen

Isaac

"What about Vinnie?" I lay on the couch in the corner of my office and tossed a mini basketball over my head.

"I already asked him," Alex said. "He's got some family thing with Greta this weekend."

"And you're sure Jade can't go?"

"She said to keep her on as back up, but the baby is teething, and she doesn't want Diedre to deal with it alone."

I threw the ball across the office to the mini hoop mounted on the far wall and sat up. "And Steven is sick, and Mushroom is going to see his mom, and you refuse to leave Dani."

Alex shrugged. "You didn't exactly give us a lot of notice. You decided, what, yesterday, that you wanted to make this trip? People have lives, man. You can't be mad about that."

I ran a hand across my face. He was right, but it was still frustrating to have my momentum . . . stalled. At least Tyler could swing the trip. He'd do most of the filming. But experience had taught me I needed a co-pilot. I could handle solo stuff, but I was better when I had someone to banter with. Theoretically, when the new road trip segments started, that role would fall to the people we were working to connect. But on this trip, that person was me.

"You're sure you can't just do it alone?" Alex asked. "Or could Tyler just do both jobs? Be your co-pilot and do the filming at the same time?"

I shook my head. "Nah. Tyler's not great on camera. And I really think the segments need a two-person dynamic."

"What about one of the interns?" Alex asked.

I fought the urge to roll my eyes. We'd had some amazing interns come through *Random I.* But the current crop was particularly . . . frustrating. Two of the five seemed more interested in Charleston nightlife than anything work-related. A third had a bad habit of hanging around the studio during filming and snorting loudly every time I said something funny. And the fifth had a blog he kept up as a "*Random I*" insider on which he discussed everything from the kinds of sandwiches I ordered for lunch to the color of my socks. It was trivial and totally inane stuff, so it didn't really matter, it was just *annoying.* And the way he framed the information like people should actually care about what color my socks were? There was an inevitable level of celebrity tied with my job, but that didn't mean I had to perpetuate it.

"I'd rather take Greg from Accounting than one of the interns."

"Greg can't do it either," Alex said. He dropped his phone onto my desk and retrieved the basketball from where it had landed in the corner. He made a shot, the ball arcing across the room and swishing through the basket. "This week is spring break, and he's got a kid. They're doing a family thing."

"Seriously? I can't even get an accountant to go on my trip? It's starting to feel like the entire office is conspiring against me. Does *everyone* have plans?" I folded my arms across my chest and stared out across the warehouse. There were definitely fewer people in the office than usual, but that couldn't be because of spring break, could it? Wasn't that something that only mattered to people who had kids in school? Greg was more an anomaly than the norm in that respect. Quite a few people had babies, but I didn't think many had school-aged kids at home. "Where is everybody?"

Alex shrugged. "It's just that time of year, I guess. It starts to warm up and people start to use their vacation days."

"And you approved them *all* being out at the same time?"

Alex tugged at the collar of his shirt then pushed his hands into his pockets. Was he uncomfortable? "Not everyone will be out all week," he said, almost too casually. "And you have good people. Everything is still getting done."

Maybe. But that didn't do anything to solve my problem. I'd done a lot of random and impromptu trips over the years. And my original team had always been able to make it work. It was irritating enough knowing I was going to have to introduce a new person to viewers. I wanted it to at least be someone I knew.

"What about another YouTuber?" I asked. "I could call Rizzo." We'd collaborated together in the past, so viewers would at least be familiar with his work. And he'd bring his own viewership, which could only help launch the new Connections segment.

"Right. Because Rizzo seems like the kind of guy who would fly all the way from California to Charleston just so he can cram himself into a Volkswagen Rabbit and drive twelve hundred miles with your sorry carcass."

"Wow. Thanks for the vote of confidence, man."

"Sorry. I just don't like Rizzo."

I couldn't exactly blame him. And if I really thought about it, Rizzo *wasn't* the kind of person I wanted on my trip.

"Hey, what about Rosie?" Alex asked.

I shot him a look. That was a random suggestion. "From web

design?" Rosie was at her desk, leaning toward Greta while they both looked at a tablet Rosie held in her hands.

"I only thought of her because she's *from* Kansas," Alex said. "That might make for some interesting conversation if she knows something about where you're headed."

"Right, but . . . would she do it?"

"It couldn't hurt to ask. She's got a pretty cool vibe. It would probably translate well to your viewers."

"Yeah, I'm sure it would. But that doesn't mean she'd be comfortable on camera. I get the sense that she's pretty introverted."

"Maybe," Alex said. "But she's also really funny. And it's not like you'd be forcing her to interact with huge crowds of people. It'll just be three of you in the car. I think she could handle it."

It was a weird suggestion, and yet, having Rosie along might actually work. She *was* funny. I'd had enough conversations with her to know that she was great at banter, that she had a quick wit and great comedic timing. At the same time, she'd turned down the opportunity to be on camera when I'd asked her to help with the Drake Martinson questions. And going on the road trip would require her to be on camera a lot more than that.

"I don't know, man. I still don't think she'd do it."

Alex shrugged. "That only leaves the interns. You could always delay the trip a few weeks, then we can plan better, and Steven could make the trip with you."

I shook my head. I didn't want to wait. I'd been waiting too long already. Now that I'd made the decision to meet Ana in person, I couldn't make it happen fast enough.

"No. It has to be now. I've already messaged her and told her I'm coming."

"Then . . ." Alex motioned toward Rosie as she walked across the warehouse floor toward the kitchen.

"Would it be weird taking a woman with me . . . to go meet another woman?"

"You'll just be going as friends, right? And Tyler will be with you the entire time."

Tyler. I'd forgotten that I'd thought about setting Tyler up with Rosie. This could be a good opportunity for them to get to know each other. "So I should just ask her?"

Alex clapped me on the back. "Go for it. I think she's your best shot at making this trip work."

@RandomIOfficial: Okay. Everything is set. Have I told you how excited I am to meet you in person?

@Briarsandthorns: You have. A few times. It's starting to worry me, actually.

@RandomIOfficial: Why is that?

@Briarsandthorns: Because I'm very ordinary, Isaac. And your expectations feel very . . . not ordinary.

@RandomIOfficial: That was a very honest answer. But I don't think you are ordinary. And I don't think I'll be disappointed.

@Briarsandthorns: You haven't met me yet, remember? I could be.

@RandomIOfficial: I have good intuition, Ana. It's guided me through life so far. I don't think I'm wrong about you.

Chapter Fifteen

Isaac

Rosie was sitting on her porch steps, her elbows resting on her knees, when I pulled to a stop in front of her house early Friday morning. She wore bright purple Converse and big sunglasses, with a striped blazer over a vintage-looking t-shirt I couldn't quite make out. A suitcase the same color as her shoes sat at her feet.

"I still don't understand why we have to take such a small car," Tyler said, shifting in the back seat.

I eased the car into park and turned to face him. "Are you kidding? This car is a classic. Have you ever seen interior plaid like this?" I ran my hand down the side of the passenger seat. "This is a car that has character."

"Says the man who doesn't have to sit in a munchkin-sized backseat with all the equipment and luggage."

I grinned. Tyler wouldn't be Tyler if he didn't complain about something, but he'd filmed from far worse locations. Perched on the back of a golf cart. Riding backward on a roller coaster. Sitting on the back of a donkey. He could handle the backseat of a VW Rabbit. "This is why I pay you the big bucks."

He rolled his eyes. "Yeah, yeah. Are we stopping for food? I'm already hungry."

"Road trip snacks are up next, but we've got to get some opening shots first."

"Want to do them here? The light's good, and her house has a good Charleston beach bungalow vibe."

"Yeah, but give me a minute first. Let me get her up to speed and make sure she's comfortable before you start rolling."

"No problem. I'll just stretch out and relax while I wait. I've got tons of space back here."

I ignored Tyler's grumbling and climbed out of the car, squashing the nerves that flared in my gut. Rosie had agreed to make the trip pretty quickly when I'd asked her the day before yesterday, but there had definitely been hesitation lurking in her eyes. I was pretty sure it was only the assurance that we could stop off and see her parents on the way home that had pushed her into saying yes. Weirdly, her parents lived in a suburb of Kansas City, just an hour or so away from where Ana lived in Lawrence. We wouldn't even have to make a detour.

She stood as I approached and pushed her hands into the front pockets of her jeans.

"You ready to do this?" I asked.

She nodded and looked at her feet where a cat was wrapping itself around her legs. "Yep. I just need to put Reggie inside."

"Will he be all right while we're gone?"

She scooped the cat into her arms. "He'll be good. My landlord will check on him for me."

I reached over and scratched the cat's ears; he pushed his head into my hand and started purring. "Thanks again for agreeing to do this. I know I put you on the spot, but I really appreciate it."

"It's not a big deal. And hey, I'll get to see my parents so . . . woohoo! Free trip." She closed her eyes and gave her head the tiniest shake, a splash of pink creeping onto her cheeks. "I, um . . ." She shifted the cat onto her shoulder. "Let me just get him . . ." She turned toward the door. "Then I'll be good to go."

She was obviously nervous, but maybe that wasn't too surprising. She'd never been in one of my videos. A road trip with a guy she didn't know all that well was a lot to ask. A road trip with a camera filming the entire thing? Rosie was a good sport.

She closed and locked her front door, the cat safely inside, and took an audible breath. "Okay. Let's do this."

I cocked my head to the side and studied her. "Actually, let's sit a minute." I motioned to the stairs.

Her eyebrows went up. "Here?"

I sat first, and she followed, placing herself a few feet away on the step beside me.

"So here's how things will go." I looked at Tyler and gestured for him to join us. "I'd like to do some introductory shots here, outside the car before we leave. I'll introduce you to viewers, we'll get a shot of the car, I'll do some basic explaining of what the trip is going to look like, then you and I will climb into the car and drive around the block so Tyler can get a shot of us leaving before we circle back and pick him up."

"Well that feels sneaky," she said, though there was a smile behind her words.

"Not sneaky. Just good storytelling."

She shook her head. "I don't know if I like seeing behind the curtain, Isaac. This trip is going to ruin the magic for me, isn't it?"

"It might," I said wryly, "but only because you're going to realize how boring it can sometimes be to get all the footage we need. Tyler will do a lot of filming, probably so much that you'll eventually forget he's there. Just try and relax. Remember that ninety percent of what he films won't make the final cut. So you don't have to worry about being on-air perfect all the time. If you say anything you don't want in the video, you can just look at Tyler and tell him to edit it out. And he totally will. There will be a lot of boring dead time, but hopefully, there will also be good conversation, and if we're lucky, something unexpected and amazing will happen. That's why Tyler will keep the camera rolling. To expect the unexpected."

"I actually do a lot better at expecting the *expected.* So if you could just give me a heads up when the unexpected is about to happen, then I'll be able to prepare myself appropriately."

I grinned, a comfort settling into my gut. This trip was going to be just fine.

"I'll do my best to warn you. So we'll talk, keep things easy, and Tyler will capture whatever happens. At the end of the day, he'll do a rough edit, taking out dead time and anything either of us specifically wants cut, then he'll send all the footage back to Mushroom and Vinnie and they'll work their editing magic on it and make it interesting."

"When will the video air?" she asked. "Will it just be one?" She reached up and tucked a curl behind her ear, but it sprung back, falling against her cheek. In the sunlight, her hair was a deep, rich brown.

I blinked, clearing away the distraction—how had I missed how curly her hair was?—and focused on answering her question. "Just one video, though we'll send all the footage back to the studio every night so they can start work on it. As soon as I've met Ana and everything is wrapped up, we'll try to get the video edited and ready within a couple of days. The only thing viewers will see before then are any live streams, if I even decide to do any. But you won't need to be in those unless you just want to be."

She nodded. "Got it."

"We're stopping for lunch in Asheville today, then driving west to Nashville where we'll eat dinner and spend the night, then we'll drive the last leg of the trip tomorrow; we should arrive in Kansas City by nightfall. That's when Ana is expecting me to arrive."

She was quiet for a beat, her eyes locked on mine. "Are you nervous about that part?"

I shrugged. "Yes and no."

"Why is that?"

"Yes because it's possible meeting in person will mess up the dynamic of our friendship. And I really like our friendship. But no because . . . I don't know. Ana is different. And I've just got a really good feeling about her. I've always been one to trust my gut, so . . . I'm going for it."

"Are we ready to do this?" Tyler asked. "I'm still hungry." He shot me a bored look and I rolled my eyes.

"Have you met Tyler yet?" I gave her a pointed look, hoping she understood my meaning.

She smiled tightly and shook her head. "Not yet."

"Tyler, Rosie. Rosie, Tyler," I said quickly, motioning between them. "This will be a theme of the trip," I said. "Tyler will always be hungry."

After filming a brief intro outside of the car, trying multiple times to get a shot of Rosie and me buckling our seatbelts with synchronous clicks—the fifth time finally worked—and leaving Tyler in Rosie's driveway to film the departing shot, we circled back to grab Tyler and were on our way.

With all three of us in the car, the Rabbit *did* feel a little cramped, but you wouldn't hear me admitting as much to Tyler. I'd picked this car on purpose. Because it was distinctive. And retro. And, despite outward appearances, good for the environment. Though the body style was right out of the seventies, the car had been entirely rebuilt to house an electric engine. A friend I'd known back in high school had recently started a business in Charleston converting classic cars into electric vehicles. But he was having a hard time getting things off the ground, and a little bit of free publicity would go a long way to generate some interest and put his business on the map.

I glanced into the rearview mirror, noticing how scrunched Tyler looked. I'd bought the car without a second thought, immediately loving the idea of helping my friend *and* acquiring an electric vehicle, which was something I'd been thinking about doing for a while anyway. But Tyler was possibly going to kill me by the time we made it to Kansas. Rosie seemed comfortable enough, at least. She was only slightly taller than Dani; her small frame made the front seat look spacious.

"Snacks next, right?" Tyler said from the backseat. "I cannot road trip without snacks."

Rosie shot me a sideways glance. "He's right. Every road trip needs snacks. Luckily, I came prepared."

She reached for her bag and opened it up before pulling things out one by one. "I only took care of the candy, though. We still need to stop for drinks and salty things."

"You have given this some thought."

She looked up, her eyes steady. "I am very serious about my food."

Tyler sighed longingly. "I think I just found the woman of my dreams."

Rosie grinned, and the tension she'd been carrying in her shoulders since getting in the car seemed to melt away. "You haven't even seen what I packed."

"You're overestimating his culinary discernment," I said. "Tyler only needs it to be edible. The specifics don't matter."

"That's concerning then because I did actually bring something that isn't edible."

"I am intrigued," I said, enjoying the banter. I tossed a quick glance over my shoulder to make sure Tyler was filming. I hadn't expected Rosie to settle in so soon.

"Since every normal person agrees that Twizzlers are the very best road trip snack, I have three different kinds, including everyone's favorite, Cherry Nibs."

"Yes," Tyler said from behind us, extending a hand and taking the Twizzlers from Rosie.

"But for you," she said, lifting up a second bag, "the one whose taste buds are obviously all dead, I have some Australian black licorice."

My eyes widened. "What? Where did you find that? How did you know?"

"You said it on a video once. Do you actually like this stuff? I was kinda hoping you had just been kidding, and this would be more like a practical joke."

My mind caught momentarily on the fact that Rosie remembered such a random detail from an old video. Off hand, I couldn't remember what I'd said or when I'd said it, but I'd loved black licorice since I was a kid. And I'd made a lot of videos over the years. I wasn't surprised I'd mentioned it at some point. "You are speaking blasphemous words, Rosie Crenshaw." I reached for the bag with my spare hand. "Have you even tried it? The Australian stuff is so much better than anything you can find here in the states."

"Of course I haven't tried it. And I won't, either, so don't get any ideas. No one actually *likes* black licorice."

"Then why do jelly bean companies keep making black jelly beans?"

"To keep us grounded in reality," she said. "Life is good . . . but not that good."

I laughed. "I swear, the Australian stuff tastes better. You have to try it."

"I . . . do not have to try it. I bought it for you, Isaac. It's a gift."

Tyler chuckled from the back seat. "This is great, guys."

Rosie's eyes widened and she glanced into the back seat, as if she'd forgotten Tyler was there and filming. She looked back at her lap, suddenly looking flustered.

Stupid Tyler. He'd thrown her off.

"Let's stop for drinks," I said, hoping we'd be able to find our rhythm again. Rosie was quick and witty; she'd make for some entertaining conversations, but Tyler may have to fade into the background a little more for it to happen. "But then you're trying it," I said to Rosie, hoping she sensed my playful tone.

"Fine," she said, a smile lifting the corners of her eyes. "But I'm only doing it for the satisfaction of proving you wrong."

Chapter Sixteen

Rosie

Isaac put me at ease in person as readily as he'd put me at ease when we'd first started chatting online. He was, quite possibly, the easiest person I'd ever talked to, even with a silent observer filming our entire conversation. We'd only been in the car twenty minutes when we stopped at a gas station—an intentional stop at a specific chain—but I already felt ten times better about the trip. I'd learned through all my therapy that half the battle with anxiety was feeling anxious . . . about the possibility of feeling anxious. But so far, I'd been able to remember that I was in control, that I could turn on my inner actress and play a role for the camera.

"So here's the plan," Isaac said as he cut the engine outside the gas station. "In addition to whatever beverages and snacks you want, we're going to each pick one additional thing. It has to be something that you've never tried before, but that you think the other person is probably going to hate."

"Can the black licorice count as the thing you think I'm going to hate?" I asked. "Because I don't think it's fair that I'm going to have to taste *two* terrible things, and you're only going to have to taste one. That is the point, right? We're going to have to try the thing the other person picked out?"

He grinned. "That is exactly the point. But I'm not giving you a pass on the black licorice. Because I think you're actually going to *like* it."

I looked back at Tyler, the first time I'd intentionally made eye contact with his camera. "I'm stating emphatically, for the record, I am *not* going to like the black licorice." A little thrill shot through me. That hadn't been too hard. I was doing this. And maybe not badly.

After Isaac checked in with the store manager, we wandered the store, Tyler splitting his time between us. I grabbed a twenty-ounce Cherry Coke and a bag of Cheddar Cheese Combos, a road trip snack that went all the way back to my childhood, then scanned the aisles for something Isaac might hate. Knowing that he liked black licorice made it hard to guess. At the end of the aisle, a display of salt water taffy caught my eye, one package in particular standing out. I grinned and picked it up. Pickle-flavored salt water taffy. *Perfect.*

I met Isaac at the counter where we unloaded our selections. In Isaac's hands? Cherry Coke, Cheddar Cheese Combos, and . . . pickle-flavored salt water taffy.

Isaac grinned. "This entire store, and we managed to pick out the exact same things?"

I bit my lip. "To be fair, Combos and Cherry Coke is absolutely the best possible road trip snack."

"Inarguably." He held my gaze for a second longer, his eyes holding a measure of interest I'd never noticed in them before. Not that I'd spent a lot of time staring into his eyes.

Some whisper shouting sounded behind us and we both turned.

Two kids, maybe twelve or thirteen, stood a few feet away, their eyes locked on Isaac. "I told you it was him," one said to the other, elbowing him in the ribs.

"Shut up," the other said, rubbing at his midsection. "I never said I didn't believe you."

Isaac pulled out a credit card and offered it to me. "Would you mind getting this stuff while I . . ." He motioned to the kids with his head.

I nodded and took his card. "Sure. Go ahead."

Tyler and the camera followed Isaac.

I watched from the corner of my eye as Isaac stopped in front of the kids, talking to them for a few seconds then leaning down so they could each take a selfie with him. Tyler kept the camera trained on Isaac the entire time. The kids didn't seem to care; it was clearly a price they were willing to pay to meet someone they obviously really loved. The smaller kid was even wearing a *Random I* t-shirt.

After a couple minutes of chatting, Isaac pulled a Sharpie out of his pocket and signed the kid's t-shirt before saying goodbye and sending them out the door.

"Will they be in the video?" I asked as I stepped up next to Isaac, the bag of snacks in hand. I handed him his card and he slipped it back into his wallet.

"Nah," he said. "Nothing significant happened."

"That's the way it works," Tyler added. "You keep the camera running just because something might."

"Does it get complicated though?" I asked as we made our way back to the car. "Don't you have to have permission to put people in a video?"

"Only if they can be identified in the shot," Tyler said. "Sometimes it's worth it to get the consent forms signed; other times, it's easier to just edit out anything that shows identifying characteristics."

It was crazy to think about all the moving parts, the back-scene stuff that viewers never had to think about when they were watching. I was beginning to recognize that the magic of *Random I* wasn't so much magical as it was a lot of people doing a lot of tedious things that all added up to something that *felt* magical. Of course, Isaac's magnetic personality didn't hurt matters.

"Did we get everything we need?" Isaac asked Tyler, his hand resting on the open driver-side door.

Tyler stared at the digital screen on his camera. "Actually, can we get one more shot of the two of you walking inside? The first take has a few people in the background that will be hard to edit out." He looked from Isaac to me. "You don't have to go all the way inside. Just walk from here to the door. And go quick while there isn't anyone else around."

I fell into step next to Isaac as we crossed the short distance to the gas station door. "It's not too late to slip back inside and pick out something *not* flavored like pickles," I said dryly as we approached.

Isaac shot me a sideways grin. "And ruin the fun?"

"Why is it that YouTube personalities have such a penchant for eating disgusting things?"

"Because it's funny," Isaac said without missing a beat. "And making people laugh is a lot of fun." He looked back at Tyler. "Did that work?"

Tyler gave us a thumbs up, so we hurried back to the car. It had been more than an hour, and we were still less than thirty minutes away from home. Alex had been right. This was definitely not a normal road trip.

"Do you ever get tired of people wanting to talk to you everywhere you go?" I asked Isaac when we were finally back on the road.

He shrugged dismissively. "Not really. People are usually pretty chill about it. And it's not like *everyone* knows who I am. Even people who have seen a handful of videos and might recognize the name of the show don't necessarily recognize me when I'm just walking down the street. Out of context, it doesn't always click for people. It's definitely not paparazzi-level stardom."

That made sense. From what I'd observed, Isaac was generally able to move around Charleston with relative freedom, though I'd gotten the impression from listening in on Jade and Greta's conversations that Alex didn't like Isaac to travel by himself. Something about other people providing a necessary buffer. If Isaac was with friends, people were less likely to approach. If he was alone? There was nothing to keep them from invading Isaac's space and taking up his time. Not that Isaac had seemed to care when the kids at the gas station had approached. But surely even for Isaac it would get tiring if that happened all the time.

I pulled our snacks out of the back, belatedly realizing that there was very little center console space to speak of. Unless Isaac was just going to hold his drink the whole time, I'd have to act as somewhat of a snack distributor. I at least handed Tyler's things back to him; he had a little bit of seat room that wasn't occupied by equipment, though he hardly looked comfortable with a portable boom mic pole digging into his leg.

"So, I guess I'll just hang onto this stuff?" I said, holding it up for Isaac to see. "You can just tell me when you want something."

"Should have brought a bigger car," Tyler said from the backseat, his voice all sing-songy and high.

"Should have brought a different cameraman," Isaac sing-songed back. He shot me an apologetic look. "Sorry there isn't a ton of room. I'll take my drink now. And we can share a bag of combos."

"I love this car," I said, handing Isaac his Cherry Coke. "It has character."

"See?" He looked at Tyler through the rearview mirror. "Rosie gets it."

"Rosie isn't six feet tall and sitting in the back seat," Tyler shot back. "Are you guys going to eat the licorice now? I'd like something to distract me from the feeling of my knees digging into my armpits."

My phone buzzed inside my purse at my feet, and I pulled it out, suddenly realizing that I hadn't yet silenced my notifications. "Give me just a sec," I said, jumping to my settings before I read the message. Even just on vibrate, you could still hear it when a message arrived. I didn't think Isaac would be sending messages to Ana while he was driving, but better to silence the notifications now just in case. Isaac was a smart guy.

If my phone buzzed every time he sent a message, it wouldn't take him long to piece things together.

After silencing everything that could possibly be silenced—sounds, vibrations, all of it—I pulled up the message that had just arrived.

Please tell me I'm not a terrible mom, Marley had texted.

I quickly keyed out a response. *You are an amazing mom. Not terrible in any way. You okay?*

Yeah, she replied. *Just tired. Shiloh is having a moment.*

What kind of moment? I texted back. *Elaborate.*

"Everything okay?" Isaac asked from across the car.

I looked up and briefly met his eye. "Yeah. It's just my nephew. He's giving his mom some trouble, I guess."

"A nephew. So you have siblings?"

"Oh. Not exactly." I turned my phone face down in my lap wanting to give Isaac my full attention. Hopefully Marley would understand if I didn't respond right away. "Marley is my cousin, but she came to live with my family when she was sixteen. I was fifteen, so we basically spent the next three years as best friends. She feels more like a sister than anything. And since I'm otherwise an only child, her kid is my only shot at being an aunt."

"Do you like it? Being an aunt?" Isaac asked.

I grinned. "Yeah. Shiloh is amazing. A handful, but an amazing one."

"I'll be an uncle in a few months," Isaac said, a genuine smile splitting his face. "Dani's pregnant."

"What?" Tyler said. "Are you serious?"

Isaac cursed under his breath. "I . . . was not supposed to say anything. Sorry, Tyler. She's still early days so they aren't telling people yet." He tossed a look over his shoulder. "You'll edit that out, yeah?"

"You got it," Tyler said from behind the camera. "I'm happy for her. That's awesome."

"Tyler went to high school with Dani and me," Isaac said. "He's known us a long time."

So many of Isaac's people had been with him from the beginning. It suddenly made me feel a little bit like an imposter. How could I ever expect to fit in to his already-close-knit circle?

"A lot of your people have been with you since the beginning, haven't they?"

"A good number," Isaac answered. "Some were with us and then left to do other things, then came back. That's what Jade did."

I nodded. "Yeah. She told me."

"I'm glad you guys have been hanging out. They're a lot of fun."

I shrugged as if indifferent to his words. "Jade and Diedre are fine, I guess, but I mostly just hang out with them for Max."

Isaac grinned. "You speak the truth. Are you going to Diedre's show next weekend?"

Diedre had started her art career selling seascapes out of a booth at the open-air market in downtown Charleston. Her reputation had slowly grown, and around the time she'd met Jade, she'd gotten her first painting into a King Street gallery. Since then, she'd slowly built a reputation as one of Charleston's finest local artists and was slated to be featured in a gallery opening the following week.

"I'd planned on going," I said. "Though I already told Jade if she can't find anyone to hang with the kids, I'll babysit so she can go and be the glowing supportive wife without the kids underfoot."

"That was awesome of you to offer."

I shrugged. "I'm happy to do it. I really like Diedre."

"Yeah. She balances out Jade's harder edges, doesn't she?"

"Exactly." I looked into the back where Tyler was still filming.

"Don't worry," Isaac said, as if reading my concern. "He'll edit all of this out. Jade and Diedre would not be happy to serve as fodder for our on-air conversations, especially since we mentioned the kids."

Tyler dropped the camera. "How about you guys get all your family talk out of the way while I eat a little and then we can film you eating pickle taffy and licorice."

My stomach rolled over at the thought. I'd only opened the black licorice bag long enough to smell it and that had felt like more than enough.

I shifted in my seat and turned to face Isaac. "I'd like to know everything there is to know about your family," I said dryly. "Start with your birth and don't skip any details."

He smiled. "Avoidance. Admirable tactic. But you know it isn't going to work forever."

"So are you the older twin? Or is Dani?" I asked, undeterred by his warning.

He shook his head, but his smile never left. "Dani is older. And she never lets me forget it."

Conversation was easy for the next half hour, though I had more than a few brief moments of panic trying to remember what things *Ana* had told Isaac about her family so I could make sure not to claim the same details. Ana had a sister—a matter of semantics, that difference—and had grown up in Lawrence, just outside of Kansas City. My parents still lived there, in the house I'd grown up in. When he asked me where *I* was from, relative to Lawrence, I claimed a closer suburb of Kansas City, where my grandparents had lived, since I knew enough about the town to sound convincing. It was a tiny lie, but one I hoped he'd forgive once he discovered the truth. The one thing I made sure not to claim as Rosie was any affection for or knowledge of Red Renegade. Since that's what had started his connection with Ana in the first place, I didn't want Rosie to touch it at all.

Also, I was getting very tired of thinking of myself in the third person. As two separate people with different histories that couldn't overlap. It was exhausting.

Thirty-six hours. That's all I had to make it through. A day and a little more and Isaac would know the truth, come what may.

I hoped for it as much as I dreaded it.

Chapter Seventeen

Isaac

Rosie didn't like black licorice.

Even the Australian kind.

She dropped the bag onto her lap and reached for what was left of her Cherry Coke. She took a long swig, emptying the bottle. "Ugh, that barely cut the taste. Are you actually serious when you tell me that you like this stuff?"

I reached into the bag with excessive slowness and pulled out an entire handful, shoving several pieces into my mouth at once.

"Nope," she said, shaking her head. "I think you have to be faking it."

"For what purpose would I be faking my love for black licorice?" I said, grabbing another handful. "It isn't exactly a popular opinion."

"It isn't *anyone's* opinion. Just yours."

"That's not true," I said matter-of-factly. "I went to high school with a girl named Tasha. She loved it too."

"Aww, a cute little two-person club. How sweet."

I tossed a piece of licorice at her nose. "I'm going to make you eat more if you don't stop making fun of me."

"But then I won't be able to eat my pickle-flavored taffy," she said.

(For the record, the pickle taffy got a hard no from both of us.)

The thing about Rosie was that she didn't play to the camera. She wasn't reacting for anyone else's benefit. Not to be funny. Not to get a rise. It was obvious she was just being who she was. It had been a long time since I'd spent time around someone as genuine as Rosie, and it made me wonder if I'd lost sight of who *I* was. Because I never stopped thinking about how my actions, my reactions, my facial expressions, my words played to an audience. I'd been putting my life on camera for more than a decade. Every experience I had filtered through whether or not it would make good television.

I envied Rosie's lack of awareness. It read a little like innocence, but that wasn't the right word. There was just a purity to her personality that, after just an hour or two in her company, I realized I envied. Maybe somewhere deep, I recognized that I used to be that way. But I'd changed.

I wasn't sure I was ready to figure out why. Or if it was for worse or better.

Regardless, who Rosie was worked incredibly well on camera. We had a great, natural vibe between us. When Tyler was too obtrusive, she would clam up a little and retreat, but when she forgot he was there, or at least got better at ignoring him, she sparkled. Her wit was sharp, her humor on point, and her smile was engaging in ways that made my heart flop around in my chest.

But I didn't want to think about Rosie's smile.

I was on my way to see Ana, and she was different from anyone I'd ever met. She got me. Understood me in ways that no one ever had before. Realistically, I knew it was possible we'd see each other in person and not feel a connection. I wasn't so shallow to think that physical attraction was the most important thing, but it did matter. Of course I worried that I'd see her and not feel that spark. But it was hard to imagine that I wouldn't. That's how perfect our connection felt online.

A swell of nerves pulsed through me, and I tensed up, breathing out a quick sigh to try to find my equilibrium. Things would be fine. *Fine.*

"You okay?" Rosie asked. She dropped her phone into her lap.

I gripped the steering wheel. "Uh, yeah. Just got a little nervous thinking about where we're headed."

"It's going to work out, Isaac," she said, the quiet confidence in her voice bolstering me up in a way I hadn't expected. At the same time, a tiny thread of disappointment snaked its way through my mind. Despite my commitment to the cause—to the trip—Rosie had ignited a small spark of attraction somewhere in the recesses of my mind. To have her encouraging me toward another woman quickly stomped out that spark. But that was a good thing. The right thing. Feeling attraction for Rosie would only make this road trip more complicated.

"Have you ever heard of Red Renegade?" I asked on impulse. I thought of the way Bridget had complained whenever I'd played Red Renegade when she was around. If Rosie felt the same way about my favorite band, it would make it that much easier to stomp that spark well and truly out.

I looked over and caught her eye for a brief moment before turning my gaze back to the road. Something had flashed across her expression, but I couldn't guess what it was or what it meant. It looked like . . . recognition.

"The band, right?" She spoke slowly, almost hesitantly, as if she wasn't really sure. "Didn't they play at the Compassion Project benefit you did a couple years ago?"

"Yeah. That was an amazing night. Do you know any of their stuff?"

She bit her lip. "I'm sure I'd probably recognize it if I heard it."

I shouldn't care what she thought. But I suddenly wanted to play a few Renegade songs just to see how she felt about them. If she reacted like Bridget, well, then I would know, and it would be that much easier to keep my mind on track. If she liked them . . . I didn't want to think about what it would mean if she liked them. Because I recognized that I wanted her to. And that was a scary realization.

"Ana loves Red Renegade," I blurted.

Rosie's eyes went wide for a brief moment before she nodded. "Does she?"

I was making things awkward. So, so awkward. "Yeah. That's actually how we met."

"I remember you showing me," Rosie said. "That day out on the patio. It was an album cover, right?"

"Oh, right. Yeah. Yes. Her artwork. She's wicked talented." I almost cringed at the sound of my own words. They sounded so . . . eager. So *convincing.*

"Does she do anything with her art? Is that her job?" Rosie asked.

I shook my head. "It could be, she's that good, but no. She's actually a web designer like you." I paused. "Um, I've never actually made the connection before now, but that's actually kind of weird. You're both web designers, and you're both from Kansas."

She tucked a curl behind her ear. "There are a lot of web designers in Kansas," she said dismissively. "I went to college with quite a few."

"Oh. Right. Of course. Actually, where did you go to school? Maybe you've met her."

"I don't think so," Rosie said quickly, her eyes focused on her phone. "Her name doesn't sound familiar. So, um, do you want to play some Red Renegade for me?" She lifted a shoulder. "Maybe I'll like it."

"Yes. Absolutely," I said, anxious to stop talking—stop *thinking*—and give my brain a second to chill. "Music sounds like a great idea."

We listened to a few songs in silence while we crossed the North Carolina border and started climbing. The Appalachian Mountains were a bright spring green, a stark contrast to the blue skies behind them. I rolled the window down for a brief moment, long enough to feel the chill in the air as we climbed in elevation.

Rosie leaned toward the window, her eyes locked at the looming mountains before us. "This is amazing," she whispered.

"Have you never been here?" I asked. As kids, our parents had taken Dani and me up to the mountains a few times a year to hike and splash in the cool highland creeks. As an adult, Asheville was still one of my favorite getaways. It was different enough from the Lowcountry for me to feel like I'd really gotten away, but it was only a four-hour drive up the highway. It was too easy not to make the trip regularly.

"I've been to the Outer Banks," Rosie said, "But that's nothing like this."

"You'll have to drive back up when you can stay awhile," I said. "Asheville is amazing. Great food. Amazing hiking. Crazy views. The Biltmore House."

"You had me at great food," Rosie said.

We made it into Asheville an hour ahead of schedule, which was impressive, and completely out of character for me. Knowing that Alex had arranged for us to eat at an eclectic taco place that was weeks away from opening three new franchise locations across the Southeast, and that they had scheduled some kind of promotion in conjunction with our stop, I didn't want to show up early. They were expecting us, planning for us. Showing up an hour early would throw them off their game. Instead, I opted to drive up to the Blue Ridge Parkway that crossed through Asheville and give Rosie a view of the mountains. We didn't have enough time to go far, but we could at least get high enough for her to see the view of Mount Pisgah.

We pulled off the parkway onto an overlook and I stopped the car.

Rosie immediately climbed out, her eyes wide as she took in the expansive view.

I couldn't blame her. I never got tired of seeing the mountains. The way they rolled into each other, their varying shades of blue and green blending until, at the edge of the horizon, you couldn't even tell where sky started and mountains stopped.

"This is unbelievable," Rosie said. "I've never seen anything like it."

I put my hands on Rosie's shoulders and gently turned her to face Mount Pisgah, looming just behind her. My hands lingered, liking the sensation of closeness, until I remembered who she was and what I was about. My hands dropped and I took a step back. "See the radio tower? On top of the closest mountain?"

She nodded.

"That's Mount Pisgah. You can drive up to the top. There's an inn there, the Pisgah Inn, and a trailhead for a hike you can take up to the base of the tower. It's only a mile or so, but it's straight up the whole way. The view from the top—it's unbelievable. Three hundred and sixty degrees of nothing but mountains and sky."

"That sounds amazing."

"Yeah. Our parents brought us up here when we were kids. I used to tell Dani that whenever I got married, I'd want to honeymoon up here." I huffed a laugh. "She always made fun of me. Said the world was so huge, why go somewhere so close to home? But . . . I don't know. It seems like the perfect place, you know? It's quiet, peaceful. Great views, great food at the inn, countless places to hike."

"Let's do it," Rosie said, her voice low and breathy. She tensed and spun around, her eyes darting to mine. "That's not . . . I didn't mean . . . not *us* do it," she said, her cheeks flaming. She pressed her palms to her face, sliding her fingers open so that one eye peeked out. "That's not what I meant, I swear."

I pushed my hands into my pockets and grinned. "I mean, this is a pretty perfect location for a proposal, but honestly, your delivery was a little lacking."

She dropped her hands from her face and swatted my shoulder.

"Shut. Up."

"Man. I know I'm charming, but four hours in the car, and you're already ready for a honeymoon. I am better than I thought."

She rolled her eyes and stomped back toward the car. "Oh my word, you are completely ridiculous." When she reached the car, she shot Tyler a menacing look. "If one second of that exchange makes it into the final video, I will quit my job and move home to Kansas and never speak to either of you again."

"That feels serious," Tyler said.

It *did* feel serious.

And I wasn't sure I was ready to analyze exactly why.

Chapter Eighteen

Rosie

The restaurant was crowded.

So crowded. And not just with patrons. Fans had gotten word that Isaac of *Random I* was stopping by for lunch—an intentional move on the restaurant's part—and the people had not disappointed. When we'd first driven past the restaurant and seen the crowds, I'd wondered if it was wise that Isaac was traveling without security. There were people everywhere. We couldn't have found a parking spot in the restaurant lot if we'd wanted to. Fortunately, our instructions were to park *behind* the restaurant and enter through the kitchen to avoid the crowds. They had a table set up for us on the outdoor patio—an area fans would not be able to access—and it would remain that way until we were finished with our meal.

Isaac and Tyler didn't seem to mind the set-up, but I couldn't stop glancing over my shoulder at the semi-circle of fans that was surrounding the patio, in some places two or three people deep. I wasn't used to eating with an audience.

"The tacos are good," Tyler said, scarfing down his fourth— fifth?—taco. "I like the sauce on this one."

Isaac nodded. "We used to come here when I was a kid, too. Actually, it was on my list of places I thought I might want to visit on my—"

"Don't," I said, pointing my finger at him. "Don't you dare."

His eyes danced with laughter, but he didn't say another word.

I had never been so mortified. *Let's do it?* What had I been thinking?

In truth, I would have loved to honeymoon on the Blue Ridge Parkway. We'd only driven a short stretch before coming to lunch, but what I'd seen was gorgeous. We'd driven through a long tunnel that wound right through the mountainside and I'd made Isaac turn the car around so we could drive through it a second time. At the entrance, mountain laurel—according to Google and a useful plant identification tool—was in full bloom, growing up and around the arching roof of the tunnel then continuing up the mountain. Flower petals dotted the road leading into the tunnel, numerous enough to look like pale pink snow. It almost looked like a portal into a different world. Like we might drive through and come out in Narnia.

I'd been swept up in the beauty of it. And fine, yes, I'd let my mind consider the possibility of returning with Isaac without any secrets between us.

But I hadn't thought I would actually say the words *out loud.*

Weirdly enough, it actually helped that Isaac was teasing me about it. Somehow, it dispelled the tension that might have sat between us otherwise.

"Hey, Isaac, I googled the little wedding dress boutique you told me about," Tyler said, his expression serious. "It's right on the way so we should be able to hit it on our way out of town so Rosie can pick out a dress." His voice finally cracked at the end of his sentence before he and

Isaac erupted into laughter.

I dropped my napkin onto my now empty plate. "I literally hate you both." I stood up, unable to stop myself from smiling, despite being the butt of their joke. "I'm going to the bathroom. You're welcome to just leave me here and I'll hitchhike back to Charleston."

"We love you, Rosie," Tyler called as I walked away.

They were *both* ridiculous. Fun. But ridiculous.

The bathroom was crowded enough that I had to wait for a stall, though that was hardly a surprise with the number of people that were outside. Still, I didn't like all the eyes that kept darting my direction. No one talked directly to me while I waited, but people were definitely watching. The line thinned as I waited, so by the time I came out of the stall, there were only a handful of people left—a group of preteen-looking girls who were clearly all together.

And it was obvious they were waiting for me.

I made it to the sink to wash my hands without making eye contact. Maybe if I ignored them, they would take the hint and *not* try and talk to me. I forced a breath, in, then out, and willed my nerves to settle. This wasn't a big deal. Still, sweat broke out across my lower back.

I took an extra-long time drying my hands, but it became glaringly obvious the girls weren't leaving until I did. With a resigned sigh, I finally turned around.

"You're here with Isaac," the first girl said. She was the shortest of the group but had an air of authority about her that supported her being the first one to speak.

"Are you his girlfriend?" another girl asked.

The girl standing next to her elbowed the one who had asked the question. "It's rude to ask that."

"Shut up. It's not like we don't all want to know."

"She can't be his girlfriend because they're on their way to *meet* the woman he's in love with. Didn't you *watch* his last video?" the leader-girl said.

I inched my way to the door, but the girls only stepped closer, completely blocking my path.

"We don't know he's in love with her. He just said she was *special* to him. Your grandma can be special to you. It doesn't mean anything," a fourth girl said. She was the only one who hadn't yet spoken.

The leader-girl rolled her eyes. "He is not driving all the way to Kansas to meet his grandma." She looked to me for confirmation. "Right?"

I held my hands up. "I appreciate your interest, girls, but we've got to get back on the road."

They parted enough for me to push my way through, but that didn't stop one final volley of questions.

"Is he a good driver?"

"Are you in love with him?"

"How much money does he make?"

"Are you the reason he broke up with Bridget?"

"Is the woman in Kansas the reason he broke up with Bridget?"

Sensing that the girls would likely try to follow me out to the terrace—where were their parents?—I ducked around the corner and slipped into the kitchen long enough to lose them. A confused kitchen staff person looked my way, but seeing as how we'd entered through the kitchen, they didn't seem all that concerned that I was back again. I waited another minute or two, then peeked through the round window at the top of the door, assuring myself the teenybopper parade had ended and I was safe to go back outside.

Tyler and Isaac had already left the table, Isaac doing a meet and greet with the fans lined up around the terrace, and Tyler recording the entire thing.

I dropped into my seat, watching as Isaac smiled and laughed and took selfies with the fans. The girls who had accosted me in the bathroom appeared at the edge of the crowd, smiling heart eyes at Isaac as he inched his way toward them.

How did he make it look so easy? So effortless?

I was still in a cold sweat and I'd only dealt with half a dozen middle schoolers. Persistent middle schoolers, but still. They'd been perfectly harmless.

And yet, they'd still knocked me off-kilter. They hadn't known anything about me yet. But if Ana and Isaac became *Rosie and Isaac,* they would know. Their questions would be personal. Specific. If we ever broke up, they would want to know why. Who was at fault? Why did it happen? Would we ever get back together?

And the very nature of Isaac's life meant that some measure of that, his fans would know. They would have to.

I pulled out my phone, hoping for a distraction, and noticed immediately that I had a dozen different messages and four missed calls. Silencing my phone had made me somewhat unreachable.

Most of the messages were completely benign. My mom, wanting to know if she should plan on me and my guests spending a night with them once we arrived tomorrow. Jade, wanting to know how things were going. Greta asking the same thing. Alex warning us that the crowd would be bigger than he'd anticipated at lunch in Asheville. Well. That was the truth. Ana also had a message from Isaac—he must have sent it when I'd been in the bathroom because I didn't remember seeing him on his phone at all—giving me an update on the trip and expressing again how excited he was to meet me. I looked up and made sure he was occupied enough not to notice me responding to him and sent him a quick smiley face. The other messages were all from Marley, as were the four missed calls.

My heart quickened as I read through the messages, starting with the one she'd sent in response to my question about what was going on with Shiloh.

It's hard to say, really, the first message read. *He just seems angry all the time, and he doesn't want to talk to me about why. I think there's a kid at school who's saying stuff about his dad. This is why I wish I'd never moved home. Too many people in this stupid town know too much about my personal life.*

Just before Shiloh had started kindergarten, Marley had reconciled with her parents and moved back to Westonburg, just outside of Nashville, believing that Shiloh would benefit from a closer relationship with his grandparents. The move had nearly killed *my* mom, who had been acting as surrogate grandma for five years, but she'd understood that Marley's parents deserved a second chance. Mom was a social worker. She'd always opt for reconciliation between families whenever it was possible.

The move *had* been a good thing for Marley and Shiloh when it came to their relationship with Marley's parents. The downside was that Westonburg was small. Everybody knew everybody. And everybody included Shiloh's biological father, Blake Shepherd, the town's golden son who had gone off to law school at UT and returned home to set up practice. He'd married someone local and had promptly started a family, living a perfectly perfect life right down to the white picket fence that lined his front lawn—a perfect life that made no mention of the fact that five years before, he'd slept with a girl three years his junior and then abandoned her when she'd discovered she was pregnant.

Until Marley had shown up with a kid no one had known about except her parents, who had also, quite intentionally, told exactly no one.

The trouble was, the older Shiloh got, the more he looked like his father. Suddenly it wasn't so easy for the golden son to deny that he'd had anything to do with Marley's baby. No matter how much Marley insisted she didn't want anything to do with Blake, the town still talked. And by the time Shiloh was ten years old, the talking had finally compelled Blake into stepping up.

But Marley had been raising Shiloh for ten years on her own. She wasn't interested in letting him in. And who could blame her? Blake had known about Shiloh since day one. Why should she suddenly let him jump in now?

After that first text, Marley's messages grew a little more panicked.

I just got a call from the school. Shiloh ran away from recess today and they can't find him.

Rosie. Is there a reason you aren't answering my texts? This is a big freaking deal.

Has he reached out to you? Tried to call?

Finally, her last message read, *We found him, thank God. He was at Blake's house. He rode his bike all the way to the edge of town to confront him. My world is so upside down right now. Where are you?!*

I glanced up at Isaac, who had nearly reached the edge of the crowd. This was not the time or place to call Marley back. I typed out a quick text instead. *I'm so sorry! My phone has been on silent all day and I missed all of this until just now. I'm so glad he's found and safe. I'll call you as soon as I can. I'm sorry I can't be there with you right now.*

I dropped my phone on the table and pressed my forehead into my hands. Poor Marley. Poor Shiloh. I hated not being in a position where I could do more. Marley didn't need sympathy texts. She needed a friend. She needed *me.*

A sudden thought popped into my head. We were staying in Nashville that night. And Nashville was only forty-five minutes away from Westonburg. That was hardly a detour. It wouldn't even need to *be* a detour. Once we were checked into our hotel, I could borrow the car and drive over to see Marley, or even Uber if Isaac didn't want me to drive the Rabbit, spend the night with her, and be back at the hotel the next morning. It wouldn't add any extra time to our trip.

I debated whether or not I should tell Marley. A part of me wanted to surprise her. Another part thought it might help her to know I was coming. But then, the road trip wasn't *my* trip. I couldn't tell her I was coming if there was any chance it might not happen. A surprise was likely the best way to go. That way, if it didn't happen, she wouldn't be disappointed over something she hadn't even known to expect.

After a few more minutes of talking and picture taking and a final shout out to the restaurant and the amazing food we'd enjoyed for lunch, we were back in the car, headed toward Knoxville, Tennessee on Interstate 40. The drive through the Pigeon River Gorge was stunning enough that we hardly talked, and Tyler spent more time filming the scenery than he did me and Isaac.

"It's a shame we don't have time to go to Dollywood," Isaac said after a particularly long stretch of silence.

"Dolly what?" I leaned my head back in my seat.

Isaac shot me a look. "Have you never heard of Dollywood?"

"Is that what the billboard was for a few miles back?"

"Cut her some slack, man," Tyler said from the back seat. "She didn't grow up in the South."

"Dollywood is possibly the best amusement park in the entire country, named most prodigiously for its creator and benefactor, the ever-talented Eastern Tennessee native, Dolly Parton."

My eyebrows lifted and I looked back at Tyler. "Did he swallow a brochure or something?"

"He's very passionate about Dollywood. So passionate, you should probably expect it as a part of your honeymoon tour."

"You are never going to let me live that down, are you?"

Tyler shot me a knowing look. "Are you sure you want me to?"

I tensed, my eyes automatically darting to Isaac before I focused back on Tyler. What was he trying to say? And more importantly, what would Isaac make of it?

"Whatever," I finally said. "I think you're both ridiculous." I turned around to face the front. "This is how rumors get started. And if the pack of middle-schoolers who nearly accosted me in the bathroom back at the restaurant is any indication, you cannot afford to start baseless rumors."

Isaac suddenly looked concerned. "Are you okay? They didn't actually accost you, did they?"

The warmth in his tone helped ease the sting of Tyler's too-pointed teasing. "Not with anything but their words," I said. "But they were very persistent with their questions. For a minute, I actually wondered if they were going to let me leave."

"Did you answer any of their questions?" Isaac asked.

"Of course not. They were all . . . personal."

"Like what?"

"Like whether or not I'm your girlfriend. Or whether or not I had something to do with you and Bridget breaking up. How much money do you make? Are you in love with the woman we're going to meet in Kansas?"

"A middle school girl really asked how much money I make?"

I shrugged. "She was wearing a shirt that said *Future Accountants of America* on it."

"Is that even a thing?" Tyler asked.

"Regardless, I didn't answer anything. I hid in the kitchen until they'd all left so I could escape back to the terrace."

Isaac nodded. "That's definitely one strategy."

"There's another one? What would you have done in that situation?"

"Fortunately, I likely won't ever be accosted by a pack of middle-school girls in the bathroom."

I rolled my eyes. "Pretend for a minute, then. I'm genuinely curious. How do you deal with the questions?"

"The key is to answer just enough that they feel like they're getting something from you. Then they'll leave you alone."

"So you just tell them what they want to know? Doesn't that feel horrible? To share your personal life just because a curious stranger asked?"

Isaac tilted his head as if really thinking about my question. "Here's the thing you have to remember. To me, the people asking questions are strangers. But I don't feel like a stranger to *them.* A lot of these people who recognize me, approach me, have been watching my show for years. Sometimes it seems like they know more about my life than I do. So even though the questions can feel inappropriate to *me* when they ask them, it helps to remember that they don't feel like a violation of my privacy to *them.*"

"Okay, that makes sense. But still. No matter how well they think they know you, they still shouldn't ask how much money you make."

"True. And that question, I would never actually answer. Not outright, anyway. But there are ways you can answer questions without actually telling people anything."

"Explain," I said, folding my arms across my chest. The whole concept made me feel defensive on his behalf.

"Just try me," Isaac said. "Ask me the questions the girls asked you earlier."

I didn't actually want to ask him point-blank if *I* was his girlfriend—we'd had enough teasing today already—so I modified the question just slightly. "Do you have a girlfriend?"

"When I'm in a relationship I'm ready to share with the world, I'll be sure to let everyone know."

Huh. That was pretty good. He answered without actually confirming or denying the presence of a relationship.

"Okay, how about this one. Is the woman in Kansas the reason you and Bridget broke up?"

Isaac pursed his lips. "That one's tougher. Okay, how about: Bridget is a lovely person, and we're still friends. We're both excited to be moving in new directions."

"Is that actually true?" I asked him.

"Sort of. I mean, I'm happy to be her friend as soon as she returns my vintage 1987 Red Renegade t-shirt."

"I saw her wearing that shirt," I said, feeling vindicated that Isaac hadn't actually given it away. "The one from their limited-edition album, right?"

He glanced away from the road long enough for me to see the question in his eyes. "Yeah, but I thought you didn't know Red Renegade's stuff."

Well, hell. How was I going to backpedal out of this one?

"No, I don't. I didn't. But Bridget was wearing it at the pool party at Jade and Diedre's, and I told her I liked her shirt. She's the one who told me what it was."

Isaac nodded, appearing somewhat appeased. "I guess she'd heard me tell her enough times how important the shirt was. I shouldn't be surprised that she remembered enough to explain it to you. But it never felt like she was actually listening."

"Yeah. She told me she only took it because she liked the colors. She still hasn't given it back?"

He shook his head. "Nope. And I'm not sure she ever will."

I was already playing with fire what with how close I'd come to outing myself. But I couldn't stop myself from asking one more question. "How *did* the break-up with Bridget go? Did you order her dinner to go?"

"I did. And she took it home with her, so thanks for that suggestion. Actually, you've given me good suggestions a few times now. It's like you're my own private relationship guru."

My stomach tightened. There was nothing worse that he could have said.

Tyler leaned up and smacked Isaac on the back. "She's a good friend, right? Giving you girlfriend advice. Coming on the road trip. She's just like one of the guys."

Ouch. This just kept getting worse and worse.

"No," Isaac said quickly, shooting Tyler a weird look. "That's not what I . . . she's not—"

"It's fine," I said, cutting him off. Things had already gotten bad enough. I didn't need to hear Isaac's excuses or explanations of me and what I meant to him. "I'm glad we're friends, and I'm always happy to give you advice."

"I appreciate that," Isaac said, still throwing daggers over his shoulder at Tyler. "You're easy to talk to, Rosie. So I'm grateful you're willing to listen."

Something had happened between the two friends. There was obviously some implied meaning to Tyler's comment that had frustrated Isaac. But what? And why? We were on our way to meet Ana. Why would Isaac have any reason to feel defensive about Tyler calling me one of the guys?

I thought back to the moment on the elevator when Isaac had offered to introduce me to Tyler. So *that* was the look he'd given me earlier that morning when he'd first asked if I'd met Tyler before. He was suggesting I might be interested in *meeting* Tyler. *Dating* Tyler.

Hot emotion pulsed through me, a combination of fear and anger and embarrassment all rolled into one. This trip was not going to end well. Isaac really *did* see me as one of the guys. Or as a personal relationship guru, whatever that meant. Which meant he couldn't possibly see me as potentially datable material.

If the sadness that swelled inside me at the thought did anything at all, it told me just how big my feelings for Isaac had actually become. I still had my doubts. Fears about Isaac's life in the public eye. But if the thought of *not* having a relationship with him affected me so keenly? Those doubts couldn't be taking up too much room in my heart.

Which meant the potential rejection at the end of this whole ordeal was only going to hurt that much worse.

Diedre's words flitted through my brain. *You're the one taking the risk, here, Rosie. No one else.* She was right, of course. And I was suddenly terrified that I was going to live to regret it.

Chapter Nineteen

Rosie

We pulled into the hotel parking lot in Nashville a little after seven p.m. Luckily, Alex's itinerary had allowed us a quiet dinner that we'd picked up on the road without having to do any correlating publicity; I wasn't sure I could have handled a second round of what lunch had been.

"Chesapeake Hotel and Lounge," I read off the bright neon sign that hung above the parking lot. "I suppose they're expecting us?"

"Nah. I just picked this place because of the honeymoon suite."

Tyler guffawed from the back seat and I suddenly wanted to smack them both. "Very funny."

Isaac grinned. "Chesapeake has hotels all over the Central United States, and they just installed charging stations in all their parking lots. We get a full charge, we help them get the word out, we stay in their best suites, and everyone goes home happy."

I stretched my arms over my head, though the car didn't actually allow me to extend them fully. I was ready to get out and walk around a little.

"I'll go get us checked in," Isaac said before climbing from the car. Standing outside, he pulled his hoodie up and over his head, an attempt, I imagined, to make it slightly more difficult to recognize him.

The hotel wasn't dead, by any means, but it wasn't exactly bustling either. I hoped, for Isaac's sake, that no one inside would notice him.

"Should I have offered to check us in?" I asked. "I don't mind. And why doesn't he have an assistant who travels with him to do stuff like checking him in at hotels?"

Tyler shifted and opened his car door. "Isaac has never been about the fanfare. The rich-person privileges. He'd just as soon give all his money away than use it to pay more people to tend to him."

"He does have an assistant though, right?"

"Back at the warehouse, yeah. But Alex keeps her busier than Isaac does. He just likes to do stuff himself."

"Yeah, that makes sense with his personality."

"Plus, he likes the attention. He's not famous enough that everyone recognizes him everywhere he goes. Just famous enough that some people do. And he likes interacting with his fans."

It baffled me how anyone could *like* the kind of attention that Isaac received, but I sensed the truth in Tyler's words. For as uncomfortable as I was when we stopped for lunch in Asheville, Isaac had been perfectly at ease eating lunch with an audience, shaking dozens of hands and taking selfies and signing t-shirts. A familiar pulse of uncertainty throbbed in my gut, at war with the earlier desperation I'd felt at the idea of *not* having a relationship with Isaac. I had never felt so conflicted.

"Hey, you want to go for a walk really quick?" Tyler asked. "If I don't unfold myself out of this car, my muscles might be permanently hunched for the rest of forever."

I hesitated, but only briefly. I didn't get any relationship vibes from Tyler, despite Isaac's powers of suggestion. A walk was likely just a walk. Nothing more. "Sure," I said.

I climbed out of the car, joining him in the relatively quiet parking lot. It was a little cooler in Nashville than it had been in Charleston, but it still felt like spring, the air warm enough that I could lose the blazer and still be comfortable in my shirt sleeves. We followed the sidewalk that lined the parking lot to where it curved and led to an outdoor terrace filled with potted plants and benches.

Tyler stopped next to the first bench. "So how long do you think it'll be before Isaac figures out who you really are?"

I froze, my heart suddenly pounding so hard I worried Tyler might be able to hear it. What did he know? Or what did he *think* he knew? I swallowed, trying to keep my voice casual, dismissive. "What? I don't know what you mean."

"How long before Isaac figures out that *you* and *Ana* are the same person?" Tyler asked, this time more pointedly.

Hot dread washed over me, making my skin prickle and my face flush. I lifted my gaze to meet Tyler's, relaxing a tiny fraction when I saw the understanding in his eyes. He wasn't out for blood. He actually looked rather proud of himself. I sank onto the bench behind us. "How did you figure it out?"

He sat down beside me. "It was a hunch, really. Just based on my observations."

"Like what?" I wasn't sure I actually wanted to know. But then, Tyler had been watching me all day while doing his filming. Maybe I was less of a closed book than I thought.

"The first thing I noticed is that you love Red Renegade," he said, matter-of-factly. "You knew those songs Isaac played. All of them. I caught you mouthing the words more than once, and when 'Wings that Weep' came on, your face noticeably brightened. Plus, you knew which album you'd seen on the cover of Bridget's t-shirt."

I winced. I'd worried about the Bridget thing; that had been a total slip. And even though I'd made an actual effort to keep myself from singing out loud, Red Renegade's stuff was so familiar to me, it was hard to pretend like I was a first-time listener. "That still feels like a pretty big leap to make based on my preferences for a band."

"Maybe. But it doesn't take detective-level observation skills to see the most obvious clue."

I met Tyler's gaze, willing him to continue, too tied up in knots to actually ask him to do so with words.

"You're in love with Isaac, Rosie."

I sighed and dropped my head into my hands, shaking my head back and forth. "You can't know that. *I* don't even know that. I—"

"The way you watch him, the way you lean into his words, it's like the two of you are tuned into each other in this weird, kinetic way."

I *did* feel tuned in to Isaac; I could at least admit that much. But for Tyler to notice? Was I really so obvious? And did that mean Isaac had noticed?

"I still wanted to be sure though," Tyler continued. "So I did some googling and found this."

He handed me his phone, face up so I could see what was on the screen. "Ana Rose Crenshaw," I read off the top of my resume. "Where did you find this?"

"The Computer Science program at the University of Kansas has it up on their alumni site."

I swore softly. "But how did *you* find it?"

"When I thought about the observations Isaac made this morning about the similarities between you and Ana and then factored in all the stuff I observed all day, I took a guess. It took a few tries of googling the right name combination, but then the resume came up and it was an obvious match."

I took a deep, cleansing breath. "Are you going to tell him?"

"Not if you give me a really good reason why I shouldn't. But Isaac is one of my best friends, Rosie. I don't want him getting hurt."

It only took five minutes to give Tyler the condensed version of how I'd ended up on a road trip to meet myself. He laughed more than once and seemed visibly relieved when he discovered that Alex, Jade, and Greta were also in on the ruse.

"So we're driving all this way so Isaac can meet someone who actually lives in Charleston and works twenty feet away from him every single day," he said, his tone dry.

"We're driving all this way so we can talk up taco joints and eclectic hotels and set up the road trip connections segment as something viewers will enjoy."

"So the plan is to tell him when we get there? To make it all the way to Kansas City before he knows?"

I nodded. "Alex said because of all the promotional stuff he scheduled, it'll be better if we finish the whole trip. Besides, Isaac needs the segment to take off. The show needs the boost."

"That's true, but Rosie, I'm not sure we're going to make it all the way to Kansas City. The chemistry between you two is legit. And Isaac is already feeling it. You saw how weird he got about me calling you one of the guys. I did that on purpose just to see how he would react, and he was just as defensive as I guessed he'd be."

"I thought it had something to do with *you,*" I said. "Isaac told me once he thought you and I should meet. That I'd like you."

"In any other circumstance, I'd be flattered to have you interested in me. But this thing with Isaac, it's real for you, isn't it?"

I nodded. "But it doesn't matter. Isaac thinks he's falling for Ana. His focus is on her right now. You know how single-minded Isaac can be. Even if he does feel something for me, he isn't going to do anything about it. There's no reason why we won't make it to Kansas."

"You're missing the point, Rosie. Isaac has gone live three different times today on Instagram, and all three times you were in the video."

"I wasn't really in them," I argued. "I was in the background. I barely spoke a word."

He shook his head. "Still, there's a . . . vibe. I've been filming Isaac for a decade, so it's possible I'm more finely tuned to the guy, but he's got fans who notice everything. I haven't checked, but they could already be talking, trying to figure out who you are and why Isaac likes you so much."

Why Isaac liked *me.* Not Ana.

The thought sent a thrill through me, but I'd be lying if I pretended the thrill wasn't also laced with fear. The last thing I wanted to do was climb onto a roller coaster because it was exciting and fun and what I thought I'd always wanted only to have it throw me through a double loop to loop I wasn't ready for.

"Hey." We both looked up to see Isaac approaching us, his eyes darting uneasily from Tyler to me then back to Tyler. "I thought you guys might have bailed."

I looked at Tyler one last time, willing him to keep my secret. He gave me a nearly imperceptible nod. We were on the same team. For now.

I stood up. "Just stretching our legs. Since there's so much room in the Rabbit."

Isaac didn't even smile. He just handed us our room keys then turned on his heel and headed back toward the car.

"What was that?" I said under my breath.

"That is what they call jealousy," Tyler answered.

I hurried my pace, leaving Tyler behind and quickly catching up to Isaac. "Isaac, wait," I called.

He didn't turn until he reached the hatch of the Rabbit; he opened it, pulling out Tyler's suitcase and setting it next to the car. "Our rooms are all on the same floor," he said, not making eye contact, "so if you need anything, you can just text me."

It was endearing that even though he was the star, the one who had the means and thus the justification to have other people doing things for him, making his life easier, he was the one unloading luggage and making sure I knew I could call him if I needed anything.

"Actually, I kind of have a really big favor to ask," I said, wanting to stop him before he unloaded my luggage.

He looked up, finally meeting my eye, curiosity evident in his gaze. "Okay."

"Remember my cousin Marley? Who texted me earlier about her kid?"

Isaac nodded.

"She lives not far from here. In Westonburg, forty miles east. Today was actually a really tough day for her, so I was hoping I might be able to borrow the car and drive out to see her. I'll be back by morning, and it won't interfere with our trip at all."

He ran a hand through his hair. "It's how far?"

"Not far. About forty-five minutes."

He pushed his hands into his pockets. "Cool. What if we all go?"

I stilled. "To see my cousin?"

"I'm actually getting a little concerned that we don't have enough interesting content. A detour, a family visit, it could be good. Another connection we could emphasize, you know?"

That was the last thing I wanted. Marley was my family. And she was in crisis. She didn't need a YouTube star and his film guy invading her personal life. "I don't think so, Isaac. This is personal. I don't really have any desire for it to be in one of your videos."

"We've got plenty of content, man," Tyler said, joining the conversation. "We always have more than you think."

Isaac nodded. "All right. I guess—"

Tyler cut him off before he could finish his sentence. "I have some editing to do tonight so I'm going to be terrible company. But why don't you two go see Rosie's cousin?"

Something that looked a little like hope sparked in Isaac's eyes. So he wanted to come?

"I could drive you if you want," he said. "The car will need to charge, so I could drop you off at your cousin's, find a place to charge up, and then come back for you."

I'd hoped to spend the night, but it was only just after eight p.m. There was still plenty of evening left. And Isaac looked so earnest.

"I don't have anything else to do," he added, his tone a little sheepish.

He *did* want to come. With me. *Rosie.*

Agreeing to the road trip to spend more time with Isaac had been a good idea. But this is what I'd really wanted. Time with Isaac without anyone else watching.

"No cameras?" I asked.

He nodded. "I need to do one final live stream checking in and noting our progress, but then, I promise. No cameras."

I lifted my shoulders in what I hoped looked like a casual shrug. It *felt* a little more like I was trying to scratch my ears with my shoulders, but neither man seemed to notice. "Okay," I finally said. "I think I'd like that."

Isaac grinned, the tension—jealousy?—that had been obvious in his shoulders completely gone. He walked toward me and pulled his phone out of his pocket. "Want to join me for this one?" he said, pulling up the Instagram app.

Tyler's earlier warning flitted through my brain, but Isaac was standing so close to me. And the look in his eyes was so warm and welcoming. "Sure," I said, pushing my hands into my pockets. "What do you want me to do?"

"Nothing. Just stand there. This one will be really brief."

He draped an arm across my shoulders and tugged me into his side, so we were both framed in the video capture of his phone. Without thinking, I slipped my arm around his back and held onto his waist. The closeness was nearly dizzying.

"Ready?" he said softly.

I nodded. "Ready."

"Hey, guys. Isaac and Rosie checking in from the Chesapeake Hotel in Nashville, Tennessee to say that even though we're tired—"

"And we've eaten all the black licorice and pickle-flavored salt water taffy," I jumped in to add, surprising even myself.

Isaac shot me a quick grin, his grip tightening on my shoulder before he continued, finishing our sentence. "We can't wait to get back on the road tomorrow. We're going to charge up the car, give Tyler the camera man time to stretch"—he flipped the shot around to catch a quick shot of Tyler leaning against the car, his face impassive before he turned it back on us—"and get some sleep and then we'll be back at it tomorrow, counting down the miles to Kansas City." He looked down at me. "Want to do the final send-off?" he asked me, the video still rolling.

I rolled my eyes and smiled. "I thought you said I only had to stand here for this one."

His eyes sparkled with mirth. "You could have just said no, Crenshaw. You don't have to embarrass me in front of all my friends."

I reached up and patted Isaac on the chest, temporarily distracted by the curve of muscle under my palm. His muscle twitched with awareness and I pressed my lips together, a pulse of desire coursing through me. Isaac was not one of those super-ripped gym rats with muscles visible for miles. But this was nice—so nice. Remembering that we were live-streaming my exploration of Isaac's physique, I gave my head a quick shake and turned my face back to the camera. "I'll do the send-off," I said, "but not for you. Only because of how much I like all your friends." I smiled into the camera.
"Don't forget to be real, remember that kindness always matters most, and pay it forward every chance you get."

"Well done," Isaac said. "You didn't miss a single word."

"Why are you so surprised?" I said. "I am nothing if not a dedicated and loyal employee."

"I'll never underestimate you again," Isaac said.

We both waved a final goodbye and then he closed out the video. "That was awesome," Isaac said, giving me a surprised look. "You've done great today."

I took a deep breath. I'd actually felt pretty comfortable, weirdly enough. Something about having Isaac's arm around me had made me forget that filming a live stream was something I was supposed to feel anxious about. Which, twenty-four hours ago, was the exact opposite of what I would have expected. Being around Isaac should have made me feel stressed. Tongue-tied. Worried about saying or doing something stupid. And being on camera should have only exacerbated all of those worries. But with Isaac, and by extension, his seventy bazillion followers, I hadn't felt any of that.

I *had* done great today. A quiet sense of pride filled my chest. From the outside, the video would likely look like nothing. Forty-five seconds of two friends bantering back and forth. But for me, that video, and everything else I'd managed, even down to evading a pack of crazy middle schoolers, felt like a momentous accomplishment.

Tyler walked past me, his laptop bag slung over his shoulder. He grabbed his suitcase from where Isaac had left it next to the car. "You've done it now," he said under his breath, pausing to readjust the straps of his bag. "If people weren't talking about you before, they definitely will be now."

Chapter Twenty

Isaac

The dynamic in the car was different while we drove to Westonburg to see Rosie's cousin. *Better* different. Though, we did have a few conversations I wished we could have gotten on camera. Rosie had surprised me in the most unexpected way. It wasn't just that she was funny. She was just so . . . real. It wouldn't take much for viewers to fall in love with her. It was also possible I was slightly obsessed with her curly hair.

I suddenly wondered what kind of hair Ana had. Weirdly enough, I hadn't given it much thought. There had been something incredibly liberating about getting to know her without the pressure of face-to-face interaction. It didn't matter if I was in pajama bottoms with mustard on my t-shirt when I messaged her. If I hadn't showered in three days or had forgotten to brush my teeth. Likewise, I'd found myself asking questions that were focused much more on getting to know her as a person instead of any of her physical characteristics.

And yet, with Rosie sitting next to me, I suddenly had an intense desire to know what Ana looked like.

I didn't want to dwell on what that might mean.

"Right up here," Rosie said, pointing to a street sign in the distance. "This is her neighborhood."

I slowed the car and pulled into the development. The houses were small but well-maintained, with tiny, manicured lawns. The porches were all covered in pots of blooming flowers. Wide sidewalks lined either side of the road, street lamps lighting it up at regular intervals.

"This neighborhood is great," I said.

"Marley saved for a long time to be able to afford a house in here. The house is tiny, but it's only her and Shiloh. They don't need a lot of room." She pointed again, at a corner house with blue shutters. "That's hers."

I pulled into the driveway and cut the engine. "Do you want me to come in with you?"

She pursed her lips. "Not yet. Is that okay? I just don't really know how she's going to be feeling, and company may be too overwhelming."

"No problem. It'll take me forty minutes or so to charge up . . ." I pulled out my phone and pulled up an app that mapped all the charging stations around the country. "And there's a charging station ten minutes away. Should I text you when I'm done and see how things are looking?"

She nodded. "That would be great. I think Marley would actually really like to meet you, and Shiloh definitely will, I just want to make sure they're feeling okay first."

Rosie had given me the condensed version of Marley's history on the drive over. Navigating custody and parental involvement in a kid's life was far out of my realm of expertise, but it seemed unfair that a kid would have to suffer so much because his parents couldn't figure out a way to get along.

Rosie reached for her door handle. "Actually, you don't have my number, do you?"

It felt weird that I didn't since we'd spent the entire day together, but I hadn't had reason to get it. In the days leading up to the trip, my assistant had been the one to communicate with Rosie about when we were leaving and how long she should expect to be gone.

"You're right. I don't have it. Here." I pulled out my phone and handed it to her. "Want to just send yourself a text?"

She quickly keyed out a message and handed my phone back to me. "Thanks for driving me over," she said, a smile brightening her face in a way that made my heart trip the tiniest bit.

"No problem."

While I waited at the charging station, I browsed social media, feeling tempted to do another live video. It would kill the momentum of the last one though, and the last one was doing really awesome, even just an hour after posting.

I glanced over a few comments—I knew better than to read them all—but I was bored and had time to kill. A majority of the comments all had a similar theme.

Where did Rosie come from? I LOVE her. Can we get more of her in the future?

OMG Rosie is the cutest.

One, in particular, caught my eye.

Am I the only one noticing what a cute couple these two would be? I don't know who Isaac is determined to go and see with this road trip, but if it's a potential GF? He ought to give up the road trip and look a little closer to home. How can we let him know? Let's start a movement. #teamrosie

Rosie *had* been pretty convincing in our live video. Even I had felt the chemistry sparking between us. But it wasn't necessarily romantic chemistry. It was more like I could just tell that the dynamic between us, and the way it was going to play to the audience, was exactly what it needed to be.

That didn't mean I needed to date her.

Especially not when I was on my way to meet Ana because I *did* want to date her.

At least, I thought I did.

A text on my phone popped up from Rosie. *Everything's good. Want to come back? Marley would love to meet you.*

Be there in a few, I texted back. The car still had another twenty minutes of charging to do. And I needed to sort out how I was feeling before I saw Rosie again.

Actually, what I really needed to do was message Ana.

@RandomIOfficial: Have you ever been to Westonburg? It's this little town outside of Nashville. I like it here.

Luckily, she was available and responded right away.

@Briarsandthorns: I've driven through it before. You're at the halfway point! Exciting.

@RandomIOfficial: Very exciting. We're stopping in the morning at a diner that's supposed to serve the best breakfast this side of the Mississippi. Which feels like a bold claim because Charleston is also this side of the Mississippi, and I just don't think anyone handles grits like a true Charlestonian. And a true best breakfast MUST include grits.

@Briarsandthorns: As a native Kansan, I have very little opinion on the subject. I have eaten many a delicious breakfast without any grits included. I think I've only tried them once?

@RandomIOfficial: It doesn't count unless you were in Charleston when you tried them. Or if you ate them with sugar on them. That's against the rules. Grits are not oatmeal.

@Briarsandthorns: That must be why they tasted so awful. How should I eat them?

@RandomIOfficial: With butter and salt, at a minimum. With cheese and bacon is even better.

@Briarsandthorns: Well that explains it. You could put butter, salt, cheese, and bacon on sand and it would taste good.

@RandomIOfficial: I am offended on behalf of all Southerners who know

how to eat breakfast.

@Briarsandthorns: Are you nervous about tomorrow night?

I leaned back in my seat and considered her question. Weirdly enough, I wasn't, really. I'd told Ana I was trusting my gut when it came to her. And I was. There was just something that felt . . . *right* about our interactions. I'd never admit it out loud because the guys at work would never let me live down sounding like some cheesy romance movie. But it felt as if we were *meant* to be together. Like there was something bigger connecting us.

Before replying to Ana, I pulled up my text messages and typed out a message to Jade. *Heads up. If you haven't already noticed. Rosie is getting some attention in the comment thread of the live video we posted.*

Jade's response came right through. *I'm aware. #teamrosie. I'm not surprised though. She was adorable in that video.*

Yeah, she's a natural, I replied. *But I don't want the hashtag to pick up steam. I'd rather viewers get excited about the actual woman I'm making this trip to see in the first place. Can you kill the hashtag for me?*

Jade texted back several laughing emojis in a row. *You seriously overestimate my abilities. Unless I'm deleting half your comments, I can't kill anything. And doing that would only make things worse.*

I ran a hand through my hair.

Just let this play out, Jade texted before I could respond. *If you and Ana are meant to be together, it won't matter what some random viewer said in some random comment. You're all about trusting your gut, right? Trust it now, too.*

It was good advice, but something about the whole thing still made me uneasy. No, something about *Rosie* made me uneasy. Because as good as I felt about Ana, I couldn't ignore the fact that when I was with Rosie in person, something felt really good about that, too.

I went back to my exchange with Ana and keyed out a reply.

@RandomIOfficial: Yeah. I am nervous. You?

@Briarsandthorns: I'm terrified. But also so anxious to just get the first meeting over with so I can eat a full meal without feeling like I might vomit. You do weird things to my insides, Isaac.

@RandomIOfficial: Thank you, I think?

@Briarsandthorns: I definitely meant it as a compliment. But I hope this feeling doesn't last forever. Apparently, I need to try some cheesy bacon sand—I mean grits—in order to know what real breakfast tastes like.

@RandomIOfficial: It's a date. See you tomorrow.

I added a winking emoji to my last message and closed out the Instagram app not even sure what I was feeling. How I was feeling. Whether or not I ought to be feeling anything at all.

A text popped up from Rosie—the address to Marley's house, followed by a quick message. *So you can find your way back.*

A cool sense of relief washed over me. I didn't want to think. And if it was time to go back to Marley's house, I wouldn't have to.

It's possible I was overly confident. After a couple of hours of hanging out with Marley and Rosie, I was more confused than ever. I liked Rosie. I liked the way she laughed. And the wry way she joked without making fun of other people. A lot of people were funny. But to be funny at no one else's expense was an entirely different level of skill. I liked the way she listened, with her eyes laser-focused on whoever was speaking. She was just . . . easy. It had been a long time since I'd dated a woman who felt *easy.*

But I wasn't supposed to be thinking about dating Rosie.

Marley stretched her arms over her head. "Are you guys going to stay?" she asked, her voice hopeful. She looked at me. "There's an extra bed in Shiloh's room that Rosie usually takes, but you're welcome to the couch." She patted the cushion next to her. "It's plenty comfortable."

"Oh, I don't want to impose on your family time." My gaze shifted to Rosie. "I can just head back to the hotel and then come back in the morning to pick you up."

"Please stay?" Rosie said. "Shiloh has a soccer tournament in the morning and they're leaving really early, but I would love for him to get to meet you. He's a huge fan. It would be dumb for you to drive all the way back to Nashville only to return here by six a.m."

"Ohhh, true. That's early."

"Please?" Rosie said again. She shot a knowing look at Marley. "Things have been really tough for Shiloh lately. It would mean a lot."

A startling realization crystallized in my gut. I couldn't tell Rosie no. To this. Or anything. I held her gaze for a long moment, reading her eyes, trying to figure out if I was making up the connection that, thread by thread, was slowly weaving us together.

She finally blinked and looked away, a hint of color filling her cheeks. Had she felt it too? For all I knew, Rosie had a boyfriend back in Charleston. I couldn't assume that just because we had on-air chemistry and I liked the way she laughed that she was into me. That she would ever be into me. The smarter decision was probably to decline Marley's invitation and drive back to the hotel, giving myself some much-needed distance.

But Shiloh seemed like a good kid, from what I'd been told about him. If I could do a small thing to help brighten his day? That was exactly the kind of thing that Isaac of *Random I* would do.

"The couch sounds great," I said, the wheels in my head already turning. It was late—too late to do anything huge, but I could still stage some sort of a surprise, sneak into Shiloh's room, maybe promise him the newest PlayStation. We'd just featured the newest FIFA Soccer game on one of our tech segments, airing it in conjunction with a prerecorded message from Rao Cortez, one of the players featured on the game. We'd given away a dozen game packs featuring the game, a signed soccer ball, and a set of the newest wireless controllers. I could probably get my hands on one more. Of course, it would be better if I could actually *give* it to him in the morning, but with so little time to plan, maybe just telling him it would be shipped right to his house would be good enough.

"Seriously, Shiloh is going to freak out in the morning," Marley said. "Thank you for staying." She looked back to Rosie. "And for surprising me. I didn't know how much I needed you here until you showed up."

The women stood and hugged. "It was lucky we're staying in Nashville."

I stood and pulled my phone out of my pocket. "I'm going to grab our things out of the car and give Tyler a quick call so he knows what to expect."

Rosie offered a grateful smile. "Thanks."

It's about branding, I thought to myself as I walked outside. I pulled Rosie's suitcase out of the car, momentarily distracted by whether or not she'd intentionally matched her shoes to her suitcase or if she'd just gotten lucky. I'd never paid attention to her shoes before, but it wouldn't surprise me if she had more than one pair of colorful sneakers. She definitely had a colorful sneaker vibe.

As I wheeled our bags into the house, I repeated my earlier assertion. Staying at Marley's house was a good move for the brand. It was about taking the opportunity to surprise a fan in person. Viewers ate up those kinds of videos. And Shiloh was exactly the kind of kid I loved to help. That's all this was.

That's all it could be.

Chapter Twenty-One

Rosie

I followed Marley down the hallway while Isaac was out at the car. When we passed Shiloh's bedroom door, I itched to go in and wake him up, but Marley had said he'd been keyed up over his tournament and had struggled to sleep in the first place. If I woke him up, *and* he found out Isaac Bishop was in his house, he'd never get back to sleep. We'd at least have a little time together over breakfast.

I lingered over the pictures that lined Marley's hallway while she pulled some towels out of the small linen closet beside her bedroom door. "He's grown so much," I said, pointing at the most recent shot of Shiloh. He was outside, the sun glinting off his dark hair, his blue eyes bright.

"Yeah, and every day he looks more and more like Blake." Marley leaned against the wall beside me, the towels clutched to her chest.

"I still can't believe he just went over there all by himself," I said. We'd hashed and rehashed Marley's day when I'd first arrived. We didn't need to go over it again, but to think of Shiloh riding his bike seven miles across town to a neighborhood he'd never been before to meet his dad? Every time I thought of it, my heart squeezed, hurt seeping into every corner. I understood Marley's reasoning for keeping Blake away from her kid. He didn't deserve a relationship with him after abandoning Marley so thoroughly. The trouble was, Shiloh *did* deserve a relationship with his dad. It only sucked it wasn't possible to have one without the other.

"I'm going to have to let him start seeing Blake, aren't I?" she asked. She lifted a finger to the picture and traced it down the side of Shiloh's framed, freckled face.

"Yeah. I think you are."

"It's just my pride, Rosie. This really stings. That I've been here all this time, working like crazy, breaking my neck so Shiloh can have a good life, and it isn't enough for him, you know? I'm not enough."

"That's not true, and you know it. He's just curious, Marley. And how could he not be? Not when Blake is so close. Maybe this will turn out to be a good thing. Maybe Blake has changed. Grown up some, you know?"

She breathed out a heavy sigh. "Maybe." She squared her shoulders and shook her head as if to toss off the weariness. She handed me the towels. "Let's talk about you now."

I fought a smile, but after the two hours we'd just spent with Isaac, it was hard to hide it.

"He obviously likes you," Marley said.

"Right? It definitely felt like there was a . . . something happening between us."

"Absolutely. We're talking explosive chemistry. Seriously, why don't you just go out there and tell him?"

I glanced back down the hallway, suddenly scared Isaac was back inside and close enough to hear us. I motioned for Marley to lower her voice. "I can't tell him. Not until we get to Kansas. We've got all these stupid stops scheduled that we have to do for marketing and crap."

"Well. At least sleep easy knowing that when you *do* tell him, he is not going to be disappointed."

That single thought buoyed me up as I said good night to Marley, delivered towels to Isaac back in the living room, and retrieved my suitcase, wheeling it silently into Shiloh's room. The kid was actually a pretty heavy sleeper. If I didn't *try* to wake him up, I probably wouldn't.

I changed into a pair of loose, cotton pajama bottoms and my favorite gray tank then tiptoed to the bathroom to brush my teeth. I reached for the bathroom door handle only for it to drop out of my grasp as the door opened from the inside.

I jumped back, my own surprise reflected on Isaac's face. "Oh. Sorry. I can just . . ."

"No, you're good," he said. "I'm done. You just scared me."

"Yeah. Me too."

"Hey, do you have a quick second? I wanted to run something by you."

"Sure." I followed him into the living room. He'd also changed into pajamas—plaid flannel pants and a Red Renegade t-shirt I'd never seen before. I itched to ask him about it. Where had it come from? Which concert tour? What year? But I wasn't allowed to like Red Renegade. Not until I'd assumed my identity as Ana.

I dropped the bag that held my toothbrush and face wash onto the chair and followed Isaac to the couch where his laptop was set up. But not before noticing the way his eyes moved down my body as I approached. My hands moved to the inch of skin exposed at the base of my tank. What would it be like for him to touch that skin? For him to . . .

Isaac cleared his throat, effectively snapping my attention back to the moment. "Right," he said. "So I just wanted you to see . . ." His words trailed off as he started clicking on his laptop.

I dropped onto the couch next to him, knowing distance was probably what was needed, but still sitting close enough for our legs to touch. It did very little to help cool the heat in my cheeks, but then, from the looks of it, I wasn't the only one who was flushed.

Isaac wouldn't meet my eye, so I followed the direction of his gaze to his laptop. A picture of some sort of prize pack filled the screen.

"What's this?" I finally said, willing a giant dose of normalcy into my voice. I was fine. Everything was fine. So the room was bursting with sexual tension. We were adults. We could control ourselves.

Isaac cleared his throat one more time, his hands gripping his knees. "This is a prize pack we gave away on the show a few weeks back. A new PlayStation, the newest FIFA soccer game, and a soccer ball signed by Rao Cortez."

"Okay."

"I was thinking I could give one to Shiloh."

Understanding dawned. "Oh, that's an amazing idea. He would love it."

"Does he have a PlayStation?"

"An older one, I think?"

"Awesome. Sweet. It obviously won't get here for a couple of days, but I've already sent an email to PlayStation and to Cortez's PR people to see if we can put together one more prize pack. I'm positive they'll say yes. The spot on the show was a big success for them."

"That's really amazing of you," I said. He was *not* making it easier for me to feel less attracted to him.

"It's nothing," he said dismissively. "Just a few emails."

"Still. Shiloh could use some cheering up right now. This will feel huge to him."

Isaac grinned and my heart squeezed. "So I was thinking I could sneak into his room in the morning once he's up and dressed, surprise him, tell him about the prizes, then get Rao on a video call to wish him good luck with his game. Of course, I'd need you to be filming the whole thing on your phone, so I can use my phone to make the—"

"Wait, hold up. You want to film it?" The warmth in my chest cooled just slightly. Because *of course* he wanted to film it.

He shrugged. "Yeah. Of course. Fans love this kind of stuff." He studied my face for a moment. "But maybe that's not the best idea this time?" he said slowly.

I truly believed Isaac's motives were pure. But did he genuinely feel like every single thing he did needed to be for public consumption?

"This is why we left Tyler back in Nashville though, right? No cameras?"

"Right, but this wouldn't be a part of the road trip, it would just be a side thing. And Shiloh would get to be on the show. He'd love that, right?"

"What Shiloh would love is meeting *you.* And not because he's part of some promotional opportunity. You don't even have to give him anything, Isaac. Just talk to him. Ask him about his soccer. Spend five minutes interested in his life and just be present. Not because you have to. But because you want to."

He scoffed and leaned back, his posture defensive. "That *is* what I do. That's always what I've—" He sighed and didn't speak for a long moment. "At least that *used* to be what I do."

I reached a hand out and placed it on his knee, willing myself not to tremble from the contact. "You do good work, Isaac. I don't mean to doubt your motives. But when there is always some promotional thing worked in, when it always has to involve people, viewers, seeing what you're doing, your motives might get lost on the people you're interacting with. What would it feel like if this was a moment that's just about Shiloh? And *you,* too. You can have meaningful moments off camera too, you know."

He kept his gaze down for a long moment even as he slid his hand over the top of mine, the one still resting on his knee. "You like to challenge me, don't you?"

I swallowed, feeling like I couldn't quite catch my breath. "Is that a good thing?" I whispered.

He met my gaze, his lips lifting into a small grin. "I haven't decided yet." He shifted forward, angling his body and bringing his face closer to mine. There was a question in his eyes. And also . . . *desire.* Lots of it. I wasn't rolling in experience when it came to reading a man's desire just from the look in his eyes, but there was no confusing what I saw in Isaac's expression. He leaned forward until his nose brushed against mine, lifting his hands to either side of my face. "What's happening, Rosie?"

Whatever it was, I wasn't going to let an opportunity like this one pass me by. Forget the road trip and the stupid promotional stops. Isaac wanted me and the blood pumping through my veins told me I wanted him too. I leaned into his touch, tipping my face until our lips finally touched. The kiss was . . . explosive. Raging. A torrent of heat and desire that nearly overwhelmed me. Isaac's hands slid down the bare skin of my arms then around my waist where his fingers slipped under the hem of my tank top, pressing against my back. I leaned even closer—any space between us felt like too much—my hands moving to his chest then over his shoulders and up to his face.

I'd dreamed of kissing Isaac before. But my dreams had been rather sedate compared to this. This was fire without the burn, a warm glow consuming every inch of my skin, a melding of passion and desire with a very real awareness that I'd never felt so at home in a man's arms.

Isaac shifted, and I leaned back onto the couch, pulling him with me. The weight of him against me sent thrills through my body, and I arched into him, my hands grasping the fabric of his t-shirt and pulling him even closer. Only then did Isaac still, his breathing labored as he broke the kiss and pressed his forehead to mine.

I released my hold on him, though my hands stayed on his chest, and tried to slow my own breathing.

"That was . . ." he said softly. He sat back on the couch, letting my hands fall away. "I, um . . . I shouldn't have done that."

I sat up. Not exactly the post-kiss conversation I would have hoped for, but he wasn't running from the room screaming, so maybe I could still count it as a win. "Technically, I started it."

He huffed a laugh. "No, I wanted . . ." He stood and started pacing around the room. "But I shouldn't have. *We* shouldn't have."

This was ridiculous. If Ana was the only reason he thought he shouldn't be kissing me, I could solve that problem with one very short conversation. We could fake the rest of his stupid road trip. Or just call the whole thing off. Alex had said my feelings were more important, that Isaac had pockets deep enough to eat the loss of any planned stops.

"Isaac, I need to tell you something."

He paced around the room, his hands on his hips and his eyes looking everywhere but at me. He shook his head. "This was a bad idea."

"If you would just stop and listen—"

"No," he said, cutting me off. "You've done enough."

Well, *that* hurt.

"There are so many things to consider right now. I have a plan. And the road trip. And Ana. And the viewers have expectations. I can't disappoint them with this."

With *this?* What was that even supposed to mean? "Disappoint them with what?" I said. "Your viewers aren't watching you right now. Is that really what you're thinking about fifteen seconds after kissing me? Whether or not your *viewers* would approve?"

"That's not what I—" He ran a hand through his hair. "But yes, in a manner of speaking. What my viewers think can make or break my entire career—everything that I've built. I can't disregard how that factors into my personal life."

"But it doesn't have to *be* your personal life. You can have boundaries, Isaac. You can do what you want to do without bringing fifty million people into your bedroom."

He scoffed and rolled his eyes. "This is not my bedroom, and I wouldn't have . . ." He waved his hand dismissively.

He wouldn't have what? Slept with me? Initiated the kiss had I not done it first?

Two things became clear in a matter of seconds. One, Isaac had felt the same charge of attraction that I had. He wouldn't be overreacting if kissing me hadn't felt like something special. And two, I *did* challenge him. And that frustrated him more than the kissing had. It was making him reactive and unkind; I couldn't hold anything he said right now against him. But I also didn't have to stand around and take it.

I stood up and moved across the room, avoiding the tense, pacing idiot in the middle of the small space. I picked up my toiletry bag from the chair where I'd left it. "You can think this was a bad idea," I said. "That we shouldn't have kissed, that it's more important that we stick to the plan and make your precious viewers happy. But just for the record? I don't care about your viewers. And I don't have any regrets."

"You don't have to care about them," Isaac responded, his tone sharp. "I do."

I shook my head. "You give them too much power, Isaac. Is this how you make every decision? Only after evaluating what your fandom would want you to do? Do you even know what *you* want anymore?" I sighed and backed up a step. "I'm just asking you to be real with yourself. Be real with me."

"You don't think my show is real?" he asked, his tone defensive. "That what I do for people is real?"

I shrugged. "That's not what I said. I have no doubt that your show is real. But I was talking about you. Not your job. Your *life*."

He dropped onto the couch, looking suddenly weary, like the fight had died out of him in a matter of seconds. "I didn't know there was a difference," he said, his voice low.

My heart dropped into my gut. It was the very thing I'd been afraid of. The reason I'd agreed to come on the stupid road trip in the first place before telling Isaac who I really was. Because I'd been afraid that for Isaac, there really *wasn't* a difference between *Random I* and Isaac Bishop. For him, the two would always be fully entwined. And yet, the way his eyes had flashed at my accusations made me wonder if that really was what he wanted. If some part of him didn't crave a little more normalcy. A little more privacy.

But no one could make the decision to do things differently but him.

"I guess there's not." I took another backward step but paused before turning away completely. "I hope Ana's cool with that."

His eyes darted to mine. "Because you wouldn't be?"

There was a vulnerability embedded in his question that made my heart squeeze and my throat dry up. It suddenly felt like any potential for a future with Isaac hinged on how I responded. The part of me that had been in love with the idea of Isaac for years wanted to tell him exactly what he wanted to hear. Anything to get him to accept me. To love me. To kiss me again. But the adult part of my brain couldn't yield. "Call me selfish if you want. But I wouldn't be."

I turned and hurried into the bathroom. I locked the door before leaning against it and lowering myself to the floor, the fuzzy pink rug in front of the sink soft against my feet.

What had just happened?

I should have just told him the truth. But the sting of how quickly he'd voiced his regret had silenced my efforts, freezing the words in my throat. Not because he'd mentioned Ana. I couldn't *actually* be offended that he'd cast me aside for her, not when she was me, and I understood his desire to see things through to the end.

But then he'd mentioned his viewers. What they wanted. What their expectations were.

I'd wanted to believe Isaac could separate himself from it all. Have some boundaries and pursue a relationship that wasn't constantly on camera. But now I wasn't so sure.

And after that kiss, that was the thought that hurt worst of all.

Chapter Twenty-Two

Rosie

I woke up to gentle nudging and the sound of my nephew's sweet voice urging me awake.

"Aunt Rosie!" Shiloh whisper-yelled. "Wake up. Wake. Up!"

I smiled and cracked an eye open. "What time is it?" He was already dressed for his tournament, his bright green soccer jersey bringing out the blue in his eyes and making his freckles pop.

"Just after six. Mom says I can't go in the living room, but she won't tell me why. Do you know why? Did you bring me something? And it's hidden out there and that's why I have to stay away?"

A wave of emotion washed over me as I thought of Isaac and everything that had happened the night before. Gooseflesh broke out across my arms as I thought of the kiss. But that was not a memory I could dwell on. Not yet, anyway. Maybe not ever, depending on how the rest of the day went. The heavy weight of dread settled into my stomach as I thought about what would happen by the end of the night. Isaac would know everything.

I couldn't dwell on *that* thought either. Not when I had less than an hour to spend with Shiloh. "It's nice to see you too," I said, reaching out to ruffle his hair.

He grinned. "Sorry, Aunt Rosie. Hi." He reached down and hugged my shoulders as best he could. "Now can you tell me about the surprise?"

"Not quite yet. But give me a few minutes to get ready and then we can go out together, yeah?"

Shiloh groaned. "That's what Mom said too."

"Your mom's a smart lady." By the time I'd finished getting ready, the smell of pancakes and bacon had permeated the house.

I met Marley in the hallway just outside the bathroom. "That's not you cooking?" she asked me as she used a towel to squeeze water out of her hair.

I shook my head no. "I assumed it was you."

Her eyebrows went up. "So Isaac is making us breakfast?"

We inched down the hallway together until we were close enough to peer through the living room into the kitchen. Sure enough, Isaac was standing at the stove, his back to us, a growing pile of pancakes on a plate beside him.

"Is he wearing an apron?" I asked.

"Yes, and it is so sexy," Marley said.

A pulse of heat snaked through me. I knew firsthand just how sexy Isaac could be. I cleared my throat. "Should we get Shiloh?"

"In a minute. I just want to enjoy the view a tiny bit longer."

"Oh my word, you're horrible," I said, nudging Marley with my elbow.

"Oh, come on. It's not like you weren't staring last night. The energy between you two was crackling."

I glanced back into the kitchen, suddenly worried that Isaac could hear us, but he had music playing—I could hear faint strains of Red Renegade—so hopefully we were safe.

"Did anything else happen after I went to bed?" Marley asked.

I bit my lip and avoiding answering long enough for Marley to gasp. "Something did happen! What was it? Did you kiss? Did you—"

"Marley, stop," I said, dragging her a few steps back down the hallway. Isaac's music wasn't that loud. If she didn't dial it down, Isaac would hear us.

"Sorry," Marley whispered. "What happened?"

"We kissed," I finally said.

Her eyes lit, but I shook my head and they immediately dimmed again. "It wasn't good?"

I scoffed. "It was amazing. But . . . that didn't stop him from regretting it anyway. He was all worried about his fans, about what they would think, about disappointing them if the road trip didn't happen as planned."

"Dude. He would not be disappointing his fans by dating you. After your video last night—you were adorable, by the way—the comments have been full of love for you. I've been reading them all morning. They love your vibe."

"Really?" Gearing myself up to be in the video had been hard enough. There was no way I'd ever intentionally go read people's comments.

"Yes, really. Tons of people have declared themselves Team Rosie. You even have your own hashtag. I mean, there is an equally vocal contingent that's rooting for the mystery girl at the end of the road trip. But still. Generally speaking, fans would not be disappointed."

"That's just it," I said. "I don't want it to even matter what fans think. I don't want Isaac to like me only because I've got a vibe his fans love. I don't want it to be about his fans at all."

She leaned against the wall across from me and folded her arms across her chest. "So what are you going to do?"

Good question. I'd spent over an hour debating that very thing before falling asleep last night. If not for Shiloh's steady breathing on the other side of the room, I might have even panicked a little. But Shiloh's presence had kept me grounded. "I don't know, honestly. See this thing through, I guess? See how he responds when he realizes it's me?"

She studied me closely. "How's your heart holding up?"

I shrugged dismissively. "What do you mean?"

Her eyes narrowed. "Rosie. You just kissed a man you've loved from afar for a very long time. A relationship with him is actually within reach. You can't tell me you're fine and have me believe you."

Unexpected tears welled up in my eyes and I shook my head, trying to clear them away. "It's . . . overwhelming. Being around him in person, spending time with him. He's exactly the same, of course. And I knew he would be. The person he is online is exactly the person he is in real life. But thinking about a relationship with him is different now. Now that I've kissed him, I realize how amazing it could be. How *right* it feels when we're together. But I never thought about the repercussions. The invasion of privacy, of sharing him with millions of viewers."

"Honey, he's never kept his relationships private before." Marley put her hands on my shoulders. "How did you never think about this part?"

"He hasn't dated *that* many women. And why would I have thought about this part? I didn't think we would ever actually date. I dreamed about it, sure. But in those dreams, I always just imagined Isaac in *my* life. I never really spent much time imagining myself in his because I didn't think it would ever actually be possible."

Marley nodded in understanding. "But now it *is* possible, and you're terrified. Because after all this effort, what if it isn't what you want?"

I nodded. "It isn't a question of whether or not I want *him.*" The memory of his hands sliding across the skin on my lower back flitted through my mind. But it wasn't just the physical chemistry. I also loved the way he made me laugh. The way we talked about music. The way he just made me feel good. Whole. Happy.

"I wouldn't give up yet," Marley said. "You're a pretty stellar human, Rosie. If he cares about you, he'll be willing to change."

"No, I don't want him to change. You can't start a relationship expecting someone to become someone they're not."

"But you can want boundaries," Marley said. "You can ask him to build some better ones."

I shrugged. "But will he?"

She squeezed my shoulders. "For you? I bet so."

Footsteps approached and we both turned toward the kitchen. Isaac appeared from around the corner, spatula in hand. "Oh. Hey," he said. "Good morning." I waited for his gaze to meet mine, but it almost seemed like he was making an intentional effort *not* to look at me.

"Good morning," I said. Regardless of what he was capable of, I couldn't take my eyes off the man. Isaac hadn't shaved that morning, and light stubble covered his jawline. He wore a fitted white t-shirt under the purple apron he'd apparently found in Marley's pantry. His hair was mussed, though that was pretty typical, and he was wearing glasses. I'd never seen him in glasses. Ever. It totally worked. He'd nailed the sexy professor on a Saturday morning vibe perfectly. "You wear glasses."

"Oh." One hand flew to the side of his glasses and he touched them self-consciously. "Yeah. I normally wear contacts. Dani is trying to convince me to wear these more."

"You should," I said, my voice cracking just slightly. I cleared my throat and tried again. "They look . . ." *Sexy. Amazing. Perfect. Sexy.* "Nice," I finally managed to say.

"Thanks." There was a distance to his tone that set me on edge. Isaac was not the kind of man who built walls around himself. And yet, there was a definite wall now. One he'd put firmly between us, apparently. He looked at Marley. "So, I borrowed your apron and made some breakfast. I hope you don't mind."

Marley shook her head. "I love breakfast. It smells amazing."

Isaac smiled, glancing down the hallway between us. "Is Shiloh awake yet?"

"I'll go get him," I said louder than I needed to. I needed a purpose. A reason to *not* stand in close proximity to Isaac for even a minute longer.

Marley and Isaac were back in the kitchen when I walked Shiloh down the hallway, my hands covering his eyes. We stopped at the edge of the kitchen table, where Shiloh would have a clear view of the man flipping pancakes at his mother's stove. "Are you ready?" I said close to Shiloh's ear.

He pushed my hands away, pausing long enough to take in the scene before him. Slowly, he reached up and tugged on my shirt. "Aunt Rosie?" he said quietly.

I grinned at Marley, who was pouring herself a mug of coffee across the room. "What's up, kiddo?" I said.

"Is *Random I* making pancakes in my kitchen?"

I chuckled. "Yep. He sure is."

The next twenty minutes went by in a blur. Isaac and Shiloh talked nonstop. About the show. About school. About soccer. About the prize pack Isaac promised to have mailed right to Shiloh's front door. Through it all, Isaac didn't get his phone out once. No recording, no photos. Nothing. Just Isaac giving of himself to a kid who really needed it.

A bolt of yearning shot through me, squeezing my heart in a way that almost hurt. I wanted this man. Desperately. Watching him with Shiloh, recognizing that, wall between us or not, he'd listened to what I'd wanted his visit with Shiloh to be, flamed a spark of hope in me that the night before, I'd all but completely squashed out. Suddenly, I wanted to just tell him everything. Get everything out in the open, come what may.

Marley and Shiloh took off a few minutes after breakfast in order to make his tournament, leaving Isaac and me to finish up the dishes. We worked in companionable silence, though my mind couldn't stop rehashing my confession. *It's me, Isaac. Ana Rose. Rosie. It's always been me.* Just when I finally felt like I'd worked up the nerve to begin, a knock sounded on the back door.

"That's Tyler," Isaac said casually.

I froze, the last dish from the sink still in my hand. Tyler was here?

Clearly reading my confusion, Isaac continued. "I had him catch an Uber to meet us here. Figured it would save us a little time and let us get on the road quicker."

"But aren't we supposed to have breakfast somewhere in Nashville?" I'd actually forgotten about breakfast until then. I would have eaten a few less pancakes had I remembered. Not to mention the fact that in order to get back to the interstate that would take us north toward St. Louis and then Kansas City, we would have to drive right back through Nashville. Making Tyler Uber all the way to us felt like a superfluous trip.

"Yeah. But now we won't have to stop at the hotel to pick Tyler up."

Before I could say anything else, Isaac crossed to the back door and let Tyler in.

Tyler entered the kitchen and eyed me curiously, one eyebrow drawn up, but what could I tell him? Isaac obviously wasn't telling me the full truth. Tyler might even know more than I did.

We finished up the kitchen and gathered our belongings with little conversation. Not until we were outside by the car, Tyler loading gear and luggage into the tiny back hatch of the rabbit.

Isaac approached me, a sheepish look on his face. "So I thought we might change things up a little today," he said, avoiding eye contact.

"Okay," I said hesitantly. "In what way?"

He ran a hand through his still-messy hair. "Tyler has just been so cramped sitting in the back, I thought he could ride shotgun today, get some close-up shots of me driving, and some shots of the open road. Are you cool with that?"

Wow. The wall between us had apparently doubled in size. "Isaac, if this has something to do with last night—"

"It has nothing to do with last night," he said coolly. "It's just business. Just getting the shots we need to make the video work."

He was lying to me. Blatantly. And dismissing me in a way that stung so deeply, it triggered anger instead of tears. Who did he think he was? To be so dismissive after what had happened between us seemed hugely out of character for him. "Whatever you think is best, *boss,*" I said, emphasizing the word I knew he hated to hear from his team members.

His jaw tightened, but he didn't say another word.

Settled into the back of the rabbit, I pulled out my phone and did my best to ignore the banter happening in the front seat. As soon as Tyler turned on the camera, Isaac turned on the charm, playing to the audience that would eventually see segments of the video. Tyler shot me a few concerned looks over his shoulder but didn't make any attempt to pull me into the conversation. Apparently, his instructions from Isaac had been clear.

I scrolled through my notifications, noticing a message that had come in earlier that morning. Somehow with the excitement of Shiloh and breakfast and all that had happened, I'd missed it.

@RandomIOfficial: Morning. Today is the day! I'm nervous, honestly. But I think you get me, Ana. You understand me in ways that other people never have. I think this is going to be a very good thing.

The message was followed by a winking emoji.

I dropped my phone onto my lap and leaned my head against the cool glass of the window, closing my eyes. It was stupid that his message to Ana could wound my pride. It was a message to *me. I* was the one Isaac thought understood him in ways that other people never had. But I couldn't help but feel like he'd written it with *Rosie* in mind. Ana understood him . . . but clearly Rosie never could. It was the weirdest, most ridiculous sensation ever to be both flattered and insulted at the same time. It was impossible to be jealous of myself, and yet, I totally was. Jealous of the woman Isaac believed he would find in Kansas City. And positive that once he did find out it was me? He was going to be disappointed.

Anxiety bubbled up in my midsection, clawing its way up my throat. My hands started to tremble and sweat broke out across my forehead. I kept my eyes closed and focused on my breathing. I was not going to freak out now. I was in control. I could control this moment and I could control my next actions. Ten intentional breaths later, I felt a little better. But I also knew with sharpened clarity what those next actions should be.

Isaac claimed I understood him in ways that other people didn't. And maybe I did. I'd always believed that what made Isaac so wonderful, so popular, was the fact that he was so genuine, so *real*, on his show. People felt like they were getting the real Isaac all the time. And in many ways, that was true. But the night before, I'd seen something more flashing behind his eyes. Something that almost looked like loneliness.

And why wouldn't he be lonely? Isaac had been living and sharing his life with the public for more than a decade. Considering how to frame his life, filtering his interactions and relationships through the lens that would play best to his audience had become second nature. Of course he was capable of having interactions without filming them; he'd demonstrated that well enough when he'd had breakfast with Shiloh. But he'd only done it because I'd told him to.

The lines had gotten too blurry. For all I knew, the only reason Isaac wanted Ana instead of Rosie—and that much was obvious—was because finding her at the end of his mysterious road trip made for a better story.

What was the cost of focusing so much energy on what other people wanted? On what had the highest entertainment value?

This time around? The cost was me.

Rosie and Ana, both.

Chapter Twenty-Three

Isaac

It had been rude to push Rosie into the backseat. I wasn't so insensitive not to realize as much. But what choice did I have? I couldn't stop thinking about her. And I *needed* to stop thinking about her. And not just because I was going to see Ana.

I'd meant it when I'd told Rosie she challenged me. She did. In ways that made my gut clench and my skin prickle. The only other person that had ever challenged me on the boundaries I had regarding what did and didn't make it onto the show was Dani. She'd been firm. Her relationship with me was not for public consumption.

I'd always been happy to respect her feelings. Mostly because Dani was not the kind of person you mess with. And since we hadn't always been close, there was no way I was messing up how good things were now by demanding she play a bigger part in *Random I.*

Besides, it wasn't her life that had become *Random I.* It was mine. I was the one who had to keep it going. I was the one that fans expected to hear from. It was my life they cared about.

Still, I couldn't get Rosie's words out of my head. Did I spend too much time thinking about what fans would like the most? It was true that I often framed interactions and experiences based on what would be the most entertaining. It was an interesting brand of stardom. Because my brand hadn't been built off of my acting skills or my savvy tech knowledge. I was just a guy that had started talking about his life one day. And for whatever reason, it had taken off. Now, there were seventy-five employees who depended on all those viewers *liking* my life. Liking what I had to say and how I said it. I got that boundaries were important. But making sure Jade and Diedre could afford to adopt a third baby was also important. Making sure Greg from Accounting could put his kid in braces and take his family on vacation for spring break. Making sure Alex had a good job so he and Dani could raise their baby without worry. It all mattered. And it all rested on my shoulders.

I couldn't really afford to be selfish. To think about what made me happy without considering whether or not it aligned with the show. Come what may, it was the nature of the business I'd built.

I pulled into the diner parking lot and sighed when I noticed the crowds already gathering on the sidewalks out front. I wasn't in the mood for this. It had been hard enough bantering with Tyler on the way over, Rosie's looming presence in the backseat notwithstanding. Ever since our kiss, it was like I'd become tuned in to her every movement. She'd obviously done her best to ignore me—a treatment I fully deserved—the entire ride over, but there was no way I could ignore her.

As soon as the car pulled to a stop, Rosie bolted from the backseat, nothing more than a mumble about needing to find a bathroom coming from her lips.

"Sheesh," Tyler said as soon as Rosie was gone. "What happened between you two?"

"Nothing," I said dismissively. "Everything's fine. Besides"—I nodded toward the restaurant owner who was waiting for us at the front door—"we have work to do."

And so we worked. Ate. Smiled. Interacted with fans and took selfies and talked on camera about Nashville's greatest French toast. The only thing that disappointed me were the grits. My Charleston-defined standards were just too high.

Rosie must not have liked her grits either. She slid them around on her plate without hardly taking a bite.

"They're better in Charleston," I said. Tyler had filmed more than enough footage and had already gone outside to pack up his gear, leaving just the two of us at the table.

Rosie looked up, her face expressionless. "So I've been told." She put down her fork and dropped her napkin onto her plate. She held my gaze for a long moment. "They're best with salt, butter, cheese, and bacon, right?"

I stilled, my eyes narrowing. That's exactly what I'd told Ana about grits. Not that it was an unpopular way to eat them. At least not in the South. But something about the way Rosie looked at me made me think—

But no. She couldn't be.

Rosie's phone dinged and she pulled it out of her bag. "I'm going to go take this," she said. Then she was gone.

I pulled out my own phone, pulling up my message thread with Ana. I'd sent her something first thing that morning.

She still hadn't responded, which wasn't like her at all. I looked toward the restaurant's door, assuming that's where Rosie had gone. On impulse, I stood to follow her, only to be waylaid by a group of fans that had been waiting to approach, not wanting to interrupt my meal. I smiled my way through one last round of introductions and forced myself to take selfies with each of them.

By the time I made it outside, Tyler was leaning against the car, his feet crossed at the ankles and his phone in his hand. Rosie was nowhere to be found.

"Where's Rosie?" I asked, a feeling of dread already pooling in my stomach.

Tyler looked up and sighed. "She's gone."

"What do you mean *gone?*"

"I mean an Uber just picked her up to drive her to the airport. She's going home."

My phone dinged with an incoming message and I yanked out my phone, feeling intuitively that it was Ana.

@Briarsandthorns: I hope you aren't going to be disappointed . . . but I fear you're going to be just the same.

I swore under my breath and leaned against the car. "Why did you let her leave without talking to me?"

Tyler shot me a snide look. "Why did you relegate her to the backseat and spend the entire morning pretending she didn't exist?"

That was fair.

The majority of the crowd that had gathered for our restaurant stop had dissipated, but the parking lot still felt uncomfortably full. Suddenly, I didn't want to have an audience. "Can you drive?" I said to Tyler.

"Not if I'm filming," he answered slowly.

"I don't care about filming. I just want to get out of here and I . . . I don't want to drive." I was too keyed up. Too . . . overwhelmed. Because I was pretty sure Ana and Rosie were the same person. And I couldn't figure out what that meant.

"Give me the keys, man," Tyler said, his tone shifting. "I've got you."

We pulled out of the parking lot and drove in silence for several minutes. "Did she say anything about why she was leaving?" I finally asked.

"Only that you guys had a falling out and she didn't want to make the rest of the trip uncomfortable. What happened?"

I leaned back in my seat and pressed my head into my hands. "I kissed her."

Tyler choked out a laugh. "I can't say I didn't see that coming."

I shot him a look. "What's that supposed to mean?"

"Oh, whatever. You were in the car yesterday. You guys were all flirty and couple-like. You were obviously into her and she was obviously into you."

"Obviously not, because she left. If she were actually into me, why would she have done that?"

"Gee, I don't know. Maybe because you're on your way to meet another woman? Or because you kicked her from the co-pilot seat mid-trip and probably made her feel embarrassed and stupid in front of me?"

Tyler made very valid points. And made me wonder whether or not Ana and Rosie really were the same person. I'd been a jerk to Rosie. She had every right to leave. Was it just wishful thinking that had made me believe they were one and the same?

"Where are we going, Isaac? Am I driving to Kansas City?"

"Yeah," I said. "I have to see this thing through."

"Do you want to stop in St. Louis like we planned? I think Alex had one more—"

"No," I said, cutting him off. "No more stops. Not unless we're charging the car or grabbing fast food to eat on the way."

He nodded. "And no more recording?"

I'd never been so certain that I did *not* want to spend any more of my day on camera. "No. Let's just get there."

Chapter Twenty-Four

Rosie

My flight landed in Charleston a little after four in the afternoon. In the airport in Nashville, I'd debated for a matter of seconds whether or not I should purchase a ticket to Kansas City. I was aching to spend some time with my parents—nothing made me feel better like sitting at their kitchen table eating my mom's casseroles and drinking my dad's herbal tea. But I couldn't be there when Isaac learned the truth about who I was. Assuming he hadn't already figured it out.

The line about grits might have been too much. It had slipped out without me really even thinking about it. In retrospect, I wondered if I hadn't subconsciously wanted to warn him somehow. Give him time to prepare. Or maybe I'd wanted him to realize it was me right then and there, wrap me in his arms and pick up the kissing where we'd left off the night before. Had my Uber not shown up at that precise moment, he might have figured it out. His eyes had already been speaking the question, even if his words hadn't been.

I'd had a long conversation with my mom while waiting for my flight. That Isaac would show up was inevitable. When he did, she was to invite him inside and take him upstairs to my childhood bedroom. The artwork all over the walls, as well as the shrine to Red Renegade over my desk, would tell him he was in the right place. And the graduation photos hanging above my desk—me in a crimson cap and gown standing between my parents—would tell him that Ana was actually me. My hair had been a little longer when I'd graduated, but the photo wasn't so different that he wouldn't recognize me.

I told Mom she could answer any of his questions about pre-Charleston Rosie, but she wasn't allowed to talk about me and how I was feeling now under any conditions. I didn't have a whole lot of faith in her ability to avoid that last subject. Mom was nothing if not wholly devoted to my happiness. She'd want to sway Isaac. Encourage him.

But I didn't want him to be encouraged.

Once he learned who I really was, he'd know exactly where I stood. It didn't matter how amazing our first kiss had been. How much I enjoyed his text messages or how easily we'd gotten along during the first leg of our road trip. Good chemistry and a shared passion for Red Renegade wasn't enough foundation for a successful relationship. I wasn't the right woman for him—the right woman to live life in the spotlight. And we both knew it.

The air outside Charleston's airport was pleasant and breezy, warmer than it had been in Nashville. A whiff of salty air floated past my nose, and I suddenly longed to be on the beach, to feel the breeze lifting the curls from my neck, the waves washing over my feet.

My landlord was already planning to take care of Reggie for a couple more days. Who said I needed to head straight home? I pulled up my Uber app and plugged in the address for Folly Beach Pier. I needed sun. And sand. And ice cream. Stat.

While I waited for my Uber to show up, I called Greta.

She answered on the second ring. "Hey! How's it going? Are you in Kansas City yet?"

I heaved a sigh. "I'm back in Charleston. I caught a flight in Nashville."

"What? Why? What happened?"

"It's a long story. Want to meet me at the pier on Folly? I'm headed there now."

"Um, yeah," Greta said. "I'm actually at the warehouse. I came in to finish a few things. I'm mostly done. Jade is here. Do you want me to bring her, too?"

"Sure. I might as well explain everything once. Tell her to come. And to bring Diedre if she wants."

"They're all here. The kids, too."

The thought of hanging out with Jade and Diedre and Greta actually felt like a balm to my weary soul. The only thing that sounded better than the beach was the beach with my friends.

Diedre sat beside me on the sand, the baby asleep in her lap, while Jade and Max dug for seashells with Greta. Diedre's blonde hair was swept up in a loose ponytail, revealing the faint laugh lines surrounding her eyes. Diedre was older than Jade by almost ten years which made her feel a little like the mom of the group. She naturally leaned into the role, and we were all the better for it. No one nurtured like Diedre did.

"What do you think you're going to do now?" she asked, her toes digging in the sand in front of us.

I'd already given Greta my unofficial two-week notice, though she hadn't been too enthusiastic about accepting it. She'd just kept telling me to take a week off and think things through but not to make any decisions just yet. I appreciated that Diedre, at least, was talking like she'd taken my decision seriously.

"Beats me," I said. "I don't really want to leave Charleston, but I'm not sure I'll have a choice."

"There are other jobs," Diedre said. "Charleston is a big city. There are plenty of companies here that might be looking to hire a web designer."

I shrugged. "I guess. But would it be weird to stay? To keep hanging out with you guys?" They were all friends with Isaac, too. There would inevitably be overlap, and the thought of that, of seeing Isaac, interacting with him, I wasn't sure I could handle it.

"It'll only be weird if you make it weird," Diedre said. "Besides, you can't let a man chase you from a city you love. So *Random I* was the reason you moved here. It doesn't have to be the reason you stay."

It was such simple advice, and yet it resonated in my heart and mind in a profound way. I didn't have to run away. Even if I didn't work for Isaac anymore. Even if I was totally mortified and we never even talked after he learned about who I really was.

I pulled my phone out of my bag and clicked through to my message thread with Isaac. After my last text, the one where I told him I thought he was going to be disappointed, he'd never messaged me back. If anything, that fact only reinforced my belief that he'd already figured out who I was and didn't want to message me. Either that, or Tyler had told him. And why wouldn't he? He would have had no reason to keep it a secret once I bailed.

I half-wondered if, once he found out, Isaac had just given up and turned around to drive home. Though surely he would have let Alex or Jade know if that was the case.

I was debating the merits of asking Jade or Alex for Tyler's number—texting him to find out if he'd said anything to Isaac wouldn't be too out of line, would it?—when a message popped up from my mom. *He just pulled into the driveway. I'll keep you posted!*

I dropped my phone onto the sand in front of me like it would burn my skin if I held it any longer. "Oh, geez," I said, my hands flying to my cheeks. "Oh, geez, oh geez, oh geez."

"Rosie?" Diedre asked, concern heavy in her voice. She shifted the baby from one arm to the other and draped another blanket over her already swaddled form. The afternoon had been warm, but with the sun having already disappeared behind us, there was a definite chill in the air.

"Isaac just got to my house," I said. "My mom just texted." I lowered my head onto my knees and took several breaths, but the narrowing of my vision told me just how little oxygen I was actually taking in.

Diedre placed a warm hand on my back. "Hey. You're fine. Everything is going to be fine."

I breathed for a few more moments, focusing on the rhythmic motion of Diedre's hand sliding up and down, up and down. She didn't say anything, which I appreciated. I *would* be fine. I just needed a minute to breathe my way into feeling centered again.

I finally lifted my head off of my knees and looked out at the horizon, to the fine line where the deep blue of the ocean melted into the navy night sky.

"Better?" Diedre said softly.

I only nodded. Better, yes. But not better enough to say actual words.

Isaac was at my house.

Walking up the stairs. Looking through my bedroom.

An image of my bed flashed through my mind with a bolt of startling clarity. I'd combed my brain for any details of what Isaac might see when he entered the private space of my childhood and had concluded that while he might see a little too much in-person evidence of my teenage angst, there wasn't anything I should be too terribly embarrassed by.

But I'd forgotten about my bedposts.

How could I have forgotten about my bedposts?

"Oh, hey, she looks green," Jade said, lowering herself onto the sand beside Diedre. I hardly heard her words; I was too focused on trying to remember whether or not the four *Random I* beanies, one in each of the original signature colors, were still adorning the bedposts of my queen-sized bed.

"Isaac is at her house right now," Diedre said softly.

"Yikes. That's gotta feel weird."

Yes. Thank you, Jade, for stating the obvious.

I pulled up my phone and considered texting my mom back, asking her to race up the stairs and hide the beanies before she let Isaac in, but it was likely already too late. And what was the point, really? I'd shown Isaac with my kiss exactly how I felt about him. It likely wouldn't surprise him to know I'd been a fan long before we'd even met.

Max walked over and pressed his sandy four-year-old hands to my cheeks. "Aunt Rosie?" he asked. "Remember when you said you wanted to learn how to find shark's teeth?"

A surge of warmth filled my heart. He'd called me Aunt Rosie. I was an only child, so there was no chance I'd ever be an actual biological aunt. But I'd loved filling the role for Shiloh, and the thought of doing the same for Max had a certain rightness to it that warmed me from the inside out. I pulled Max onto my lap, catching Jade's smile over his head, and snuggled him against me. "I do remember that."

"Do you want me to teach you right now?" Max asked. He tilted his head up and looked at me, his eyes flashing in the light coming off the pier.

"It's getting dark, kiddo," Diedre said. "And Rosie has a lot on her mind right now. I'm not sure she. . ."

"Actually, I think I'd love to hunt for shark's teeth." I shifted, releasing my hold on Max so he could stand up. "I could use the distraction."

"Yes!" Max said, his enthusiasm sparking joy in my chest I hadn't expected. "I know just how! And I know the best spot. Come on!" He started to run toward the water before Jade caught him and pulled him back. "You're gonna put your sweatshirt on before you teach Aunt Rosie anything," she said, shooting me a knowing grin. I wondered if she'd suggested he call me Aunt Rosie or if he'd just decided on his own. Either way, I hoped he'd never stop. "And you better not get your shorts wet. You'll be miserable on the way home if you do."

"Mimi," Max said in an exaggerated tone that made him sound fourteen instead of four. "I know how to do it. I won't get wet." He turned to me, his expression serious. "Can we use the flashlight on your phone?" He looked back at Jade. "Will it hurt the turtles?"

Diedre was the one that answered. "The turtles won't start laying their eggs until next month, so you can use the flashlight now."

"Yes!" he said again, reaching for my hand. "Come on, Rosie. Just follow me and I'll tell you where to go."

Oh, my heart. His confidence was the cutest.

Max walked beside me, tugging my hand gently along as we approached the water. It was low tide, so we had a good ways to go before we were anywhere near the waves.

Max stopped and shined the light down onto an area that boasted a thick covering of broken bits of seashells. "This is where we might find one," Max said. "The waves bring them up with the shells."

"Yeah? What does a shark's tooth actually look like?" I asked. This was good. Exactly what I needed. To think about something as joyful and simple as time on the beach with my favorite four-year-old.

"They're shiny on one end, but rough and dull on the other," he said. "And they're pointy like this." He held his fingers up into a triangle right in front of his face, framing his grin.

"Got it. So do we just dig through the shells to find them?" I asked.

Max shook his head. "Nuh-uh. We squat down like this and watch as the water runs back into the ocean. And when we see one float by . . . we *grab* it."

It seemed hard to believe that shark's teeth would just randomly float by, but Max seemed pretty confident in his knowledge of how the hunt worked. The way his inflections rose and fell like Jade's, it was likely she was the one who had taught him how to find them. And Jade was Charleston born and raised. She'd know if anyone did. I crouched down next to Max, shining the flashlight onto the shells and sand swirling under our feet, watching the push and pull as the waves rolled in and then receded.

Max dropped his hands into the water, his chubby fingers sifting through the shells. "Isaac told me that you have to be patient."

I looked up at Max. "Is he the one who taught you how to hunt for shark's teeth?"

Max sniffed, his tiny nose pink from the chill in the air, and nodded. "He broughted me to the beach while my mommies went to pick up Nora."

My heart squeezed at the thought of Isaac spending time with Max, helping Jade and Diedre out in such a personal way. And I was willing to bet not a single second of his time with Max had made it on camera. I'd meant what I said when I told Isaac I wouldn't be okay with every aspect of his personal life making it on the airwaves. But had I jumped to conclusions about just what that meant? I'd seen ample evidence of Isaac respecting boundaries, investing in the people around him and not just in his show. Would I truly not be willing to give him a chance? Assuming he even wanted one.

"Got one!" Max shouted as his hand darted out of the water. He held up his prize, a shiny black shark's tooth about the size of my thumbnail.

"Already?" I asked, surprised that he'd found one so quickly, and in the first place we'd stopped.

Max huffed like he couldn't believe I'd doubted him. "I told you I know how. Come on. Now you find one."

I dropped my gaze back to the beach, one hand sifting through the moving shells like Max had done while the other held my phone, flashlight shining down on the sand.

"Open your eyes bigger," Max whispered. He used his fingers to open his eyes really wide. "Like this," he said.

I barely suppressed my laughter, knowing Max needed me to take his lesson *very* seriously. "Got it. Eyes are open." It hardly mattered that my feet were going numb, both from the chilly spring water rushing over them and the hunched position I'd assumed.

Minutes passed in silence as I looked and sifted through the shells and sand. When a particularly chilly breeze whipped across us, blowing my hair into my face, I stood, stretching my back. "I don't think I'm as good at this as you, kiddo."

Max shook his head. "Don't give up yet! Isaac says half of finding a shark's tooth is believing you'll find it. Maybe you just aren't believing hard enough."

I ruffled my hand across his hair. "I'm sure Isaac is right. But I think we need to come back out when it's daylight."

He sighed a giant kid sigh. "Okay." He held up his hand. "Here. You can have the one I found. It can remind you to believe."

I took the shark's tooth and cradled it in my hand, unexpected tears welling up behind my eyes. *Oh, geez.* I was *not* crying over a shark's tooth. Only, it had been an overwhelming couple of days. I'd been all over the emotional map—fear, anger, resentment, bitterness, hope, elation. I'd felt all that and more. Max giving me a shark's tooth was so simple, so genuine, it was just enough to push me over the brink of reason. "I'll keep it forever," I said, my voice cracking. "Thank you, sweetie."

We walked hand in hand back up the beach to where the others were shaking out blankets and gathering up the remnants of the impromptu ice cream picnic we'd had earlier. Max darted off to Diedre, who had his socks and shoes at the ready. I turned my face back to the ocean and closed my eyes to the cool breeze blowing off the water, grateful the moonlight wasn't bright enough for my friends to see the evidence of my mini meltdown.

By now, Isaac had surely discovered who Ana really was. The fact that he hadn't called or texted, or even that my mom hadn't messaged filled me with unease. What did he think? Had he been disappointed? Relieved? Excited?

Worse to think about: had I ruined everything by telling him I'd never be okay with his very public life? I'd meant what I said. At least, I thought I had. But I was beginning to think it was also possible I hadn't given him enough credit. Isaac had a relationship with Max that was never on air. A relationship with his sister that had very clearly defined boundaries. And he respected them. Was I truly so certain that he couldn't do the same thing for me? For any woman he loved?

I sighed and turned back to my friends. Maybe it didn't even matter.

Maybe I'd already ruined the only shot I'd ever had.

Chapter Twenty-Five

Isaac

I stood on Ana's front porch and wiped my hands down the front of my pants. The house was older and bigger than I had expected, in a mature neighborhood with lots of stately trees and driveways full of practical cars that looked like retirement. It was not the kind of house I would have expected a twenty-six-year-old web designer to be living in.

Tyler stood behind me, camera rolling. I'd debated whether or not I wanted to film the first moments I was finally face-to-face with Ana. Especially after everything that had happened with Rosie. She didn't think I was capable of having boundaries, of keeping some parts of my life private. But that wasn't true. I wouldn't take advantage of anyone, put anything on air that made anyone uncomfortable.

But she had been right about me losing sight of what I wanted. Too often, I *did* think too much about whether or not the things I did, the choices I made, made for good entertainment. The lines between what I was and wasn't willing to do, to share, in order to entertain my fans, and, let's be honest, make a buck, had clearly gotten muddied.

That's why I'd been so thrown off by Rosie's kiss. Because I had an expectation in my head of what this road trip would look like. I'd imagined this connection with Ana being the perfect representation of the kinds of connections the road trip segment would help other people make. In my head, my relationship with Ana was a love story.

Making out with Rosie had nearly ruined that vision.

Not that there weren't a million other things to consider.

Tyler had rightly reminded me of the contingent of fans that would be thrilled if I ended up with Rosie. The *#teamrosie* hashtag had only picked up steam as more and more people watched the video of the live stream she and I had recorded together. There was also the possibility of Rosie and Ana being the same person. Though, the closer we got to Kansas City, the more I doubted that it could actually be true. Why would she have gone through all the trouble of weaseling her way onto the actual road trip if she were Ana? Why not just fly to Kansas and wait for me to show up and surprise me then? The number of people who would have had to have been involved to get her *on* the road trip? It was almost *too* complicated to imagine it being possible. The much simpler, and thus more logical, conclusion was that Rosie's line about grits had been a coincidence, and Ana was an entirely different woman.

I did my best to ignore the throb of disappointment that pulsed in my chest whenever I had that thought.

There was also the possibility that Ana, assuming she was a different woman, and I wouldn't work out after all. Rosie had already demonstrated that the public nature of my life was a liability. What if Ana felt the same way?

"You all right, man?" Tyler asked from behind me.

I looked over my shoulder. "Yeah. Sorry. Just . . . mustering my courage."

"Just knock. It's going to be all right."

I took a deep breath and raised my hand to the doorbell, sending a deep, throaty gong sound reverberating through the house. It sounded more fit for a castle than a house in the suburbs of Kansas City.

"Dang," Tyler said from behind me. "That's some doorbell."

The door swung open and my heart nearly dropped to the concrete beneath my feet. Except . . . this woman could not be Ana.

"You must be Isaac," the older woman said. She had curly, salt and pepper hair and a kind smile. "Ro—Ana told me to expect you." She extended her hand and I shook it, still not exactly sure what was happening. "Come on in," the woman said. "I'm Ana's mom."

The house was warm and welcoming and smelled like chocolate chip cookies, eliciting a rumble from my stomach. We'd gotten stuck in some heavy traffic outside of St. Louis and lost close to two hours of our trip, so we'd opted to skip dinner so that we didn't show up at Ana's house too late. A decision I was glad we made now that I knew she lived with her parents. Or her mom, at least. Still hadn't seen any evidence of her dad, though I thought I remembered her telling me her parents were still together. We'd had that in common.

"Is Ana here?" I asked her mom, looking down the hallway into what was probably the kitchen.

Her mom held her hands up. "No. She's not. But don't ask me any questions because I'm not supposed to tell you anything."

I glanced at Tyler, feeling uneasy; this was not how I'd anticipated this moment going. But he didn't seem at all ruffled by the weird turn of events.

"Okay. Um, am I just supposed to wait for her, or . . ."

She shook her head again. "Up the stairs, second door on the left. That will tell you everything you need to know."

"I don't understand—"

She cut me off with a quick shake of her head and a wave of her hand. "Nope. I've said my lines. Don't ask me anything else or I'll cave, and I was told I could do no such thing." She backed up a few steps. "I'll be in the kitchen if you need me."

I looked directly into the lens of Tyler's camera. "I guess we're going upstairs."

I immediately knew the room belonged to Ana. Her artwork was all over the walls—stuff I recognized from her Instagram profile as well as several drawings that I'd never seen before, though it all had the same vibe. A series of Red Renegade posters adorned one entire wall, as well as a montage of vinyl covers mounted on display shelves in the order the albums had been released. A few spots were missing. Holes in her collection, maybe, or just the albums she'd taken with her when she'd moved away from home?

Because she *had* moved away. It was clear this room had once belonged to a high school student and hadn't been updated since. A graduation hat and tassel hung on the corner of the mirror above the dresser and a cork board hung above the desk with a collage of graduation cards and photos. I stepped closer, knowing that Ana had to be somewhere in the photos.

Only . . . the woman in all the photos was *Rosie.*

My heart started pounding in my ears.

It was Rosie.

All along, she had been right there in the warehouse. Close enough to talk to, to touch. I pressed my hands against the desk and took a slow, deep breath, trying to wrap my head around it.

I looked at Tyler. "It's Rosie. Ana is . . . they're the same person."

Tyler only grinned.

My eyes narrowed. "You already knew."

"I guessed," he said simply. "And I was right."

I turned away from the photos, taking in the room with new eyes. Rosie had lived here. Rosie loved Red Renegade as much as I did. *She* was the artist behind the work that had initially caught my attention.

I walked toward the four-poster bed in the middle of the room, noticing the beanie hats that adorned each post. They were the first beanies *Random I* had ever produced. I'd designed them and ordered them from a wholesaler myself, dropping the first six grand *Random I* had made with nothing but a hope that my fledgling fanbase would decide they liked me enough to wear stuff that had my name on it. For the first year, I'd handled the shipping out of my parents' garage, printing mailing labels off the same printer Dani had used to print her acceptance letter from the fashion design school she'd attended in New York.

Six grand had only bought me two thousand beanies, five hundred of each color.

Rosie had one of each.

Which meant Rosie had been watching my show a very long time.

Something like a laugh bubbled up inside me and moisture pooled in my eyes. I dropped onto the bed, laughing and—was I crying?—shaking my head. I almost couldn't make sense of what was happening in my head, and more importantly, in my heart. More than anything, what I felt was *relief.*

"What's the word, man?" Tyler asked, likely worried about the amount of dead time I was adding to his shot.

I looked up and smiled, sniffing in a way that couldn't be attractive. But I didn't care. Rosie was everything I'd ever wanted in a woman. Her smarts, her wit, her humor. Her love for Red Renegade. Her funky glasses and killer curly hair. But even though I hadn't realized right away—not until she'd challenged me back at Marley's house—she was also everything I *needed.* I needed someone like Rosie to balance me out. To keep me grounded. To help me remember what really mattered in life. My voice cracked when I finally spoke. "I wanted it to be her," I said, wiping my eyes. "I . . ." I laughed and pressed my hands against my face. "I just can't believe it. It was her. It was always her."

Tyler's shoulders lifted as he chuckled. "I've never seen you like this, man."

I shrugged. "I've never felt like this." I motioned to Tyler's camera. "Hey, can you turn that off?"

He immediately stopped recording and lowered the camera onto the dresser before coming to sit next to me on the bed.

"You okay?"

I sniffed. "Yeah. Just . . . surprised. And relieved, I think? So many more things make sense now that I know."

"I bet."

"Is her name really Ana?"

Tyler nodded. "Yes. Ana Rose Crenshaw."

That was good. It was comforting to know she hadn't lied about her name. At least not directly. "Who else knows?"

"Alex, Jade, and Greta. I didn't know when the trip started, but after filming you guys all day, I got suspicious and confronted Rosie."

"At the hotel in Nashville?"

"Yeah."

It was the first clue I'd gotten regarding my true feelings for Rosie. When I'd seen her sitting on the park bench with Tyler, jealousy had practically swallowed me whole. It was crazy to think that I felt that strongly after one day in the car. Less crazy when I thought about Rosie being Ana. Because I'd been getting to know her via direct message for over a month. My mind hadn't known they were the same person, but we'd connected so easily, the vibe between us almost electric. Maybe in some way, my heart had already known it was her.

"What are you going to do now?" Tyler asked.

That was a good question. "I don't know." I suddenly wondered how this moment would have played out differently had I not been such a jerk to Rosie at her cousin's house. Would she have followed me up the stairs to her room, waited for me to look around and make the connection on my own? Or would she have just told me? Would I have kissed her again here, right in the middle of her room? Would Tyler have filmed it?

A momentary twinge of sadness over the fact that *that* would have made a very good conclusion to the road trip video washed over me, but it was quickly replaced by a much more pressing disappointment.

Rosie wasn't here. And she could have been. She could have been in my arms right now. Except, would she want to be? Is that why she'd left? She'd told me in no uncertain terms that she wouldn't be okay with the way I lived so much of my life for my fans. But I didn't *want* to live my life like that anymore. She'd woken me up to that. Helped me see that I'd been prioritizing all wrong. I'd just never had someone like Rosie to challenge me on it. I ran a hand across my face. I really *had* been dating the wrong kind of woman.

I stood. "I have to go home."

Tyler nodded. "You do."

"I have to find her. Tell her . . ." I sighed. "Man, I wish she was here right now. That she could just see—"

"That she reduced you to a crying, sniveling snotface that can't stop grinning like a lovesick fool?" Tyler said dryly.

"Thanks for that, man. Really."

He grinned. "All I'm saying is she was pretty pissed when she left Nashville. I've got the footage, and your tears may work to your advantage. *Especially* if you show it *after* a montage of clips showing all the ways the two of you connected over the past twenty-four hours."

"You think I should make her a video?"

He shrugged. "Or just edit your road trip video with Rosie instead of Ana in mind. It could still be about connections. Just not the connection you expected."

"That's good," I said, pacing back and forth in front of the dresser. "Except, it doesn't need to be the regular segment. I don't want anyone to see it unless Rosie is comfortable with it. This video isn't going to be about the viewers. It's just going to be about her."

"Knock, knock," Mrs. Crenshaw said from the bedroom door. She held a tray holding a plate of cookies and two tall glasses of milk. "Sorry to interrupt. I was just waiting downstairs and when you didn't come back down right away, I thought you must be having a very serious conversation and thought you might need a snack."

I smiled. Ana's mom—no, Rosie's mom—was exactly as she had described her. *She is warmth personified,* she had once messaged. *And she loves best through casseroles and cookies.*

I crossed the room and took the tray from her hands, setting it on the dresser beside the camera. I turned back to face her, trusting that immediately pulling her into a hug was a gesture she would understand and reciprocate. She patted my back in a warm, motherly way. "There, there," she said.

When I finally released her from the hug, she looked up and studied my face. "I take it those were tears of joy that made your eyes all red?"

"Mrs. Crenshaw, can I tell you something?"

She nodded. "Of course, dear."

I took hold of her shoulders. "I am desperately in love with your daughter."

"Well that's a relief," she said. "Because she's been in love with you for years."

We stayed with Rosie's mom—her dad was out of town on a business trip—for another couple of hours, enjoying the cookies and milk and then, when she discovered we'd skipped dinner, a casserole she pulled out of the freezer and warmed up for us.

"Please tell me you're going to call her as soon as you leave here," Mrs. Crenshaw said as Tyler packed up his gear. "I'm sure she's beside herself with worry."

"Actually, I think I'm going to wait and talk to her in person."

Mrs. Crenshaw's hand flew to her heart. "Oh, you can't do that. Her anxiety will eat her up if she has to wait all that time. You know about her anxiety, don't you? Has she been honest with you about that?"

She hadn't, really. Though we'd danced around the topic in our messages a few times. Hearing her mother mention it so plainly explained a lot. Why she'd been so hesitant to meet me in person. To tell me who she was. But then, Rosie in person hadn't seemed anxious at all. She'd been easygoing and chill. Or at least, she'd seemed that way. Though I knew enough about anxiety to know that what I saw on the outside wasn't necessarily a reflection of what she was feeling on the inside.

"She hasn't told me much, actually. I guess I've still got a lot to learn."

Mrs. Crenshaw nodded. "She's good at hiding it."

"But, when we were driving, she didn't seem . . . she seemed so . . . relaxed, I guess?"

Mrs. Crenshaw raised a hand to my cheek and a bolt of longing for my own mom shot through me. I owed my parents a visit. They lived too close for it to have been so long since I'd last seen them. "She's come a long way. She manages it well, only dealing with flare-ups every once in a while. When she's with people that make her feel accepted and loved, she opens right up. I expect you did that for her."

I nodded. I didn't want Rosie anxious and worried. But I also didn't want to have the conversation brewing in my head over the phone. But maybe I could say something, give her some indication that regardless of what *she* wanted—I might lose sleep if I spent too much time worrying about that—I was in with a capital *I*.

I pulled out my phone and scrolled to the Instagram thread where we'd been messaging for the past month. I reread her last message, the one where she'd told me she was pretty sure I was going to be disappointed. She'd sent it minutes after leaving Nashville.

I typed out a quick message and sent it before I could overthink it.

"There," I said, smiling at Rosie's mom. "That should hopefully set her mind at ease until I'm back in town."

"Good man," she said, giving my arm a quick squeeze. "Now hurry home."

She didn't have to ask me twice.

Chapter Twenty-Six

Rosie

I sat on my front porch, my feet still sandy from the beach, and debated whether or not it had been long enough to call my mom. The last thing I wanted was to call while Isaac was still there. She wasn't responding to my text messages which meant he might be. Mom would talk his ears off if he let her.

I opted for sending one more text. *This is killing me, Mom. Please call me once he's gone.*

It took about three minutes for her to finally call. "Demanding little thing tonight, aren't we?" she said, her voice teasing.

"I'm demanding?" I said, Put yourself in my shoes. "Is he still there? Please tell me he isn't standing right beside you and I'm on speaker phone."

"He's gone," Mom said. "He left about an hour ago."

"An hour? Why did it take you so long to call?" I stood from the steps and started pacing back and forth in front of the wicker bench to the left of my front door.

Mom let out a weird, breathy laugh. "Oh, you know. I just . . . got caught up doing other things."

"Mom, please," I said, my voice wobbly. "Can you just tell me how it went? What did he say? Was it awful? Was he surprised?"

"Slow down with the questions, Rosie. Are you breathing? You don't sound like you're breathing."

"I'm breathing," I said. "I promise."

"He's a very nice man. So handsome and easy to talk to," she said, her tone shifting just enough for me to know she was stalling.

"Mom."

"And that smile. It's enough to make a woman's heart stop."

"Mom."

"I liked the other one—is his name Tyler?—as well. He was very nice."

"Mom, I know what you're doing. Why are you stalling? And why won't you answer my question? Is it bad? Are you trying to keep from having to give me bad news?"

She sighed. "I'm trying to keep from having to give you *any* news. Isaac asked that I didn't. He wants to talk to you in person."

I groaned and leaned forward, dropping onto the wicker bench, a cloud of dust and pollen puffing up from the seat cushion. Of course he would want to talk to me in person.

"That's it? You won't tell me *anything*? Can you at least tell me what he said when he found out?"

"I don't know what he said. I didn't go upstairs with them. I didn't want to be on camera, so I left them to it."

A little twinge of disappointment snaked through me as I thought about him filming the entire experience. Not that I hadn't expected him to film it. It was the entire point of the trip. But a small part of me had hoped he'd decide not to.

"Did you get his message?" Mom asked. "I told him to send you one.

I thought it was cruel for him to make you wait the entire time he was traveling home without getting some clue of how he was feeling. I told him that would be the worst possible thing for your anxiety."

Oh. Great. Mom couldn't tell *me* anything, but she was more than okay sharing my mental health history with Isaac. Fantastic. I might scold her, except she'd told me that Isaac had messaged. And that was a far more pressing issue. I switched the phone call to speaker phone so I could navigate my way to Instagram and check my direct messages. Sure enough, there was one new message from Isaac. How had I missed it before? I'd been checking my notifications, but somehow, Instagram had failed to send me one for this message.

I clicked it open.

@RandomIOfficial: I'm not disappointed. Wait for me, Rosie. I'm on my way home.

My body stilled even while my heart started pounding, surely tripling its speed. This was big. He'd called me Rosie.

Isaac knew who I was, and Isaac wasn't disappointed.

"Rosie?" Mom said. "Are you still there?"

"I'm here," I said faintly. "I got his message."

"Well, what did he say? I just told him to send one. I didn't make him show it to me."

"It says he isn't disappointed."

"That's it?" Mom said.

"Yes, but there's context. Because I messaged him when I left Nashville and told him I thought he would be."

"Why would you do a thing like that?" Mom asked.

I quickly gave Mom a rundown of everything that happened in Nashville, only leaving out the intensity of the kiss. It had only been the night before, and yet, kissing Isaac in Marley's living room felt lifetimes away. So much had changed since then.

"Tell me something, Rosie," Mom said, her tone soft. "Did you tell

Isaac you thought he'd be disappointed because you're you? Or was it because *you* don't want him?"

Leave it to Mom to distill the complexities of my heart into one simple question.

"I don't know. I think I *do* want him. I'm just . . . scared, you know? His life is . . . it's just a lot."

"But everyone's is in some way or another, isn't it?"

I leaned my head back on the dusty cushion. "How do you mean?"

"I just mean everyone has to deal with something. If you were to marry a surgeon, for example, you'd have to deal with his crazy schedule, with long shifts and weekends on call. You marry a police officer or a firefighter, and you're worried about their safety, hoping they come home at the end of each shift. If you're a military spouse, you're enduring deployments and moving every couple of years. I guess you could find yourself a boring accountant who just sits in a cubicle all day, but I promise he'd have something to throw you off, too. A health condition, or a bad snoring habit, or, I don't know, something. And let's not pretend like marrying you will be a plate of cupcakes. With your anxiety? It'll take someone special to take you on."

"Gee, thanks, Mom."

"I'm just saying. Every relationship takes work. Sacrifice. You have to find the person who feels worth the struggle."

Her argument made sense. I couldn't deny that a big part of my hesitation with Isaac had always been fear. But at the same time, the thought of walking away from him completely—and not just from the road trip—that felt even scarier. "What if it's too late?"

"Pish," Mom said, her tone light. "He just told you he isn't disappointed. Why would he have said that if it's too late?"

"I don't know. Maybe he isn't disappointed, but he still just wants to be friends."

Mom huffed out a breath, sounding as though she wanted to say something else but swallowed the words instead. "I promised I wouldn't say anything and so I won't," she finally said. "But don't get yourself worked up, Rosie. Just be patient. This is all going to work out."

As luck would have it, I didn't have to be patient long. Late Sunday night, while I debated whether or not I had the courage to actually show up to work on Monday morning, my phone rang.

"Oh good, you're still awake," Greta said, as soon as I answered the phone.

"Hopefully not for too much longer," I said. "Also, I'm probably going to work from home tomorrow, just FYI."

"Stop talking about work," she said shortly. "I need you to come down to the warehouse."

"What? It's almost midnight."

"I realize that. I wouldn't have asked if it wasn't important. Just hurry. And come wearing something other than pajamas. Okay, love you, bye!"

I stared at my phone, as if expecting it to explain everything that Greta had left out of her phone call. This could only have something to do with Isaac.

I did the math, calculating back the number of hours that had passed since he'd last been at my parents' house. According to Mom, he'd left her house a little after ten p.m. on Saturday night. Twenty-four hours was plenty of time to drive back home, but they would have had to drive all night. Of course, he could have caught a flight. But then he would have been home much sooner than twenty-four hours. That thought brought little comfort. Because I still hadn't heard from him.

A text from Greta popped up on my phone. *Stop overthinking. Just come. I promise you won't be sorry.*

I powered through my nerves and forced myself to get ready, choosing my outfit carefully. Greta had said not to wear pajamas, but I wasn't about to wear anything that wasn't casual. Not at midnight. I slipped on my most comfortable jeans and my favorite Red Renegade v-neck, then pulled on my royal blue blazer with the cropped sleeves. I stood and looked into the full-length mirror that hung beside my bedroom door. I looked cute. Confident. Like myself. That was the most I could hope for.

Greta was waiting for me outside the warehouse. "You okay?" She asked.

I shook my head. "Not really. I'm freaking out a little."

She squeezed my hand. "Don't freak out. This is a good thing, I promise."

Inside the elevator, Greta pushed the second-floor button instead of the third.

"Why are we going to the studio?" I said, nerves coiling my midsection into a knot.

Greta only shot me a look. "Just go with it, all right?"

I followed her through the annex and into the studio, then through a side door and down a long hallway to the chop shop where all the editing magic happened. The room was empty.

"Just stand right here, okay?" Greta said. She took my shoulders and turned me to face the giant wall of screens that occupied the back of the room.

The screens flickered to life, and suddenly I was back in the VW Rabbit, smiling at Isaac while we buckled our seatbelts with a simultaneous click.

Was I just watching the road trip segment? It could have been, except . . . all of Isaac's intro had been cut out, and there wasn't anything about any of the planned stops we'd made. This was just footage of the two of us. Listening to Red Renegade. Picking out identical snacks at the gas station. Eating black licorice and pickle taffy. Laughing over the dad jokes Isaac told whenever there had been more than a minute or two of silence.

It wasn't a wonder Tyler had figured me out. Whenever Isaac was talking, I was staring at him with open devotion written all over my face. But the thing was, whenever Isaac was looking at me, his expression was just as enthusiastic. The video cut to the live video Isaac and I had filmed together outside the hotel in Nashville. We really *did* have a vibe. The video shifted again to Isaac standing nervously on my parents' front porch. My gut tightened, which was saying something since I was already a knot of nerves.

Isaac wiped his hands down the front of his pants then glanced at the camera, his eyes bright with excitement.

My heart swelled as they moved inside, and I caught sight of my mom. I laughed as she bumbled her way through sending them upstairs, sticking devotedly to the script I'd given her. It had probably taken all her self-control not to say more. And then Isaac was at my bedroom door, walking into my room, looking at my artwork, running his hands along the shelves that held my Red Renegade album collection. When he turned to the collage of graduation photos above my desk, I had to force myself to keep my eyes open. His face morphed from confusion to awareness to disbelief. And then to something else.

He dropped onto my bed, laughing and shaking his head. Tyler zoomed in on his face; only then did I notice the tears collecting in his eyes. Isaac sniffed and wiped at his eyes, then looked directly at the camera. *I wanted it to be her,* he said. *I wanted it to be her.*

"I wish you'd been there," a voice said from behind me.

I spun around.

Isaac leaned against the chop shop door, his shoulder resting against the door jamb and his arms folded across his chest.

I swallowed, willing my nerves to stop climbing up my throat. "Hi."

He took a few steps forward. "Hi."

"That was . . ." I motioned my head toward the wall of screens. "I liked it."

"Sorry it took so long." He grinned. "I caught the earliest flight I could, but I'm not as quick as the editing guys; they had to teach me a few things, and there was a lot of footage to get through."

"You did this yourself?"

He nodded. "I wanted to."

"So this isn't . . . there will be a different video for the road trip segment?"

"This one is only for you. For . . . *us?*" He said the word like a question, as if he wasn't sure if there *was* an us. "As for the road trip segment, there's another video. But it won't post until you've watched it, until you're comfortable with every single shot. You could tell me not to post it at all and I wouldn't do it. I need you to know that."

I started to shake my head. "I'm sure it's—"

Isaac lifted his hand and caught my chin, stopping my movement. "Don't," he said softly, his tone warm and accepting. "You deserve veto rights. You're in the video. And you're important to me. It isn't too much to ask."

His hand moved to my shoulder then slid down the length of my arm until his fingers curled around mine. "You were right about a lot of things, Rosie. I have lost sight of what I want my show to be. But *Random I* will never be more important than the people I care about. I might need reminders every once in a while." He ran his free hand through his hair. "I don't always think things through before I want to jump in with both feet. But I can respect boundaries. I can keep things private."

I wanted to believe him, to trust him. But something still held me back. "That isn't what you said at Marley's house," I said, my words shaky.

He breathed out a sigh. "I know. But I was scared, Rosie. Kissing you was . . ." He shook his head. "I freaked out. I had no idea how to reconcile what I was feeling for you with what I already felt for Ana. I complained about viewer expectations, but only because that felt easier than sorting out my own feelings."

I rolled my eyes playfully. "I could have made it a lot easier on you had you just listened to me. I tried to tell you," I said. "Right after we kissed. I wanted to tell you right then who I was."

He narrowed his eyes as if trying to remember. "You did say you had something to tell me," he said, recognition flashing in his eyes.

I nodded. "But you didn't want to listen."

He leaned down, his forehead close to mine, and wrapped his arm around my waist. "Will you give me a chance, Rosie? Take a risk on a guy with a weird job and horrible taste in candy?"

"Ugh, really horrible," I said, leaning into him.

"I like your shirt, by the way," he said. "How did I not know you love Red Renegade? I can usually spot a fan a mile away."

I shrugged. "I knew if I made it obvious, you'd want to talk to me. I could barely handle talking to you about sweatshirts."

"Yeah, I saw the signature beanies on your bedposts. You've been into me for a long time, haven't you?" he said, his voice teasing.

My eyes widened and my jaw fell open. He had *not* just said that. I dropped his hand and pushed at his chest to move away, but he looped his arms behind my waist and held me to him. "Sorry," he said, a sly grin on his face. "I couldn't resist."

"I saved my babysitting money for three weeks to buy those hats," I said.

"I appreciate it. I stored them in my garage and printed shipping labels on my parents' old inkjet. The thing burned through ink so fast, once I factored in all the replacement cartridges, I barely broke even."

I chuckled. "And look at you now." I nestled into his chest, enjoying the feel of him under my hands. His warmth, his solidity. I felt safe with his arms around me. Comfortable in a way I'd never been before. The only thing that would make the moment better was actual kissing. If Isaac didn't get around to that part soon, I'd be making the first move.

Again.

"What made you send that first message?" he asked.

I scoffed. "Bridget wearing a Red Renegade shirt. She called them noise, Isaac. And said she only wore the shirt because she liked the colors." I patted his chest. "Someone had to rescue you."

He leaned forward—*finally!*—and brushed his nose against mine. "I didn't realize how badly I needed rescuing until I met you," he said.

If I just tilted my head up the slightest bit, my lips would be on his. I just had to lean . . .

"You can't kiss me until you answer my question," Isaac said, his tone playful, but laced with a measure of earnest hope that kept me from feeling annoyed that he was withholding kisses. "Will you take a chance on a guy like me?"

I slid my hands up the smooth planes of his chest, clasping them behind his neck. "You aren't wrong that I've been into you for a long time. I was *that* fan. The girl who watched every video. Bought all the merchandise. Scored a hundred percent on all the Buzzfeed quizzes I took about you."

"What's my middle name?" Isaac asked, his eyes narrowed.

I rolled my eyes. "Sterling. But stop interrupting me. I want to kiss you but you're making me say this first."

He pressed his lips closed, hardly concealing his smile, and nodded his head. "Sorry. Continue."

"It was only once we started messaging that I discovered that being *into you* doesn't even begin to compare to being *in love* with you." I bit my lip and lifted my gaze to meet his. More like lifted one squinty eye to meet his gaze while I squeezed the other eye shut. Leave it to me to find a way to be bold and brave and terrified and hiding at the same time.

Isaac's eyes were open and warm and full of . . . *love*? It looked like love. "Are you telling me you love me?" he said.

"Isaac," I said, holding his gaze. "Please kiss me now."

Our first kiss had been an unexpected and frenzied passion—a reaction to a moment that had taken us both by surprise. But this kiss was a promise. A declaration. A commitment. Passion pulsed beneath it though, flaring to life when Isaac pulled me flush against him, his kisses growing more heated.

My hands slipped up the arms of his t-shirt, curving around his biceps. A low moan escaped Isaac's lips, eliciting a visceral response that I couldn't have stopped had I wanted to. I leaned into him, willing him to hold me tighter, to kiss me deeper. I could not get enough of this man.

A throat cleared behind us and we pulled apart. Isaac slid his hands up to cradle my face, giving me one last gentle kiss. "I love you, too," he whispered softly. "Just in case you couldn't tell."

He kept his arm around me as we turned to see Alex standing in the doorway. "I hate to break up the party, but Dani's on the phone wanting a full update, and since it's already past midnight, I feel justified in interrupting."

"How many people are here?" I asked.

"Almost everyone," Isaac said. "The editing team. Greta. Alex." He motioned to the doorway. "Jade was here all day, but she wanted to get home in time to see the kids before they went to bed."

"They were all helping you?"

He shrugged, his tone playful. "They wanted to help. Turns out everyone who works for me was already on Team Rosie."

The next day at work, what seemed like half the warehouse crowded into the chop shop to watch the final cut of the road trip video.

"Remember what I said," Isaac said, squeezing my hand. "Anything you don't like, we can take out before it airs."

Vinnie sat down beside us, offering me a wide grin and two thumbs up as he lowered himself into his chair. The gesture brought a surge of warmth to my chest. Vinnie had believed in me from the start.

The video included some of the same parts that had been in the one Isaac had made for me, just with more stuff about the car and its retrofitted engine, the places we had lunch and breakfast, and the hotel we'd booked in Nashville. The way it was edited, you couldn't really tell that I'd bailed halfway through the trip—they'd just used footage from the previous day scattered throughout so it appeared as though I'd made it all the way to Kansas. There were plenty of flirty clips between Isaac and me, all of them building nicely to the moment in my old bedroom when he admitted he had wanted it to be me. The video concluded with a shot of Isaac sitting on the hood of the car inviting people to send in their own stories and apply to be featured on the show so they could make their own meaningful and lasting connections.

It was fine. Great, really. But it wasn't *right.* I shook my head. "You can't end it like this."

Isaac raised his eyebrows. "Like what?"

"The whole segment is about making connections. And yet, at the end of the video, you're alone."

He squeezed the hand he was still holding. "What do you suggest?"

I scoffed. Wasn't it obvious? "I need to be in it. We need to be together."

Isaac studied me for a long moment. "Are you sure you're okay with that? You don't have to, Rosie."

I pursed my lips to the side. "What video editing software do you use?"

"Pro Direct," Vinnie answered from his corner of the room.

I walked toward his desk. "Perfect. I know that one. Can you pull it up for me?"

Vinnie glanced up at Isaac who must have nodded his approval because Vinnie immediately pulled up the video, then yielded his chair to me.

I scrolled through the video until just after the clip of Isaac in my old room when he'd admitted that he'd wanted Ana to be me. I tried not to dwell on the fact that he'd cried actual real tears when he'd found out. It might make my heart explode, and that would grossly interfere with what I was trying to accomplish. I froze the shot and added a filter that fuzzed out the image until it looked like gray and white static you might see on an old tv, then added in a low volume audio track of staticky white noise. On top of that, I layered on some text that read: *Censored for privacy. But just because I know you're curious...there was kissing.*

Isaac chuckled behind me. "That's great."

"Now we end it with a shot of the both of us sitting on the hood of the car. You could be eating licorice or something to tie the moment back to the first half of the trip. We just both need to be there."

"Together," Isaac said.

I nodded. "Connected."

"How did you know how to do all that?" Vinnie said. "You just did stuff in Pro Direct that I don't even know how to do."

I shrugged. "Oh. Um, I did a little video editing in college."

Isaac laughed and wrapped his arms around my waist, apparently not even caring that his entire editing team was staring at us. It was exactly the kind of attention I generally shied away from, but for once, I didn't mind so much. As long as I was in Isaac's arms, they could stare all they wanted.

"You are entirely unexpected, Rosie Crenshaw," Isaac said.

"But in a good way, right?" I said.

He leaned in and kissed me one more time. "In the very best way."

Epilogue

Isaac

I had no doubt in my mind that *Random I's* viewers and fans would love to be a part of the day that I had planned. The road trip to Kansas had been a big hit—it had the highest views of any video I'd ever posted—and Rosie was a fan favorite.

But today was not about my fans.

Today was about Rosie. And all the ways she'd changed my life for the better.

Dani poked her head into my bedroom door. "How are you? Are you good?"

I nodded. "Nervous. But good."

"Rosie's parents just got here. Mom and Dad are entertaining them downstairs. And Mom said to tell you she picked up the ring, but she's with the twins now, so she gave it to Dad. He's holding it for you."

"Got it," I said. "Mom, twins, Dad, ring. How are the twins, by the way?"

She yawned in response. "Exhausting. I swear they never sleep at the same time. Or for longer than an hour."

"And yet, you and Alex make parenthood look so easy."

"Alex makes it look easy. The man is some sort of magic baby whisperer. Me? Not so much."

I put my hands on her shoulders. "You're doing a great job, Dani. You're a great mom. Those babies are lucky to have you."

"I know. And I'm lucky to have them. But man, I'm tired." She reached up and straightened my tie. "You look good, little brother."

I rolled my eyes. "You're only older than me by five minutes."

"Five minutes is three hundred entire seconds. And every single one of them counts."

I followed Dani downstairs where I hugged my parents, retrieved the engagement ring I'd had sized to fit Rosie from my dad, and ushered everyone out onto the back patio so Rosie wouldn't see them when she first arrived. The engagement *party* couldn't be a surprise until after the actual *engagement.*

Jade and Diedre were there with their kids, as well as Greta, Vinnie, Tyler, and a few other friends from work who had gotten to know Rosie over the past few months. Max ran over, and I scooped him up to give him a hug.

"Where's Rosie?" Max asked, quickly wriggling himself back to the ground.

"She'll be here soon."

Max *always* asked about Rosie. I'd been his favorite at one point, but Rosie had easily nudged me out of the top spot. I'd have to work harder to spoil Dani's twins just enough to keep them loving me the most.

"Tell her I found her another shark's tooth when she gets here. This one is as big as my pinky finger."

"That big? That's amazing." Max also always had shark's teeth to give to Rosie. She had at least a dozen that she kept in a little jewelry box on her nightstand. A pulse of longing moved through me as I thought about

Rosie and the way she interacted with Max, and the possibility of one day having our own kids. I ruffled Max's hair. "I gotta get back inside, kiddo. But we'll be back outside soon, all right? I'll make sure you get a chance to give Rosie her shark's tooth."

I turned off the lights on the back patio, leaving everyone with nothing but the faint winter moon to light the space around them. At least it was a relatively warm night. December was like that in Charleston. Cold one day, and then in the seventies the next. It was hard to keep up. "All right, guys. She'll be here in another five minutes or so. Try to stay quiet if you can."

There were four children five and under on the patio. Odds probably weren't very good. But I didn't plan on wasting any time once Rosie arrived. I moved back into the living room where I'd hung twinkle lights across the ceiling, crisscrossing back and forth to make a canopy of indoor starlight. The room was filled with a hundred roses in ten different colors. Cliché, maybe, but roses were Rosie's favorite. Red Renegade played softly in the background—a carefully cultivated playlist of their most mellow songs.

Everything was ready to go.

All I needed was Rosie.

Not two minutes later, she sounded a quick knock on the front door before letting herself in. "Isaac?" she called. "Where are you?"

"In here," I called, hoping my voice was enough to lead the way.

"I'm having second thoughts about this dress," she called as she approached. "Dani told me—" Her words cut off when she rounded the corner, her eyes wide as she looked around the room. "Oh, wow."

I crossed the room and slipped my hands around her waist. "Why would you ever have second thoughts about this dress?" I didn't know fashion like Dani did, but the dress looked like it had been made for Rosie, melding to her curves and flattering her figure. But then, it probably had been. "You look amazing."

"You really think so? I mean, I love it. I *really* love it. Your sister is a wonder. I just wondered if it was too . . . I don't know . . . too much for someone like me. Like, can I really pull this off?"

"Oh, you're definitely pulling it off."

She kicked up the heel of her left foot. "She even persuaded me to try heels. What do you think?"

"I think I'll take you in sneakers if that's what you're comfortable in, but you look amazing in heels, so whatever you want is good by me."

She leaned up and kissed me. "That was a very good answer." She looked around the room again. "What is all this? I thought you were taking me out tonight."

"I'm taking you . . . out to the back patio. But not yet."

She studied me closely, a smile playing around her lips.

"Isaac? Are you—?"

Before she could finish her question, I dropped to one knee, pulling the ring box out of my pants pocket. "I know I'm a handful," I said. "And this is a big ask. But I don't want to do life without you. Will you marry me?"

She reached forward and cupped my cheek with her hand. "You and all ten million of your friends?" she asked playfully.

"Nah," I said, my lips lifting into a grin. "Just me. I'll see my ten million friends at work. Maybe invite them over for Sunday dinner every once in a while."

She tilted her head as if to consider. "I can handle Sunday dinners."

"So that's a yes?" I pulled the ring out of the box and slipped it onto her finger. "It originally belonged to my grandmother. Mom said we could get it re-set into something more modern if we wanted, but I thought you might like the vintage vibe."

She nodded, wiping a tear from her eye. "It's perfect." She pulled me to my feet and wrapped her arms around my neck, pulling me into a kiss to rival all the kisses we'd shared before. Which was saying something. Because we'd had some good ones.

She leaned back, breaking the kiss, and wrapped her arms around my waist, nestling her head against my chest. "My answer is yes, in case you were wondering," she said. "In case I didn't make myself clear."

I chuckled. "I think I got the general idea." I kissed the top of her head. "Come on. Everyone's out back waiting to congratulate us."

She perked up. "Everyone?"

I nodded. "Your parents, my parents. Dani, Alex, the twins. Greta, Jade—"

"Okay, I get it. Everyone. Let's go see them!"

Dani asked me once if it felt like I'd had to give anything up to be with Rosie. It was true I didn't do near as many random live streams when we were together, and I talked less about my personal life on the show. But in retrospect, those things hardly felt like sacrifices. They felt more like gifts. Like finding Rosie had helped me settle into the man I was supposed to be, and not just the entertainer I already was. She made me better in every single respect. And that was more than I could have ever asked for.

@RandomIOfficial: Today was a good day. I liked marrying you.

@Briarsandthorns: Me too. You're pretty cool.

@RandomIOfficial: The food was good. And the music.

@Briarsandthorns: RED RENEGADE FOREVER

@RandomIOfficial: Want to move in? I've got this king-sized bed that has plenty of room for two . . .

@Briarsandthorns: YES. But only if you promise your ten million friends will never be invited into the bedroom.

@RandomIOfficial: THAT is a promise I am happy to make.

@Briarsandthorns: Then get over here and kiss me, husband . . .

@Briarsandthorns: Oh, hey. There's a surprise for you in the glove box of the Rabbit. An envelope. If there is red licorice inside, we are having one baby. If there is black licorice inside, we're having two.

@RandomIOfficial: IS THIS A TRICK QUESTION?!

@Briarsandthorns: I don't think I asked a question.

@RandomIOfficial: But you're telling me either way there is going to be a baby?

@Briarsandthorns: I feel like until you've consulted the licorice we probably shouldn't be having this conversation.

@RandomIOfficial: Red licorice. Only red. Are you for real about this?

@Briarsandthorns: Very real. Happy impending parenthood. :)

@RandomIOfficial: I was about to say I can't believe you told me via DM, but I actually can.

@Briarsandthorns: I mean, this was where it all started…

@RandomIOfficial: Here is the real . . . the rawness of you and me . . .

@Briarsandthorns: Keep quoting lyrics to me and we just might be friends forever.

@RandomIOfficial: I'm going to walk to your desk and kiss you now.

@Briarsandthorns: Bring the licorice. I'm eating for two now.

@RandomIOfficial: I'm on my way . . .

Acknowledgments

Every book has a story of how it came to be—how an idea grew from something tiny into something that could fill the pages of an entire novel. I knew what I wanted this book to be long before I figured how to make it so. Sending a woman on a road trip to meet herself felt like a ridiculous and hilarious premise. But the execution of such a premise? That proved much more complicated than I originally anticipated. There were speed bumps (ha) and roadblocks (haha) and detours (too much?), but with the help of my brilliant friends and an extraordinary editor, here we are. I love Rosie and Isaac's story, and I hope you enjoyed it too. Becca, thank you for always telling me my ideas are good and my words are worthy. Melanie, thank you for reading my words in their roughest form and helping me see where to polish. Emily, thank you for being my sounding board, my first and last reader with every manuscript. I am a better writer because of your brilliance. Cindy, thank you for beta reading with lightning speed and for always having meaningful insights. To my husband who has supported me as this writing gig has shifted from a part-time hobby to a full-time job, thank you for believing in me even when I do not believe in myself. I love you, of course. Forever and always.

About the Author

Jenny Proctor grew up in the mountains of North Carolina, a place she still believes is one of the loveliest on earth. She lives a few hours south of the mountains now, in the Lowcountry of South Carolina. Mild winters and of course, the beach, are lovely compromises for having had to leave the mountains.

Ages ago, she studied English at Brigham Young University. She works full time as an author and as an editor, specializing in romance, through Midnight Owl Editors.

Jenny and her husband, Josh, have six children, and almost as many pets. They love to hike and camp as a family and take long walks through the neighborhood. But Jenny also loves curling up with a good book, watching movies, and eating food that, when she's lucky, she didn't have to cook herself. You can learn more about Jenny and her books at www.jennyproctor.com.

Manufactured by Amazon.ca
Bolton, ON